The

Sultan's Turret

Also from Orbit by Seamus Cullen:

A NOOSE OF LIGHT

The Sultan's Turret

SEAMUS CULLEN

Futura

An Orbit Book

First published in 1986
by Futura Publications, a Division of
Macdonald & Co (Publishers) Ltd
London & Sydney

All characters in this publication are fictitious and any resemblance to real persons, living or dead, is purely coincidental.

ISBN 0 7088 8179 3

Typeset by Leaper & Gard Ltd., Bristol, England
Printed and bound in Great Britain by
William Collins, Glasgow

Futura Publications
A Division of
Macdonald & Co (Publishers) Ltd
Greater London House
Hampstead Road
London NW1 7QX
A BPCC plc Company

For Geoff, Cindy and Ellen

Awake! for Morn in the Bowl of Night
Has flung the Stone that puts the Stars to flight:
And lo! the Hunter of the East has caught
The Sultan's Turret in a Noose of Light.

Rubayyat of Omar Khayyam

BOOK
ONE

CHAPTER 1

The hot wind surged up the steep hillside, spreading the pungent odour of oranges everywhere. Dust swirled, caught in the capricious eddies, making bellowing camels blink as they struggled under their burdens. Women in dark robes trailing on the ground, their faces swathed in veiling cloth, stopped to admire a huge mound of North African dates. Wisps of smoke bore delicious smells from small shops and whipped them among throngs of pedestrians and elegant riders fighting to keep their thoroughbreds under control. Down the hillside, deeply ravined, the River Durro sparkled in the strong light. Across the river and up the steep southern slope, the majestic towers of Alhambra were rising, caught by the sun near the final stages of frantic building. Birds sang, the songs filled with laughter. Here and there, a woman's voice seemed to blend with the birdsong, adding a tender, plaintive note.

The young girl held up her hand. Behind her a few paces in the narrow alley, an 'older' woman, quite fat and panting for breath, halted uncertainly. The young one crouched, flattening herself to the white wall, her head bent forward, listening. Again she cautioned the older woman before creeping to the end of the building. She crouched even lower at the sound of approaching hoofbeats. The girl had contracted herself into a blob of indistinct cloth at near ground level by the time the first mule flashed past. She counted ten riders, each on a muscular and energetic mount, their bodies swatched in kaftans, heads hidden in wrappings of cloth known as tailesans. No weapons showed, nor could she hear the clink and squeak of armour; to all about they must seem a normal group of travellers. To young Dinah, they didn't smell right. At the flash of the last mule's white and luxuriant tail, she turned and ran back to her companion.

'What game are we playing now?' the corpulent and winded woman groaned from behind her veil. 'Our young lady will be the death of me yet.'

'It's not a game,' Dinah hissed. 'Will you stop treating me like a child, Farida!' Dinah stamped her slipper and the one called Farida sighed wearily.

'Yes, my lady,' Farida moaned, clasping her hands beseechingly across her ample busom.

'And my name is Dinah,' the young one reminded her. 'You are not a slave, I am not a princess . . . and I have no idea what wearies you so. You do nothing but tag along with me wherever I go.'

'I *am* a slave, you know that,' Farida retorted. 'And at my age, it is sheer slavery to have to keep up with your restless feet. You will be . . .'

'. . . the death of you yet,' Dinah finished sarcastically. 'Your teeth will be the death of you. Pretty soon, you will not be able to stand on your two feet . . . you will eat your way into the grave.'

'That is most unkind,' Farida whispered dramatically; she pulled herself as erect as she could, holding her abdomen in. 'May the Queen of Heaven be blessed that others find me not unpleasing . . .'

'And *that* is another thing . . .' Dinah cut herself short and held up a warning hand. She grabbed Farida's hand and whipped her into the nearest open doorway; holding a hand over the veiled mouth, Dinah pressed the large body into the shadows just as hooves clattered up the alley. Sharply defined in the overhead light, the rider stood in the stirrups, pulling his tailesan back from his face in a sweeping gesture. A flash of light sparkled in the black, ferocious eyes as the handsome, cruel face swept the area. The reins pulled the animal's head sharply and it wheeled on its hindlegs to canter back down the alley.

'Game!' Dinah spat victoriously. 'I knew they didn't smell right. I knew it, I knew it . . . they're looking for us.'

'Us?' the poor woman squealed softly. 'Why us?'

'Why us?' Dinah repeated, catching the woman's inflection perfectly, the slightly breathless concupiscence . . . hinting at the terrible, unthinkable splendour of being harshly raped ten times. Young as she was, Dinah had mastered the emerging Spanish of the Mozarabs — something few non-Christians in Arabic Spain had bothered to do. Dinah repeated the question in Arabic without the vocal innuendo. Farida looked puzzled. She knew just enough Arabic to get along in the kitchens — and absolutely no Hebraic or Aramaic.

'Not us, really,' Dinah assured her, softening, sympathetic to the older woman's distress. 'Just me.'

'I suppose slaves are not entitled to know why that should be. I will be crucified if anything happens to you, I am supposed to protect you . . .'

'Farida, stop this! I've had just about all I wish to hear. You are to protect me from myself . . . to see that I encourage no young men. You are hardly a squadron of cavalry to protect me from a marauding gang of very professional Berber soldiers and abductors.'

Farida emitted a sound like a panic-stricken mare about to drop her first foal. Or worse, lose the contents of her intestines. Dinah shook her with twice the strength one would have expected from one as slight and girlish.

'Berbers . . . African savages?' the woman moaned finally.

'Exactly. Almohades, I'm sure. Now, keep quiet and I'll explain on the way home . . . we are going nowhere else until

I speak with Grandfather.'

The way was clear when they left the alley and began climbing the steep walk just inside the high wall. Dinah took Farida's arm and helped her up the most difficult parts, her eyes forever flickering round to make sure no riders were in the area. They passed very few souls on foot.

Lecturing Farida much as a patient mother explains to a thick-headed child how fire can burn a hand, Dinah reminded her that Solomon ha-Levi was a very important man as far as the sultan was concerned. His son, Dinah's father — referred to in Arabic as Musa ibn Suleiman — was the court physician now, but for how many years before that had Grandfather Solomon been the most honoured physician and diplomatic advisor to the great king of Granada? Yes, it is true that not many Jews play such important roles in the courts of Muslim rulers. In fact, not in well over one hundred and fifty yeas when her ancestors Samuel and Joseph ha-Levi, father and son, were prime ministers here in Granada. The sultan, Mohammad ibn Nasr al-Ansari, depended on the ha-Levis in a great many ways. If the Almohade riders captured Dinah, think how they could weaken the sultan's hand in terms of advantageous alliances. Or force an unwanted alliance upon him with that rogue, ibn Hud.

A tall Gothic eunuch stood guard at the gate to their house. He smiled and nodded as Dinah slipped by, dragging the simpering Farida behind her. Crossing the large courtyard filled with fig trees, flowers and lush ferns, they mounted the stairs, circled the balcony and entered a small south-facing study; the windows were wide open and the scent of oranges wafted up the steep incline from the River Durro below. Dinah sank down on the soft cushions and leaned her elbow on the sill. She looked directly across the valley which was more like a ravine. The walls and turrets of Alhambra gazed back at her, dazzling her eyes with their reddish glow, their stunning perfection.

'One little Jewish girl could cause all that fuss?' Farida asked querulously. Dinah smiled tolerantly and did not answer. To the Mozarabs, the local Christians accepted by the Arab rulers, everything was black and white.

'What would they have done to us . . . those barbarians?' Farida shuddered hopefully. 'Where would they have taken us?'

Dinah began laughing and shook her head; the hood fell back and she stripped off the veil that had covered her face from the eyes down. Unfastening the dark grey robe, she slipped it from her shoulders and let it fall to the cushions and the lush carpet beneath. A shower of brilliant red hair swept down past those strong shoulders and the arms lightly dotted with freckles extending from the sleeveless short jacket. The light coming through the open casement made her intensely green eyes sparkle as though the fire came from inside. She kicked off the slippers and tucked the small, perfectly formed feet under her. Once more she shook her head at the palpitating woman still wrapped in her outer robe, still hidden behind a veil. No point in telling her the Almohades would have kicked the fat girl to one side when they abducted her mistress; that was not the story poor Farida was trembling for.

'They would have thrown us over their saddle pommels, they would have whipped their mules to a frenzy and born us off to some great and impregnable fortress . . . like the Alcalá de Guadaira.'

'And then? Would they harm us, would they treat us like miserable slaves and do terrible things to us?' Farida slipped her robe off and dropped to her knees in front of Dinah. The veil came off next and the young girl smiled into the troubled blue eyes which seemed to swim in salty seas of anticipation. She was really pretty, Dinah admitted, with that dark blond hair and the classic features seen on so many of the people with Gothic and Roman blood. And so stupidly fat!

'Do you mean would they rape us? Is that what you mean by "miserable slaves"? They would not rape me, I'm too young, only a child, not yet thirteen. They would have to rape you for both of us. Hundreds of them: soldiers, cooks, grooms, slaves . . .'

'No, not the slaves,' Farida protested, her hand coming up protectively to cover her mouth.

'They don't let you pick and choose, silly ninny, you have to take them all. And I would be forced to watch. The men would pass me one by one and force me to look at those frightening things of theirs . . . and then, one by one at first, then three, four, five at a time . . .'

Farida moaned and collapsed like a fat sheep struck by lightning. Dinah turned her attention back to the stunning walls and buildings across the valley. Teams of men were on the move everywhere, crawling over walls, carrying stones, lifting heavy tubs of mortar, hammering and clanging, shouting and bellowing, whipping teams of mules and oxen hitched to heavy wagons. The sultan was dedicated to building beautiful things, particularly palaces. Surely, this would be the grandest of them all.

'Why do they treat slaves like that?' Farida whined; she sounded like she had just awoken from an erotic dream.

'If you don't stop this nonsense, I'm going to send you away.' Dinah put on a grim face to hide her incipient smile. 'You are not a slave. Your family has worked for ours on the estate for a very long time. When your father could not pay the jizyah, my father paid it for him. You were sent here to work for us in this house until the amount was made up . . . stop calling yourself a slave. If you were a slave, you would have to do some work around here or be beaten until all the fat fell from your miserable bones. If you stopped eating so much and did some work, you might appeal to men and not need all these fantasies about rape. Who'd want to rape you, who could find his way through all that?'

'You'd be surprised,' the older girl sniffed. 'The Moors and the Arabs love well-rounded, generously made women.' She sniffed even harder as Dinah's head went back, her mouth opened wide, the laughter ringing back from the richly decorated walls.

'What is jizyah?' Farida demanded, cutting through the laughter. 'I know you told me, but I can't remember.'

'I've told you a number of times.' Dinah brought herself

under control. Adonai, give me the strength, she thought. Well-rounded, generously made women . . . just look at her, O Lord. A shapeless mountain of flesh. Perhaps it would be worth it to be captured . . . if they would starve her half to death . . .

'Please, I promise to remember this time, my lady.' Farida sounded sincere.

'Do you remember what the Dhimma is?' Dinah asked sweetly, knowing the girl didn't. Only twenty, still single and acts like a grandmother when she has to walk a short way. Farida made a pretence of searching her memory, then shook her head.

'Something to do with a book?' she chanced.

'Well, there is hope,' Dinah admitted. 'We are known in Islam as the "Ahl al-Kitab", the People of the Book. The Jews have divinely revealed scriptures as do the Christians and Mohammedans. Thus we are tolerated. The "Dhimma" is the contract under which we are tolerated. We are known as the "Dhimmi", the people subject to this pact. We do as we are told, we do not do what we are told not to, we wear certain clothes to distinguish us from the "true believers" as they call themselves.' Dinah turned over the left side of her robe. There was a yellow circle of cloth stitched to the breast, an identifying label demanded of all Jews throughout Islam. 'The jizyah is a special tax we have to pay. With due humility, of course.'

'Even your noble family?' Farida was genuinely shocked. 'Can the sultan not . . .'

'Of course he could and he has offered many times,' Dinah answered with pride. 'Until the system is abolished in favour of full tolerance and freedom for all non-Muslims, we prefer to pay just like all the rest.'

Bare-footed and pensive, Dinah rose gracefully to her feet and paced across the room. Farida followed her progress, wondering at the sudden change in demeanour. She envied Dinah in every way, her clothes, her sense of style and colour, but particularly that slender, lithe body. In the ankle-gripping silk trousers, her legs moved with the grace of a cat's. When she turned, Farida blinked. Since yesterday — or was it the day before? — the girl's chest had filled in markedly. She was no longer a little girl. Farida nibbled her lower lip, wondering if she could ask an indelicate question.

'You want to know if I've reached a woman's estate in these past few days?' Dinah queried tauntingly, as though she had cloven a path straight through to the other's mind. 'Yes, the moon finally gathered me up and saddled me with every woman's burden. And you wonder why I'm so preoccupied? It is because we have not heard from my father in far too long. I'm worried . . . something tells me he's in great trouble.'

'You can read my mind can't you?' Farida accused, moving back a short way as though to remove herself from a frightening experience.

'In your case, just the face. It tells me everything. Now, be a good girl and go down to the kitchen and see what preparations are being made for this evening's meal. My poor grandfather has been gone since early morning . . . as you know, he cannot eat in the palace; Jerusalem and Mecca are not fully agreed on the niceties of dietary laws. Make sure the meal is appetising and ample. Oh,' Dinah smiled warmly and stroked Farida's face lovingly as the heavy body fought to rise. 'When you've seen to everything else, please see if there is some cool fruit and something cool to drink. Just leave it here, I'll be back in less than an hour.' Guessing the girl would ask where, Dinah pressed her palm against the mouth about to open. 'Right here in the house . . . no more questions, please.'

Watching from the balcony which squared the upper storey over the court, Dinah waited until she heard the slap of sandals diminishing down the corridor to the back of the building. The smile faded and her eyes became troubled again. Her feet hardly made a sound as she sped down the short hall leading to her grandfather's study at the eastern side of the dwelling.

Solomon's room was large, spacious and thoroughly cluttered at the same time. Dinah adored the room, her favourite in all the house. Because she had been denied entry save when invited by her grandfather? That was long ago, before her mother had died; after all, she was merely seven then, who'd want a silly little girl poking about in a serious room such as this? And the smell! It was strong, full of woodland scents, strange chemicals, the acridity of metals, the elusive memory of incense and . . . and . . . yes! the smell of purification. Her grandfather smelled like purification. As though he bathed his soul as regularly as his body. He bathed his body more frequently than the Arabs and heaven knew they were fastidious to a fault. She looked at the charts hanging from every available bit of space along all four walls. The heavens, the earth, map after map. Human bodies standing erect, flesh stripped away, the fine, accurate drawing detailing bones, veins, organs. One long table was covered with containers, retorts, a crucible and more things than she could name readily, although she could seem always to divine the purpose of all this strange equipment. And there was that other room downstairs with the heavy furnace . . . and not the one for heating bath and kitchen water. No one was ever allowed in there. Here, against the eastern wall, under a high, broad window, was another table; this one covered in manuscripts, one book piled on another. Dinah already knew nearly every one by name, knew what each contained, be it in Arabic or Hebrew. She drew a stool close to the table and sat down. Her father's last letter was still lying in the corner of the table. She had read it over and over, discussed it with her grandfather and even cried. Her grandfather became very stern, a side of him she seldom saw; you'd think she were a boy the way he rebuked her weakness. Still, nothing answered the question about her father.

She glanced down the short letter briefly and then concentrated. He had left six months ago. Her idiot cousins got themselves into some sort of trouble, just what had never been clear. They had gone to Ghazna . . . Dinah jumped down and sped across the room to a large map. Tracing with a finger, she crossed the Mediterranean to

Sinai. Then across land to the Red Sea. Another boat ... her finger followed the coast past the gulf entrance to the shore of Ghazna. With good winds, eight, maybe nine weeks?

Back at the table, she glared at the letter again. Her father and cousins were meeting a caravan returning from Cathay to exchange goods; then that caravan would go on to Egypt. Moses and the cousins starting back with some things to leave in the Chazar kingdom. Did they get there ... was it possible they could be prisoners in Ghazna?

About three hundred years earlier, even before the time of the great Samuel ha-Levi, many of the family had gone to this new and vital kingdom in Central Asia. Mahmud the Great was king for years — he was only twenty-seven when he succeeded his father. Dinah's grandfather had described what a fantastic man Mahmud had been. His kingdom rivalled the best of Baghdad, scholars collected from everywhere and there was no religious persecution, no forced conversions. He even used Hindu troops against his Islamic enemies ... an open-minded visionary, grandfather had termed him. They would be dealing with their own family there; who would take members of his own family as hostages for ransom?

Captured by the Chazars? Ridiculous, the Chazars had been converted to Judaism long ago. She smiled, remembering the patriarch's story. Six hundred years earlier, King Bulon of the Chazars won a great victory through the good offices of the One Supreme and Only God. The one worshipped by Jews, Christians and Muslims. He felt a great conviction that he should convert to the 'true' religion ... but which one was true? First he called a Muslim to a private consultation and the Muslim he chose was learned — so learned he was a 'Hafiz', a man who knew the Qur'an by heart. The king asked him if he had to choose — if there were no Mohammad, no Qur'an, would he become a Christian or a Jew? At the time, the feeling of enmity between Christians and Muslims in that area was ferocious. The Islamic scholar chose Judaism. The same question was put to an anchorite who immediately opted for Judaism for the very same reason. The Jew smiled. But, he said, there is a Torah, there has been a Torah since before your people were a people. I will not choose, there is nothing to choose. Since then the Chazars were Jews . . . would they capture those two thick-skulled cousins? Still, that letter had arrived over three months ago.

Face puckered, lips compressed and brow creased, the young girl stared out the window to the east, then through the south-facing window and the view of the fortress-palace with its majestic snow-covered backdrop of sierras. She must concentrate, force her brain to think this out. Why was it only by chance, now and then, that she got visions, sudden realisations of what had happened or was about to happen . . . or was able to read a person's mind without even being aware of it? Why couldn't she make this gift work for her when she needed it? What went on in Farida's silly little mind was hardly important.

Idly, she opened a manuscript. Her grandfather's elegant script stared up at her. His hand was as pure as his heart, soul and mind, she told herself. 'Isaac ben Abraham, known also in the Land of Oc as Isaac the Blind, assures the student that transmission of the Hokmah Nistarah — The Hidden Wisdom — is unbroken from Adam. God taught the Secrets of Numbers and Correspondences to Gabriel; Gabriel taught this Mystery of the Tree of Life to Adam and so it has passed down to the first son in each generation.' There were more explanatory notes and then another entry concerning a long visit to Gerona where Solomon, as a very young man, had studied in the company of such famous scholars as Moses ben Nachman. In Egypt with Moses Maimonides, in Spain with ibn Rashid and ibn al-Arabi, one of the greatest Sufi masters the world had ever known. There, in the margin, in the style of the Talmudic masters, her grandfather had inscribed as a commentary a brief poem by the master, al-Arabi: 'My heart is capable of every form/ A cloister for the monk, a fane for idols/ A pasture for gazelles, the votary's mosque/ The tables of the Torah, the Qur'an/ Love is the creed I hold: wherever turn/ His camels, Love is still my creed and faith.'

She remembered clearly her grandfather quoting that poem to her, saying: 'The Christians and the Muslims could easily put a man to death for such apparent blasphemy, perhaps even the Jews. But what has he said save the very thing said by the saintly Hillel at the time of Christ's birth?'

Her hand slid across the table and she stroked the large pile of scrolls. Hour after hour she had spent here during Solomon's long absences, reading about these terrifying mysteries . . . the Sacred Qabala, could it really make such incredible miracles happen? She opened the scroll further: 'Book of the Final Mystery' it was called. By Solomon ben Ysrael ha-Levi. 'The foundation of the Tree of Life is Yesod.' She shivered with excitement and moved on.

An hour later her hands darted under the edge of the table instinctively to prevent her from falling sideways. 'I fell asleep!' she gasped with shame and annoyance. Under her hand she become aware of a large metal object. Her fingers moved up and down . . . it was a key. Slipping off the stool she bent over deeply and twisted her neck. A large iron key, it was, held fast to the underside of the table by curved steel clips. She sank down, squatting on her heels, her breath caught up behind her throat: she was mesmerised by the key . . . it seemed to shimmer with a life of its own. Now, her chest pumped frantically. It was the key to the forbidden room downstairs! She had never seen it before, but she knew with absolute certainty. Impulsively, her hand shot out and she yanked it free.

CHAPTER 2

Solomon stood in the empty assembly hall, leaning against the recess of the large window looking out over the vast western plain — the *Vega* — which swept on for miles and miles to the almost hazily invisible low hills beyond which the sun would soon sink. In one hand he held a letter with an official seal on the wax closure. One carefully manicured finger-nail tapped the paper slowly and rhythmically.

The sultan's confidential advisor and, in his son's absence, temporarily court physician again, was very tall and well-built, just short of appearing too slender; even in the short-sleeved jubbah of fine lightweight wool, a great deal of hidden power seemed to emanate from that slender frame. Despite the long silver hair and beard, Solomon looked far too vital and virile to be approaching seventy. The sleeveless robe and the soft, fitted cap were pale lemon yellow. Although it had never been mentioned, Solomon knew his liege would be offended if someone so close to his inner government wore the yellow circle over the left breast of his robe required of Jews. Still, perhaps with a touch of irony, Solomon showed a marked preference for pale yellows in his court dress.

The patriarch's eyes were deeply set and wavered between light blue and blue-green, easily discernible as mirroring his granddaughter's. The nose was long and aquiline, slight and narrow at the nostril and surmounted by a sharp ridge just below the eyebrows, a shape more often ascribed to Romans than to Semites. The heavy, highly arched eyebrows were white and thick, lending a commanding mien to his face; beneath the moustache, his mouth was soft and full, hinting at kindness and passion, as the high sweeping brow bespoke intelligence — and perhaps wisdom.

The deeply set eyes flickered away from the landscape he so loved and lighted on the letter in his hand. The man was certain of the contents. Too many rumours had already reached them concerning the dedicated Christian king from Castile. Virtuous to a fault, a kind man and a generous one by all accounts: his people referred to him already as San Fernando ... and the man was only forty-six, forty-seven. He exhibited every tendency of a peace-loving man, a man who would go out of his way to avert suffering and hardship for ordinary people; he was also deeply religious: ever since this madness called the crusades had started, motivated Christians were morally obliged to wage war against The Infidel. The Islamic obligation was the same: *jihad*, the holy war or struggle until the entire world of Infidels saw the light and converted to the 'True Faith'.

Solomon laughed softly with a detectable tinge of bitterness. In the middle, as always, were the Jews. No holy war, no crusades, just simple measures: persecution, humiliation, massacre, wholesale theft of property, expulsion; but convert and say the magic words and all is forgiven. No more persecution, no more assaults, no more restrictions and outrages ... you can even marry a nice Muslim lady. Why laugh, look how many have converted ... how many Christians too.

Annoyed with his wandering and impotent thoughts, he returned his attention to the letter. Did Fernando know the difference between Arabian civilisation and North African barbarity? Did he suspect what a great and peaceful king ruled Andalucia now, a man who thought of the prosperity of his people, not of war and conquest. Of course he did . . . but it would not stop the southward march of his forces. They would attack Jaen. They would devastate the countryside. While the noble-minded Christian king agonised over the plight of innocent non-combatants, the old, the women and children, his less conscientious and primitive soldiers would lay waste to the land, raping, looting and burning as they went. The three letters, w-a-r stood for woe, atrocity and rape.

The large door across the room, carved exquisitely by a master craftsman, swung open and the king strode in. Voices carried from the large hall outside: 'Malik karim, malik karim.' Beseeching courtiers and supplicants greeted the monarch ceremoniously as 'noble king'. The noble king entered, waving guards and the press of people back. When the door closed, all was quiet again. Only the two men stood facing each other, more like equals than second class subject and king. One Yemenite of the Khazrej and Ansar tribes, one Israelite of the priestly Levi tribe, both pedigrees of ancient distinction, looked at each other and shrugged, smiling like old friends who chance upon each other by lucky accident. Not quite as tall as the Jewish patriarch, Muhammad ibn Nasr al-Ansari, known as al-Ahmar, was equally imposing in his own way — and every inch the thoughtful monarch.

Darkly handsome, his black beard speckled with silver quite early for a man in his mid-forties, the sultan wore a simple robe much like Solomon's but in deep blue. A very simple turban surrounded his head. Ignoring the gilded throne on its dais, he signalled Solomon politely, pointing to a delicate divan nearby.

'And don't start calling me noble king, if you don't mind, you old sorcerer, I feel far from noble today,' the king suggested agreeably. 'What's that?'

'A message from the captain leading the provision train to Jaen, I believe,' ha-Levi answered, proferring the sealed letter.

'Well, open it and read . . .' the king stopped and looked up. His counsellor was still standing. 'More bad news?' He had unshakeable faith in Solomon's cognitive powers. He didn't think the seer had to open a letter to know its contents.

Solomon broke the seal and unfolded the paper. His eyes seemed to make one sweeping glance only; he lowered the letter and sat down next to al-Ahmar with extraordinarily youthful elasticity.

'The good Saint Ferdinand is on the verge of attacking Jaen. His wily officers set a trap for the goods train and our men have started a rapid retreat . . . though I'm sure some of the hotheads were keen to stay and make dead heroes of themselves.'

'Does my wise advisor think our men are so inferior to the Castilians?'

'No, sire, but 500 horsemen would not make anything but a small dent in that army . . . they're hardened, they've been campaigning constantly and they have the taste of blood as well as vastly superior numbers.'

'What are you suggesting?' the king demanded, bridling. 'We simply hand the Castilian the keys to Granada and all our domains . . .'

'Please, my lord, it is not that simple.' Solomon sighed, folded the letter and wagged his head reflectively a few times. More as though speaking to himself than to his sovereign, he reviewed the current situation. While many Christians from the north did not differentiate between Moors and Arabs, Solomon was sure that Ferdinand was quite aware not only of that difference, but of the differences between Yemenites and Syrians, between Shi'ites and Sunnis. It was only logical that al-Ahmar and Ferdinand shared many objectives, concepts and sympathies in common. They were both concerned primarily for the welfare of their people. They would both like to drive the last of the vicious, barbaric Africans — the Almohades — out of Spain. Together, they could do it . . . together, they could bring down Seville. Both kings desired peace, both were deeply religious and charitable men. All of Spain would be well-served if they worked hand in hand. Spain would suffer irreparably if they became sworn enemies.

'Being a bit less charmingly diplomatic for a moment, dear Solomon,' the king interrupted, 'what I think you mean is *not* a partnership, but one al-Ahmar bending the knee and recognising the Castilian as his overlord . . . as have the Beni Hud and a few others, just to save their skins, purses and a few shreds of pride.'

'My lord, I have given this a great deal of thought. You are not a petty king, a village chieftain calling himself king. Ferdinand knows your reputation. As a man of peace, you have long been a splendid and well trained warrior, thanks to your Uncle Yahya. Ferdinand will not treat with you as a petty prince.'

'Come, old wily one, just what are you advising me to do? Hand my empire over to this Christian without a struggle . . . to go down in history as a cowardly dog?' The king sounded stern but Solomon was not fooled.

'I know you too well, dear "malik karim", the welfare of your people means more to you than praise for bravery. I believe, if we handle this as adroitly as is possible, the crushing war machine of the north will skirt all this part of Andalucia. With your diplomatic skills, we will be able to avert endless bloodshed . . . unnecessary bloodshed. If we fight him, the Castilian will eventually wrest everything from us, leaving a trail of carnage. If we help him, we will save untold thousands of lives and farms, he will come to depend upon us far more than we depend upon him. And when the Umayyads, the Beni Hud, the Abbadites and Almoravides are mere memories fading away, the Nasr Dynasty will be merely reaching its zenith.'

'It sounds ideal and I have absolute faith in your visionary powers, good chancellor, but if Ferdinand puts my kingdom to sword and torch, I cannot stand idly by and call myself king. I am obliged to defend my people,' al-Ahmar declared vehemently.

'There is no argument there,' Solomon assured him. 'At

least a token struggle is politically mandatory. You must be seen to do your duty and the populace must realise they cannot beat the Castilian. If they don't discover that, they will insist they could have beaten him.'

'You recommend marching immediately?' the king asked with surprise, Solomon's apparent change of tactic coming as a shock.

'Let events come to us, if you will, my lord. We wait until the lion's maw is opened wide before we jump in. A citizen army of farmers and merchants, tradesmen and craftsmen, will hardly be a match for the hardened professionals in Ferdinand's standing army . . . long standing, I might add.'

'Do I detect a subtle rebuke?' the sultan inquired. 'The kingdom would have been better served had the king concentrated on soldiers instead of husbandmen?'

'My lord, my people gave up mass murder many ages ago. On the contrary, I think and have thought for a long time that you are a wise, a good, an ethical prince . . . a veritable star in the Yemenite crown. Ferdinand is the victim of his destiny. We must make the necessary show of hostility, then the obvious one of conciliation. Then we help him to aim himself correctly on the path to his destiny. Toward Seville and the last stronghold of the Berbers . . . not toward here where the civilised tradition of Córdoba now abides.'

'Will we send out a force to protect the returning supply train? What does the letter say, are they desperate?'

'I don't think they will be pursued too far, your majesty. The Castilians will not overstretch their lines like that right now. When the troops do return, we must find a way to reward the cool heads who turned the train and brought it home safely, while at the same time praising the hotheads for their devoted show of courage.'

There was a discreet knock on the door and Solomon rose to stride lightly and rapidly across the room. Holding the door slightly ajar, he bent his head forward and listened intently for a moment or two before easing the door closed and returning to his monarch.

'Two different police details have brought news of a

strange sort. What at first seemed one visiting merchant here, a few more there, suddenly coalesced into a force of ten riders on extremely powerful and carefully bred mules. One informant swears they are unusually large, more like African breeding.' Solomon paused, cocked his head and waited for al-Ahmar's response.

'A force of ten Almohades inside these walls . . .?' the King was on his feet in a bound. 'A raiding party . . . for what?'

Instinctively or intuitively, Solomon's head turned and he stared across the Durro valley to the hill on which his own house stood. There definitely was a cloud of dust.

'My liege,' he whispered, his throat constricted, 'would you think me mad if I asked you to despatch a detail of household cavalry to my house immediately . . . and would you excuse me . . .'

The sultan was beside the older man, his eyes narrowed. 'Go at once, take them with you. But don't let those villains capture you . . . I see the plot now . . .'

Before he could finish the sentence, Solomon had fled from the audience chamber.

Galloping up the hill, the captain of the guard had everything he could do to hold Solomon far back enough to allow the armed cavalry to lead. They rounded a corner of the wall to see three mounted men furiously trying to control their frenzied beasts. Four men were sprawled on the ground, blood pouring from numerous wounds. One more leaned against the wall of Solomon's house, a broken sword on the ground next to him, his tailesan torn from his head and held up to his neck to staunch the flow of blood. His eyes were glazing over and he had the bewildered look of an imbecile — or a man who had been terrified nearly to death. Suddenly, two more men came limping from the house, also covered in ghastly wounds. There was not a sign of the other mules.

One of the cavalry men raised his sword, yelled with demonic glee and rode toward the mounted raiders.

Solomon roared and the horseman drew his mount up sharp, turning quizzically in his saddle. He saw Solomon on the ground, crouching over the dazed man leaning against the wall. Bounding to his feet, he shouted to the captain of the guard.

'Take these men back to Alhambra and see that their wounds are dressed ... give them every care, but guard them carefully. There are a good many questions to be answered.' Without waiting for an answer, he turned and raced inside the building. As he passed through the court, he heard stifled sobs above. The cook, two other servants and that silly fool Farida were cowering near the balustrade, clutching each other and whining.

'Where is Dinah?' he roared at them like a maddened bull.

The stammering and cries blended but he detected something articulate which sounded like '*that* room'. Racing down the hall, turning and still at speed he made for the last door beyond the kitchen. Flinging himself against the door, he found it locked as he guessed it would be. He also became aware of the eerie, chilling sound that made the hair all over his body stand erect.

With imperious scorn, banishing the terror which had obviously infested the Berber soldiers, he stood tall, then crouched and smashed the heel of his hand against the large lock. Even to his surprise, it split asunder and fell to the ground. He pushed the door in and ignored the terrible waves of nausea, forcing himself against the sound of a hell risen to earth.

The room was filled with noxious vapours and Solomon found it difficult to discern anything clearly ... save his granddaughter's form, lying prone and face down in the centre of a double chalk circle. With the alacrity of a leopard, the patriarch leapt over the circle, landing with his legs splayed, his body crouched protectively over the child's. Glaring, he fixed his eyes on the dense cloud hovering over a triangle chalked on the floor a short distance outside the twin circles. His scrutiny was greeted by a derisive laugh;

there was as much begrudging mirth in that sound as there was anything cruel or inhuman — yet . . .

'The danger has passed, you old fool,' a vibrant voice mocked him from the thick cloud of vapour. Solomon scooped the girl's body from the floor, gathering her close to his breast. Even in the gloom, the large ring on the third finger of his right hand flashed with unlikely light. The hexagram — the Seal of Solomon — was aimed at the source of the voice.

'You Chosen People will never learn, will you?' the voice teased. 'We Muslims are like the Christians in our choice of stars . . . five points, not six. You think that will stop me, you careless dabbler?'

'Who are you that calls me such names?' Solomon demanded fearlessly. 'Did this girl summon you here . . . if so, how?'

'See? That's how careless you are. You don't even know.' A shimmering green arm emerged from the vapour, the muscles rippling with preternatural strength; an accusing finger pointed to a spot just outside the circles. A scroll was lying on the floor, its edges singed as though it had been hastily withdrawn from a fire. Solomon immediately recognized it as his own book on Qabalistic lore. He was about to stretch out his foot to draw it inside the circles when the laugh echoed again. The pointing finger wiggled suggestively, and the scroll bounded inside the circles, landing next to the old man's foot.

'Before I perform the banishing ceremony,' the patriarch warned, 'I demand to know your name . . . who are you?'

'You did not summon me, she did not summon me and you cannot banish me. I'm not one of your playful Israeli spirits who bound in and out of this world every time some careless idiot like you draws pictures on the floor, burns some incense and mumbles a lot of inane gibberish.'

'Why do you call me a careless idiot, whoever you are?' It was now obvious Solomon was losing control of his temper.

The vapour vanished, the room glowed with a greenish light and, standing fully revealed and solid before the chancellor was an incredible figure. Muscular, green-skinned, beardless but with bright red hair crudely cut and long enough to sit on his shoulders, the demon folded his arms over his chest and regarded the old man disdainfully.

'Why?' he asked. 'With your precious granddaughter unconscious — you fool, you don't know how close she was to death or worse — with the hellish stench that filled this room just before you — and I — arrived . . . all this and you ask me why? She made one small mistake, oh mighty Solomon, because you didn't bother to teach her adequately. She didn't perform the banishing ceremony first and something unsavoury lurked behind an open door between worlds.' The demon pointed downward. Like Saint Michael, his foot was holding a squirming creature pinned to the tiled floor. 'She summoned the right one, well enough, but the wrong one slipped in behind him.'

'Let me up!' a small querulous voice barked, the words coming out more like a series of inhibited belches. The demon looked down.

'Can you feel it or smell it still?' he asked with a tender solicitude which belied the foot pressing the creature down. The small mannikin shook his head violently. 'Don't lie . . . if that monster gets back in here he may blow us all to hell.'

'I promise,' the little one said. 'I swear by all that's earthy.'

The demon relented and the small thing sat up, rubbing its pot belly. It was a gnome, Solomon realised suddenly. Dinah had summoned a gnome? he wondered to himself.

'That's right,' the demon assured him, snatching the thought from Solomon's mind. 'Not a bad choice, either,' he added with a touch of admiration. 'And as to your next question, she wants to find her father and his lame-brained nephews . . .' The demon swung toward the door as the sound of running feet reached them.

'Bubbi . . . the door,' he commanded. The gnome leapt up and shot to the door, picking up the lock, slamming it against the wood, the lock sticking there, the door slamming, the key turning and the gnome back sitting in the triangle as though he'd never moved.

A heavy fist hammered on the stout wood. 'Are you all right, my Lord Chancellor?' the captain's deep voice echoed off the outer walls.

'Yes, captain, do not worry ... I shall be there soon.' The demon's lips moved; there was no sound but Solomon distinctly 'heard' him say: 'Ask if they have found the other mules.' Solomon did so.

'Oh, yes, sir,' the captain said in a muffled, fearful voice. 'Behind the house in one great mound. Eyes wide with terror, lips and noses still frothing ... each and every one with its entrails torn loose ... as if a mighty claw had shot up from beneath the ground and torn their bellies apart.'

'Keep an eye on your prisoners, captain, and calm yourself. I will join you shortly.' Solomon was finally beginning to feel a nameless terror chill his marrow and he tried not to communicate it to the obviously shaken soldier. When the footsteps were no longer audible, the demon laughed softly once more.

'Well, Bubbi,' he addressed the gnome, 'you seem to have acquired some rather awesome powers, have you not?' The gnome wriggled slightly with pleasure at such lavish praise from so truly awesome a personage, then looked down shyly without answering. Solomon was conscious of a sudden liking for the impish creature his dangerously foolish granddaughter had conjured up.

Solomon bowed his head slightly in a token of gratitude and esteem. The demon smiled in the manner of a parent who, after many years, is recognized as intelligent by his child.

'The evil spirit who entered here unbidden — and yes, the carelessness was mine — you drove him hence?' The demon nodded the minutest assent. 'He wreaked his vengeance on those poor mules?' Again the demon nodded slightly. 'And the soldiers ... the Almohade agents ...'

'Were here to abduct your daughter. I believe she knew about it earlier ... part of the rite she was working here was a plea for an amulet of protection. I set them against one another so I could be free to drive out the fiend.' Laughing, he pointed to the burden in Solomon's arms. 'Set her on her feet, she will recover now. Be a bit weak for a while. And as soon as her wits are gathered, will you lose no time in preparing her properly for what she came here to do?'

'I cannot do that!' Solomon shrank back without moving his feet, as if he had moved deeper inside himself. He stuttered with indignation. 'The secret . . . the inner holy doctrines are transmissable only through the first son . . . since Adam . . .'

'And who was Adam's first son?'

'Why Cain, of course,' the seer replied automatically.

'You don't see the irony?' the demon chided. Solomon flushed and looked down. 'Your son Moses . . . you taught him, didn't you? What did he do with the knowledge?'

'This is his only child . . . his wife died . . . he will not take another . . .'

'And if you don't teach her, the smartest one in your family, your great learning dies with you . . . to say nothing of the next time she tries something, ill-prepared as she is: she may well die, because I can't do your job for you. Think, you fool, use your head and forget your complicated rabbinical prejudices.' Solomon winced when the green fury paused. 'Put her down, I say!'

Solomon let Dinah slip down until her bare feet touched the ground. The demon's arm shot out and sparks flew from his fingers. The girl's eyes flew open. She looked at the green figure with hair red but darker than her own and opened her mouth to scream. Just then, she caught sight of the gnome; he was looking up at her adoringly, his hands crossed over his heart, pressing it as though to show its maddened beat. Her face broke into a glorious smile.

'Dinah!' The huge, overgrown boy — for the demon looked more that than a man, save for the area of his groin where extremely large parts were suspended (indeed the penis was even striped with bands of silver) — this large boy snapped his fingers to attract the girl's attention. Green eyes like saucers darted from the adoring gnome, to the outlandish appendage, back to the gnome, up to the green face.

'Dinah,' he repeated, 'your grandfather is going to teach you the mysteries you have rather perilously tinkered with . . . and you are not to do anything like this again until you are fully prepared. Is that understood?' A look of defiance moved slowly over her no longer smiling features. His sharp, snarling laugh banished the rebellion. 'Do you not remember what entered this room . . .?' Her cry broke his sentence in half. She grabbed her grandfather's arm and held on tightly, shuddering.

'Who are you?' the old man asked once more. 'Why are you doing all this for us?'

'For *her*!' The green boy corrected. 'She is extraordinary. Have you been so preoccupied you didn't think about her vision? She can see Bubbi here — as you can — with no smoke of incense. She can see me whether I will her to or not. How long did it take you to perfect yourself that far?'

Solomon looked down at the girl who was now standing freely and exhibiting no fear. He put his arm over her shoulder and hugged her.

'She was born that way, Suleiman,' the demon announced, using the Arabic form of the old man's name. 'Or should I call you Salaam as your mother did?'

'She called me Sholem, but it means the same. You're telling me the child is naturally gifted?'

'With a potential beyond your wildest guess. We want you to do everything to help her fulfil that potential . . . is that asking too much?'

'Again, who are you . . . the "we" you speak of?'

'My name is Musa — Moses — the same as your son. My great grandfather is interested in this gifted girl . . . so is Isa ben Maryam.'

'Isa ben Maryam? That is the name of the Christian messiah . . .'

'Yes, but this is a different one . . . my great-grandfather's godson . . .'

'And who is your great-grandfather? He is still alive?'

The demon smiled and shook his head. 'He is not alive in

any sense you would deem viable . . . but he still exerts a lot of influence — particularly on men's minds. He wrote a book . . . Mishqat al-Ahzia.'

'A Niche for Shoes? Are you serious? Or are you mocking the great al-Ghazali who wrote A Niche for Lights?'

'Mishqat al-Anwar,' the demon repeated. 'Think about it.'

'Mishqat al-Anwar,' the seer muttered, repeating it two or three times more. Dinah looked up, puzzled, trying to read his troubled face. Suddenly he gasped. 'Anwar? Anwar ibn Mohammad al-Hazza?'

'That's right . . . Anwar the Shoemaker.'

'One of the greatest saints . . . over four hundred years ago . . .' Solomon was visibly stunned. 'And Isa . . .?'

'One of the invisible ones . . . like Khidr, the one in the green robe who appears mysteriously when he is needed. But we must be off now . . . Bubbi!' The gnome jumped, tearing his eyes away from Dinah. 'Tell her how to summon you back . . . for the time being, I don't want her to try this again.' The green arm swept the room.

Dinah was to make the likeness of a frog out of very dark mahogany. The mouth should be open and the frog kept in a small cask full of earth from the farthest corner of the garden . . . well, full but leaving room for the frog to sit on top. When she wanted Bubbi, she was to spill a few drops of the rich, sweet wine used for ceremonial purposes into the frog's mouth . . . but if the wine had been already sanctified, she must never forget to drop a mustard seed in first and pronounce a banishing or de-sanctifying incantation. Otherwise, he would be so badly burnt it would take ages to recover. His wife Momo would not like that. Furthermore, he would never be able to return to Dinah again.

The burbling, burping voice reached the end of the detailed instructions. There was a bright flash and the room was plunged into darkness. The lock fell off the door and it swung open lazily, admitting the late afternoon light.

'Stand directly in front of me,' Solomon ordered, 'and press your body close to mine. Do exactly as I tell you, child.'

He pointed to the four cardinal points of the compass: she was to keep them in her mind and visualise a large hexagram in each, all joined together by a bright ring of fire. She was to visualise this with such fierce concentration, the illusion would seem to take on a positive reality of its own. She was to pay unwavering attention to the banishing ceremony; it would purify the room and she must commit it to memory.

He felt the girl rise to her toes; the tangible forces in the room seemed to multiply. He had done this ceremony so often the hexagrams and the linking fire did seem to appear. Solomon ben Ysrael ha-Levi blinked his eyes and gasped. There were four stars glowing around them, bright as the stars in the sky. Perfect ones, with six points, radiating a heavenly light. And the fire! It was hot enough to cook an ox! This mere child was manifesting what many would call the impossible, what the ancients spent a lifetime to develop, what the illuminated called an aport. Solomon gazed down at her head. A glowing aura surrounded it.

With deep and reverent awe he began the ritual. 'Ateh Gibor L'Olohim Adonai,' he intoned.

The girl's voice was perfectly synchronised with his, as though she had heard the words in his mind just before they reached his lips: 'Thou art mighty forever, O Lord . . .'

CHAPTER 3

'Please be seated, noble minister,' the sultana smiled engagingly and motioned to the cushions near her. 'So, this is the fabled grandchild I've heard so much about. An outstanding scholar, is that true?'

Solomon was one of the few, the very few, men in his court who al-Ahmar permitted in the women's quarters whenever he wished. It was considered one of the greatest marks of confidence; the chancellor accepted it with a dubious shrug. Possibly his sovereign considered his servant beyond the screacking cry of passion. It was certainly not true as far as this delightful lady was concerned. There were others — though the sultan was extremely modest: a few concubines to keep up appearances, only a singing girl here and there to entertain guests — but there was only one sultana. She had an excellent singing voice herself — the sultan never asked anyone else to sing for him — and her nickname, 'The Nightingale,' was in such general use her actual name was never heard.

'Where are the monkeys?' Solomon asked, hoping to distract her from a performance on Dinah's part. She was still quietly seething, absolutely furious with him. There was no other safe way: the child had to stay under guard at the palace until the treaty with Ferdinand was agreed. The next attempt to abduct the child and use her as a bargaining hostage might prove fatal . . . to her and the future of Spain. For the life of him, he could not yet deduce what ibn Hud, the other Yemenite king who still was nominally sovereign of Seville as well as Murcia and other principalities, was up to. More likely it was that rogue prime minister of his, Yusuf ibn Yakub al-Ziyad — al-Ziyad indeed. The upstart claimed direct descent from Tariq al-Ziyad, the man who conquered Spain for the Arabs.

'Are you still with us, noble minister?' the queen asked sweetly. His granddaughter reached up surreptitiously and pinched his elbow. Although his skin had been darkened to polished mahogany by years of travel under desert suns, he still blushed, and warned himself not to let his thoughts distract him so.

'Sorry, my lady, an important affair of state . . .'

'I know how burdened you are, noble sir. The sultan sings praises to your enterprise and diligence all the time. I said, I had to get rid of the monkeys. We let them run about a small private garden Muhammad gave me for my own use . . . they were forever scratching and *everyone* started scratching for fleas or staying too long in the baths to soothe themselves with unguents and hot water.'

'Perhaps birds would be more congenial . . . peacocks, maybe?' Solomon asked, sincerely desiring to be helpful.

'That terrible whistling screech? Minister, you can't be serious, I'd be driven insane in less than a week.' She gave him no chance to prepare elaborate and poetical apologies. 'You must stop distracting me and tell me all about this pretty girl . . . actually, she is beautiful. From whence came the red hair and green eyes? I am no geographer, but I do remember what you call the Promised Land is very close to Arabia . . . have you seen green eyes and red hair on many Arabs, dear child?' She asked Dinah.

'Only on demons, your majesty,' Dinah answered seriously. 'It seems they all have very red hair and . . .'

'I forgot to mention that Dinah has a very vivid imagination,' Solomon rumbled, flashing the briefest warning to the girl.

'Allah be praised,' the queen of nightingales chuckled musically. 'How drab life would be without it. While she is our guest, Dinah and I can amuse each other by inventing new tales to add to the legend of Haroun al-Rashid, may Allah give him peace.'

'I'd like that,' Dinah said enthusiastically.

'Thank you very much, your gracious majesty, is the correct form of address. Where did you leave your manners, child?' her grandfather rebuked.

'Good Solomon, please. In this area, poor as it is, I reign. Even the king bows to my distempers here. Dinah is to treat me like any member of her family. Whatever will I be able to learn from a clever young lady who has studied, even learnt to read ... Dinah,' she turned to the youngster with girlish enthusiasm; in the blink of an eye, Solomon was watching two happy children beginning to play together. 'Dinah, will you read to me just a little ... please?'

Dinah looked up to her grandfather, hoping he would not make her perform. His stern rebuke gazed back at her. The look said: for your own protection, for the safety of your family, you are entrusted to the queen of a great realm ... not many have that privilege ... please stop being a spoilt little thornbush and do as you're told.

'I'd be pleased to, my lady,' Dinah answered, nearly choking on the lie. Nightingale called a serving girl and sent her to ask the chief eunuch for a book of poems ... love poems. Almost immediately, the large, fat scowling face glared down at them. He thrust forth a copy of the Qur'an.

'Not that!' the queen protested, coming perilously close to blasphemy. 'I said love poems, something musical the child will enjoy reading.'

Solomon saw it even as the eunuch had approached; he had easily read on his face the intense hatred the two visitors had engendered in his twisted mind. A converted ex-Christian from France, he hated Jews with a vengeance only converts seemed able to muster. He thought of Saul of Tarsus . . . a Jew. He converted himself to Christianity . . . practically inventing the religion single-handedly and along with it, anti-Judaism.

'She loves it,' Solomon sighed softly. 'Besides, dear lady, this inspired book of revealed truths is filled with sublime poetry.' He nodded to Dinah who took the book from the offended hand. Solomon smiled . . . the eunuch hated them but could not read the book he professed to revere. Still, neither could the mighty sultana . . . few Muslim women could; in fact, among the Jews, Dinah was a rarity.

The classic cadences of the surahs were given a perfect rendering by the child, her voice pitch, the changes in emotive strengths, the lilt of emphasis so haunting and exact she could easily have shamed some of the religious leaders of the court. Dinah closed her eyes and rested the book on her knee. The melody flowed on, one surah sounding more impassioned than the last. She did not stop for nearly ten minutes, never once again looking at the pages before her. Even the hard-hearted eunuch backed off in surprise, although he showed no awe or respect if he felt any.

'She is a hafiz?' whispered the queen, awe clearly written on her features. 'She knows the Qur'an by heart?' Solomon nodded with humility. 'How?' the queen fairly squeaked. 'Honoured Solomon, she is not even Muslim.'

'She taught herself. Granted, God gifted her with a perfect memory, may the Lord be praised. When she was trying to teach herself Arabic — to read and write, I mean, she spoke it from infancy — I gave her a copy of the Qur'an and the Traditions of the Prophet. I told her there was no better source for perfecting her knowledge not only of the language, but what the language meant spiritually. She took me seriously and stored it all in her heart.'

'Can she do that with any other language?' the queen asked with genuine reverence.

'Hebrew — there, I was her teacher, but she needed me only for that one, the first language. After that, the concept of language was hers. Now she can read, write and converse in Arabic, Hebrew, Aramaic, Castilian and, of course, our everyday Ladino dialect of it . . . yes, she knows Latin and Greek, but not to speak . . . the same with Persian.'

'When you discussed her with me before, you said she was only about thirteen . . . I don't understand.'

'Well, she tends to be a bit lazy now and then. I had hoped she would have mastered a few more by now, it would certainly be helpful in the merchanting part of our enterprises . . .'

'Solomon ha-Levi! Don't you dare trifle with me . . .' the queen exploded. The patriarch laughed and shook his head.

'Madame, she started all this when she was not quite three. I assure you, she startles me all the time . . .' he paused to cast a quick glance at the girl . . . 'not least the other day when those Almohade marauders were after her. She was on her way home with a girl who is supposed to take care of her . . . she heard the Africans and hid. She sensed who they were, what they were after and ran straight home.'

The queen brightened and clapped her hands happily. 'She is a magician as well? Wonderful, she will be able to teach me to read with no difficulty.' She drew Dinah to her and hugged the girl. Solomon was happy to see the girl's response was eager, warm and genuine. Lord, he prayed silently in his heart, may you only see fit to create a place in this queen's heart for one more child. She needs a surrogate mother so much.

'Your majesty,' Dinah pronounced solemnly, 'there is no *magic* way to learn. You will lose patience with me, you will scold and perhaps have me flogged, but I will not give up. I will make you learn. Learning and knowledge are the only things which can set women free.'

'DINAH!' her grandfather roared, half rising to his feet. 'How dare you speak that way to her majesty?'

Nightingale moved herself in front of Dinah protectively. She glared a warning at the patriarch and asked Dinah over her shoulder: 'That sounds very good, Dinah, just what made you say it?'

'A woman named Rab'iah al-Adawiyah who lived over

four hundred years ago, your majesty. She invented losing oneself totally in the love of God. She became one of the greatest saints in Islam. People came from everywhere to be her pupils, to study with her as Sufic disciples. She was revered and looked up to by everyone . . . not just a woman, but a great person, greater than most men. Knowledge freed her from the slavery of women.'

Solomon began to quake with angry concern, but the queen merely shook an impatient finger at him. 'Why do you say we are slaves, child?' she asked softly, waving the attentive eunuch out of earshot.

'Your majesty . . .' Dinah stated solemnly, endeavouring to control her rising emotions.

'If I always call you Dinah, will you not call me Nightingale? We would sound more like friends, don't you think?' This quick shift of attention banished the upsurge of emotions. Dinah smiled and nodded.

'There are slaves, dhimmi and women,' Dinah offered. 'If a slave works hard, pleases his master and saves, is enterprising, he can buy his freedom. The dhimmi, be he Christian or Jew, merely has to say: "La illah il Allah, wa Muhammad rasul Allah" and he is a convert . . . no course of instructions, no papers to sign . . . just that one expression: "There is no God but God and Mohammad is the Messenger of God." Just that, and he's free. Only a woman cannot be free.'

The sultana rose, noticing the agitation on the minister's face. 'Please stop fretting, good Solomon, I am not displeased. It seems I shall learn a good deal more than reading and writing.'

'Grandfather, please do not be angry with me,' the girl pleaded, reaching for his hand. He threw his arms about her and kissed her, lifting her high off her feet as he did, using but little of his still prodigious strength.

'My child, I am no believer in slavery for anyone. No righteous Jew ever should. I did but worry you'd upset the queen.'

'You will be back this night for my lessons?' she asked with great anticipation.

'Tonight and every night until I have to leave for Jaen . . . and that may be very soon. Remember, you are to try nothing . . . nothing until I tell you you are ready.'

As they walked to the door she whimpered, remembering the encounter with the fiend who invaded the ritual she was working. She did not have to tell her grandfather what worried her. He reached inside his robe and took out a tiny casket and a small vial.

'Here is the talisman your new friend told you to make. It is all done save two things. With the tiny knife you will find inside, carve the open mouth on the frog. Ask the queen if she will give you ten paces by ten paces of her large private garden. Use the earth from there to surround the frog. And tell your small friend that that part of the garden is his. That will bind him to you with great loyalty.'

'But what if the queen sees him working in the garden . . . and what part of the garden do I ask for?' She tugged at his sleeve as he was about to move off.

'What part? Walk around it over and over. Until you find where the magnetic forces are strongest. It seems you have all the psychic powers needed to detect them. As for the queen seeing your friend, she cannot . . . he won't be working the garden on "this side".'

'Grandfather, what in the world does that mean?'

'It means you are going to have to do some more learning on your own . . . you can't ask me for every answer. Don't worry, you'll discover what that means soon enough.' He pointed to the small silver flask. 'Aren't you going to ask me what's in there?' he suggested mockingly.

'Don't be silly, that's the wine . . . oh, has it been sanctified?'

'See . . . you're learning already. No, it is not sanctified, but there is a tiny packet of mustard seeds in the casket just in case you run out of wine. Remember, don't bother him too much, he has a wife and family to take care of.' He kissed her and dashed away.

* * *

'What did you say?' The sultan had been eating slices of orange dipped in wine and honey; he nearly choked when he asked the question, his throat wheezing as he coughed. He and Solomon were in a small study the king used when not required to attend court meetings. It was sparsely furnished, almost overpowered by the large table the king used for reading and writing. The two men sat across from each other, two silver cups of dry, cold white wine before them in addition to bowls of fruit.

'I said they got along marvellously. Dinah loves your noble queen and she in turn seems fascinated with the child . . .'

'I mean about reading and writing,' al-Ahmar choked again on orange and spleen.

'Your good wife asked Dinah to read to her. I thought the child gave a very feeling performance, making sheer poetry of the Qur'an. The queen insists on being taught . . . that's all.'

'Did you not tell her it was forbidden?' demanded the king.

'Tell whom, her majesty or my granddaughter?' Solomon asked with naive simplicity. Al-Ahmar sat back and studied the classic features of the greatest diplomat he had ever met. The king was wary of falling into a trap. 'If I tell my granddaughter to disobey the queen . . .'

'My wife, dammit!'

'Muhammad, my friend and lord, you tell her majesty what is forbidden in the harem, please, not I.'

'You fox! You crafty fox!' the sultan spluttered.

'Allah be praised,' Solomon offered affably. 'Were I not, you'd hardly have me in your employ. Now, have we learnt anything from those renegades we captured this afternoon trying to abduct Dinah?'

'That reminds me,' the king grinned, 'the captain said you were locked in a room downstairs in your house. One filled with strange noises, even more terrifying atmospheres that leaked out and chilled him to the bones. What was going on?'

'We had a very unwelcome guest ... one I had to get rid of with no interference ... but that's another story for another time, if my prince will permit.'

'The guards have bastinadoed the two strong enough to be coaxed into revealing the necessary information. Useless ... they simply lose consciousness. Solomon, torturing human beings goes against my nature ...'

'Allah be merciful, who suggested torture? That is no civilised way to ...'

'Don't be upset, I ordered them to cease immediately. How those fellows can be so obdurate, I don't know, do you?'

'I think ibn Hud recruited them from the Jond, the African militia that patrols the frontiers around Seville. They are savages; four hundred years of Arabic influence has not civilised them. It is something bred into those tribes — they are like men of iron ... but, like all hard things, there is a soft spot, an Achilles heel as the Greeks called it.'

'You lay the plot at ibn Hud's feet?' Ahmar asked. The seer nodded. 'We should be in the same camp ... yet? A Yemenite, from a tribe similar to mine, and still he is always my enemy; he would rather side with those African barbarians.'

'I suspect that his vizier, one Yusuf ibn Yakub who calls himself al-Ziyad is pouring poison into his ear.'

'With your son and nephews missing, your granddaughter under threat, would you prefer not to undertake the secret embassy to the Christian king in Jaen?'

'Thank you, sire, but no. However, I don't think the time is quite right yet. Chasing our goods train is not sufficient reason for a military campaign. There will be a valid excuse soon, of that I am sure. When it ignites tempers here, then I will be off. The show has to be first-class or we will look foolish indeed.' Solomon raised the glass, saluting and bowing his head deferentially toward the monarch before enjoying the cool, crisp flavour. Ahmar was an ideal Muslim, meticulous about his religious observances, but, like many great princes, in private he did enjoy wine. But never to excess. Lord be praised, he added.

'Will you allow me about fifteen minutes with the heartiest of the prisoners? I would also like to attend the wounded once more.'

'Of course,' Ahmar agreed without pause. 'Do you think you can get something out of him? How?'

'I'll work that out as I walk to the prison, but it does occur to me that what the strongest can take in terms of their bodies, they may not be able to where the mind is concerned. We shall see. With your august permission, I shall return shortly.'

* * *

As they reached the lower level of the fortifications beneath the armoury tower — the one referred to as the Sultan's Turret because of Ahmar's habit of pacing up there when he was agitated or planning something and wanted to avoid distractions — Solomon turned to the shorter, powerful Nubian slave carrying the minister's medical chest on one shoulder.

'Are you sure you want to stay, Joseph? This will not be pleasant, I fear.'

The handsome young black stepped along lightly and gracefully, his athletic body rippling with life and energy; he shrugged, frowned slightly, then smiled so broadly his perfect teeth reflected the blazing sconces on the walls.

'If I do not attend my master on every occasion, how will I in turn master the physician's art? Can the true physician ever pick and choose, say I will treat this but not that?'

Solomon smiled, his ears pleased with the sound of the youth's voice. This lad did great justice to the Arabic tongue; in fact, he must have worked painstakingly to cleanse each and every colonial fault from his speech. He had been captured one day during a brief skirmish with an Almohade raiding party between Illora and Alcalá de ibn Said, the very area now being troubled by San Fernando's troops. Three days later, Ahmar had called for his trusted minister in his rôle as temporary court physician. The youth had been seen splinting the leg of a young cat which had been savaged by one of the stable dogs. 'Take him, he's yours,' Ahmar waved to him generously. 'He seems very bright, perhaps you can make a military surgeon of him ... we can use as many as we can get.' When Solomon protested he'd prefer a student who was a freeman and thus permitted to live in Solomon's household, Ahmar frowned. He'd enjoy his freedom more if he worked hard to earn it; the king added that ministers who try to play saint and change the order of the world prove very tedious ... sooner rather than later.

'That is fine in terms of dressing the wounds of these prisoners,' the patriarch agreed, 'but after that I shall be delving into an area you may not wish to know about ...'

'Magic, Master?' The youth's eyes sparkled with gleeful anticipation and he touched Solomon's sleeve beseechingly.

'Hmmmn, something like that. Generally, our rabbis frown on such things as magic ...'

'But you are also a rabbi, Master. The greatest and wisest one in the glittering kingdom of Granada. So if you are doing some very special thing, I would rather lose my right hand than be denied the privilege ...'

'Joseph,' the older man scolded, 'you have developed much too silvery a tongue — nay, more like quicksilver. You work yourself around me like waves of warm, invisible oil. Fine, light, scented oil. Why did you convert to Judaism?' Solomon demanded, intending to so rattle the boy he'd get a proper and truthful answer.

'The truth?' he asked timorously. Solomon nodded emphatically, knowing only too well this question was a parry — the young verbal swordsman was gaining time to weave another elaborate story.

'Before I was captured in Nubia, I had met an old man from near the sea. He told me of his tribe and the one true God they worshipped. His was one of many tribes ... and they all went back to Adam. When I was captured and taken first to the north coast, then eventually to Seville, no one asked me a thing. But in Seville, the commander of the military asked me about religion. I thought: here am I a slave of these people . . . why? Must I have their religion too? They captured my body, but I would not give them my soul. Quickly, I had to choose and, naturally, I chose the one which had fascinated me in my free boyhood. True, it was different from the magic of my people, it had none of the spirit gods one depends upon for survival . . . still, I chose it. I worked in the kitchens of one of the military chieftains and his cook was very good to me. He let me sneak away as often as I needed, for I needed to find a rabbi to teach me my chosen religion. I found him and I learnt; that was five years ago when I was thirteen. I have never regretted the choice although the rulers of Seville were very unkind to me. If it was not easy to be a Jew there, it was less easy to be a black Jew. I liked the challenge.'

'You are extraordinary and I am amazed at your ability to master difficult subjects with such ease. In that way, you remind me of my granddaughter . . .'

'The one with the gorgeous green eyes and the lovely hair like beaten copper and gold?' Joseph asked without thinking. Solomon halted and turned on the bold fellow.

'How do you know that!'

'Master, in running here and there to do services for you, I do look up at times as I run up the hill. Often I have seen this child of heaven gazing out over the vega . . . or up toward the turrets here. Is it a crime to gaze on such beauty?'

'The crime is not yours, Joseph. You were away on a secret mission for me to our friends in Alcalá de Guadaira when the men we are about to attend tried to capture that beauty you so admire. It is she who should be more careful.'

Guards came to attention when they rounded the last corner; they noticed a distinct chill in this part of the subterranean passage despite the warmth of the evening. Four men were stretched out on clean straw pallets on the floor of the rectangular guard room. Five had died, but these four were going to recover as far as Solomon was concerned. There was one slightly wounded man in an adjacent cell: the leader of the gang.

In less than fifteen minutes the physician and his apprentice had changed dressings, cleansed and applied antiseptic salves, judged temperatures and respirations, pulses and general state of health. Solomon rose and signalled the sergeant of the guards.

'I want them fed four times a day from now on. As before, broth of rich meat stock, green vegetables, raw or nearly raw, rice and, if their bowels are normal, start feeding them fruit as well. A half glass of rich wine with each meal . . .'

'But noble chancellor,' the guard gasped, his face registering the most dramatic shock imaginable. Poor Joseph had to lean over one of the patients, his back turned, to muffle his laughter. The shaking of the lad's shoulders in helpless mirth made it difficult for Solomon to order his own expression.

'Please do not concern yourself, good soldier, they will not be choosing to disobey the Prophet, they will be taking this potion as a prescribed physic to enrich the blood and improve circulation whilst stimulating the gastric juices; in accepting such limited quantities for the good of their bodies, they will not be endangering their immortal souls . . . unless, of course, they should continue the practice willfully once they leave my care. Besides, you are aware, sergeant, that Almohades are considered apostates and heretics by the Abbasid Khalifate, are you not?'

'I don't know what that means, your honour,' the soldier answered miserably.

'Don't distress yourself, sergeant, it merely means they have done all the damage to their immortal souls that can be done.' He patted the troubled man's shoulder and called Joseph to him. Joseph placed the silver-inlaid oaken chest on the floor. Bending over it, Solomon extracted two iron hexagons and handed one to his assistant. Next, he took a scroll, a fringed shawl and a slender wand made of lignam vitae from the chest.

'What do I do with this?' Joseph asked, regarding the Star of David with quizzical reverence. His master shot him a warning glance, indicating the guards with the minutest inclination of his head.

'Sergeant,' Solomon called out, 'will you open this cell door, please?' The soldier obeyed immediately. It was obvious he held the king's counsellor in very high esteem; so much so that the dearest wish in his heart was that one day this great statesman and physician would wake seeing the light, would say the words that would gain him admittance to the embrace of Islam so that he would be assured of paradise everlasting. Oddly enough, this was also the sultan's wish.

It took Joseph a few moments to adjust his eyes to the relative gloom. One nearly burnt out torch flickered anaemically on the far wall. Opposite, his wrists chained to rings embedded in the stone, a soldier with a bandage on his shoulder sat on a pile of disordered straw. From a tiny aperture high on that wall, the palest yellow light hinted at where the outside world might be.

'Unchain him, sergeant,' the chancellor asked politely.

'Sir, are you sure?' the sergeant hesitated about obeying *that* command with alacrity. 'He is vicious, sir, he mauled one of the guards before we chained him. I would have to stay, perhaps call another guard to guarantee your safety.'

'I wish to speak to him, to ascertain who his masters are and what they are up to. I cannot have a reasonable conversation with a helplessly gyved man. Free him, please. Lend your sword to my assistant if you are worried, then leave us. Take all your men to the far end of the corridor after you lock this door. The muezzin will cry the evening prayer in about one-quarter hour. Before your prayers, come release us.'

When the door bolt was rammed home from the outside, the prisoner's face become animated with manic glee. He leapt to his feet, crouching, his eyes on Joseph who stood carelessly, one shoulder leaning against the wall, the sword dangling listlessly from his fingers. With a muffled growl, the

Berber fairly rose in the air, attacking with incredible swiftness. The indolent Nubian was not there when he reached the wall, slamming into it. The flat of the scimitar blade struck the back of his head with such force, the walls echoed the sound painfully. The man slid to his knees, clutching at the wall for support, his nails scraping as consciousness deserted him momentarily. When he cleared his eyes, he was on his bottom, his legs splayed and he was looking up at a fantastic fighting machine balanced effortlessly on the balls of his feet, body held in a tight crouch, the point of the sword at the prisoner's throat, the blade flat against the chin, forcing the head up.

Faster than the eye could follow, the sword drew back and the fierce whistle of cloven air made the prisoner know that the point had almost touched his throat; the width of two palms closer and his head would now be rolling across the floor.

'Once more like that, barbarian,' Joseph said calmly, as though he had never moved a muscle, 'and I will carve you into so many small pieces there will be no burial necessary. Just a few bowls to carry the scraps out to the stable dogs.'

The prisoner's eyes narrowed slightly, indicating he might be entertaining another charge and, as abruptly, turned his attention to Solomon.

'What have you got to beat the soles of my feet with which the others did not?' he asked derisively. Solomon could hear by his tone that the bravado had been forced. Obviously, though a professional soldier himself, he had never confronted anyone with Joseph's speed before.

'Almohade, I am a physician, I treat men's bodies, my life is dedicated to healing, among other pious works.' As Solomon pronounced this sentence, Joseph found self-control difficult. His master was never so amusing as when feigning pomposity. 'I shall do nothing to your body, but I will look into your heart and soul. Go over there like a good fellow and sit down on your bed.'

Again, with almost invisible swiftness, Joseph made the sword's blade spin around his forearm like a wheel: instantaneously it was in his hand and pointing toward the straw. The prisoner snorted ungraciously but obeyed quickly enough.

'You asked before about the Star,' Solomon whispered. 'When I summon what I shall now summon, stand near me and if you feel threatened by either an unseen or manifest power, hold that hexagram before your face and do not look directly at whatever it is . . . under no conditions address the entity, look squarely at it or answer anything it might put to you. Do you understand?'

'Yes, Master,' Joseph answered with mock servility.

'Here,' the master handed the assistant a wedge of chalky rock. He pointed to a spot with his foot. 'Draw a neat circle with that chalk; it should be one and one-half times your height in diameter. When you've done that, draw another inside the first the width apart of your palm.' The sword still in his right hand, Joseph followed the instructions precisely with his left. Solomon grunted. He had known the lad was completely ambidextrous . . . but with his eyes as well? The sage swore he was watching the wily prisoner with one, the stone floor with the other. When the circles were complete, the sage took the chalk and pointed to an incense-burning pot and a small tripod with folded legs stored in the chest.

As Joseph adjusted the tripod, Solomon drew a hexagram that filled the area of the inner circle, the apex pointing north. He lettered in the Tetragrammaton, Agla and El in the various sections, then lettered in Adonai Hah and many more sacred names, separating them with square crosses in the area between the circles. Outside the circles, between them and the prisoner, he drew a triangle pointing north and lettered in similar inscriptions. Finally, satisfied that the working was correctly laid out, he motioned to Joseph to step inside the circles and place the incense burner in the northern apex of the hexagram. From inside his robe, he drew a small flacon of dark liquid and a sack of powdered incense. He poured some of the powder into the incense pot and the balance in the centre of the triangle. Nodding to himself, he stepped inside the circles and drew Joseph close to him. Leaning forward, he poured a small amount of the liquid over the incense; a thin wisp of smoke rose, quickly improving the dank atmosphere.

Joseph waited silently, listening to the soft susurration of Solomon's voice creating an invocation in Aramaic, a language he did not know; in fact, even his grounding in Hebrew was quite spotty.

'Will the prisoner rise?' The man on the straw bed looked up, his face suggesting the old man had gone mad. Solomon waited, showing no signs of annoyance. 'I am now in contact with a world you perhaps do not suspect exists,' the sage-turned-magus intoned in a voice that sent bumps up and down the Nubian's spine. 'I have asked you to stand; I will also ask you to tell me who sent you here, who ordered you to violate my house and abduct my granddaughter.'

'I have nothing to say,' the soldier answered with scorn, his broken Arabic almost unintelligible. 'What now? You have woolly-top cut off my head? Hah! A martyr's death would suit me perfectly, a good soldier could ask no better ... straight to paradise, the Prophet guaranteed it. But what would a despicable Jew know about that?' he challenged, sneering.

'Perhaps more than you think, my dear fellow. For if you do not answer me now, I will summon fiends from hell to make you talk ... the Prophet promises no paradise for those who consort with the evil powers of darkness, and consort you will, like it or not. Paradise? You will be forever damned.'

With fantastic accuracy, the magus smashed the flacon in the dead centre of the triangle, directly on top of the small heap of incense. The mass burst into flame, sending up tendrils of red, blue, orange and green fire; then suddenly a thick cloud of smoke rose, displaying all the colours to startling effect. It lifted to a height of just over five feet and hovered; to the prisoner's surprise he could still see the two men perfectly through the billowing cloud.

'Serafina,' Solomon intoned, 'this uncircumcised barbarian, this infidel who poses as a Muslim, refuses to leave his seat and pay you proper homage ...' A head appeared, scattering the upper smoke and forcing the balance closer to the floor. The head was a salamander's, the fire spirit the magus had summoned.

The head disappeared and a heavenly woman — as delicate and sylph-like as the imagination could conjure — slid from the flames and stood enticingly before the astounded prisoner; she took his head between her hands and drew it toward her, pressing his face into the joining of her thighs. His gasp sounded almost like a death rattle, as though his heart had stopped; a second later the calm was shattered by an unholy roar. The prisoner went flying straight up and slammed into the ceiling, only to drop like a meal sack. At the last fraction of a second, the woman disappeared and a salamander larger than a huge crocodile was standing with legs fully extended. The prisoner landed on the saurian's back with no sound at all. He rolled off and looked up. Then screamed.

'I'm often told I have infinite patience,' Solomon announced with due modesty. 'In your case I shall make an exception. Tell me who your masters are or my large friend is going to make a very rapid meal of you.'

'I shall die in the cause of Islam and a martyr's death is far superior to answering your questions, you pompous, overbearing Jew. When we take this city you better not be here ...'

An eerie noise shattered his voice, drowning the words. The horrendous sound made it seem the walls were coming apart, split asunder by a force as great as lightning. Joseph's head was arrested by Solomon's strong hand just before it could snap a look over his shoulder. The salamander now screamed in sheer panic, shrinking to the size of a tiny lizard. With an abrupt and sharp screech, the fire and the salamander disappeared. The prisoner's mouth gaped open; he gained his feet uncertainly and backed up to his straw bed, his feet slipping as he clambered backwards, struggling to press himself through the wall. The weak torch sputtered as a foul wind passed it. When it reached the terrified prisoner, he gasped, panting to fill his lungs with decent air.

'Having a bit of trouble, are we good Solomon?' A black mass rolled slowly past the two men in the protective circle. The unspeakable spirit of evil filled the space between the two in the circle and the prisoner, who was by now deathly white.

Solomon sensed Joseph was about to back away from the essence in the black mass before them. He held the lad's arm firmly and began intoning the banishing rite.

'Don't be hasty, Solomon, you have nothing to lose. I just happened to be passing by, is all. This wretch has some answers for you? And he wants to be dispatched to the glories of paradise forthwith, as the embellishing poets say? When I get finished with him he will be received nowhere but in hell! See this, you scum?'

Mouth locked open as with rigor mortis, the panic-ridden prisoner saw one of the most horrendous objects he'd even seen or imagined. The phallus was a disgusting shade of brown, hard and tough as leather and covered with terrible pustules oozing a foul-smelling pus-like substance which began dripping on the stone floor. Rats squeaked in frenzy and began racing past, throwing themselves at the far wall with mindless panic. As the witnesses stared, transfixed, unable to tear their eyes away, the vile appendage began to swell, expanding in length and width. The arms of a skeleton reached from the thick cloud and grabbed the prisoner as though the bones had been covered in great bands of muscle. Solomon heard the sharp intake of breath beside him. From the corner of one eye, he could see Joseph's eye, twice its normal size, the exposed white reflecting the unwholesome light.

The remnants of a once fine robe flew through the air. The beast in the cloud grabbed the man's penis and stretched it in a totally inhuman way. A skeletal foot flew out of the cloud and kicked the straw pallet. It leapt up, extending legs, four in all, made of its own straw; in the blink of an eye, a short straw couch stood nearly four feet off the ground, looking rigid and solid. The bony arms slammed the prisoner down on the couch, the breath knocked out of him loudly as his abdomen struck the straw. Before he had a chance to move, his own penis, extended to a frightening degree, defying the limitations of human flesh, whirled about couch and occupant, from shoulder blades to below the waist, fastening him as securely as leather thongs.

The huge phallus struck him so hard across one cheek, it sounded as though the jawbone had been smashed.

'Take another look, you apostate, heretical bastard son of a dog! This is going to be rammed up inside your pitiful, tight and unyielding fundus, do you hear me? It will split you in half as I take my pleasure . . . do you think *both* sullied, apostate, despicable halves of you will then be welcome in heaven?'

The prisoner screamed, his body lashing about wildly, his muscles in a spasm of terror far beyond his control. Solomon knew that at any moment his mind would snap.

'Azazel, Archduke of Hell, begone. I hereby banish you to the darkness from whence you came. My ancestor, Solomon, son of David, bound you over for all eternity more than two thousand years ago. I did not call you forth, I did not free you, so begone.'

'Just a moment, he's about to talk,' the voice from the cloud took on a new, a conciliatory note. 'You will owe me nothing, this simple favour will put you under no obligation . . .'

'I am not a fool, Azazel, Archduke of Darkness. You have put yourself here without my beck and you will leave with my command; I have not released the bond of Solomon. You are banished . . . now!'

The patriarch stretched out his hand, beaming the silver ring emblazoned with the Seal of Solomon, the wizard's mightiest sword and armour. The cloud evaporated and Joseph gasped. Before him stood one of the most hauntingly beautiful creatures a man's mind could possibly devise. All of eight feet tall, designed like the archetypal dream of an angel, this beautiful vision stood sadly, every part of him an aspect of divine perfection. And over it all, an invisible but palpable stamp of utter and unredeemable corruption. Tears rolled down the heavenly cheeks, soaking into the long blond locks that framed the breath-taking face. One angelic hand partially turned palm up in a silent plea. Solomon's voice rumbled on and the vision began to fade. As Solomon repeated yet again the banishing ceremony, chanting the words, 'I did not summon thee,' a brilliant light flashed before them. The angel was gone and before them glowered a beast just as huge. Hands and feet ended in claws of fierce proportions; the head was that of a virulent, enlarged bat, teeth sharp and gleaming; short horns surmounted the head and huge batwings swept out as though to enfold the two encircled in chalk.

'You may not have summoned me,' a vile, suggestive whisper caressed them, 'but your granddaughter did ... oh, not quite enough for full freedom, old fool, but I have one foot through the door now ... the other will follow, the other will follow, the other will ...'

The voice died and the vision was gone, leaving the room, cooler, the air cleaner.

A mad jabbering reached them from the floor. The prisoner was lying on his collapsed pallet of straw, writhing miserably, his nails scratching the stone, the fingers bleeding from the violence of his attack. There was no more couch, he was no longer bound in that totally unnatural way. In reality, nothing had happened to him, but his mind was gone now, burned out of him through a terror so total few normal men could have withstood it. The voice, the scratching, everything stopped at once. Solomon reached him in one bound, flipped him over on his back and began to pound his chest with fingers clasped, using the heels of his hands like a mallet.

'Joseph, put your mouth to his and fill his lungs with air. Do it over and over, pausing a few seconds between each deep breath.' It was useless; his heart had stopped and would not revive, no matter how hard they tried.

Walking across the gardens through the twilight, Joseph could not stem the endless questions. He had familiarity with the unusual abilities of the shamans who were more powerful than tribal kings in his own birthplace, but this experience had taken his breath away. Could his generous master teach him?

'Did you hear the last thing he said? That angel turned monster?' Solomon asked.

'That your granddaughter had released one foot — how?' Joseph whispered in awe.

'By playing with something that would have been better left alone. You haven't even the vaguest idea of the extent of the damage. With children, a little bit of knowledge is more dangerous than a whole lot of ignorance.'

'But, Master, I would never do anything you told me not to,' Joseph argued, his voice wheedling.

'And if you brought the sky down on our heads, you would glibly say, "But you never told me not to do *that*." Will saying so make it all right again? Put the sky back up there?'

'But, Master, if you teach the wonderful Dinah to be more careful, and you teach me to be expert as you are doing with medicine, then I can watch over her . . . as that terrible monster from hell said just before he disappeared — you know, about getting another foot here — why the more of us who know how to fight him . . .'

'Too bad you didn't hear what the prisoner said just before *he* disappeared,' the sage commented acerbically.

'But I did,' protested the Nubian. 'He said: "Yusuf ibn Yakub will have my head for this."'

'So . . . it was ibn Hud's dirty work.' Solomon stroked his beard reflectively, turning into the palace gate.

CHAPTER 4

The sultana moved among the roses and irises, a razor-sharp, slender knife in one hand, a leather glove on the other. Three of her personal maids followed her as she moved along, selecting first this bloom, then that. Each girl reached a basket forward as the knife did its work with great efficiency. The Nightingale was a natural gardener, a woman of sensitivity to every nuance of nature. They rounded a corner of the vast garden to see, at the very end, at the corner of the garden wall, a young girl bending diligently to the task of weeding a small vegetable patch.

'How strange is our delightful young Dinah. The vast vega that rolls westward as far as Seville and beyond produces such an abundance of fruit and vegetables, with little time or care for flowers, yet this enigmatic child favours only vegetables in the small patch I gave her. And yet, I know she adores flowers ...' The queen moved on, disappearing between rows of bushes, shaking her head as the girls set up a chorus of minute clucks in agreement with their mistress.

'They're gone now,' Dinah whispered. Bubbi shot straight up, like a carrot completing its entire growth cycle in a split second.

'I wasn't actually hiding,' he explained with all the dignity he could muster while slapping bits of rich loam from his dark brown leggings and homespun shirt. A tiny cap much like a pot with a peak at the crown was askew on his head. Dinah giggled and set it straight on his head.

'No,' she agreed, jesting, 'you just wanted to see how the roots were doing.'

'Dinah, if I've told you once, it must be a dozen times: you may not be the only person around here who can actually see . . . in the special way you can. I don't think even your grandpa can do it — but that doesn't mean . . .'

'Yes,' she soothed him, 'that doesn't mean that one of those silly, cackling girls following Nightingale about doesn't have special magical eyes; perhaps they're in her plump little backside and they watch us as she walks away . . . hmmmn?'

'You are going to laugh at something just once too often one of these days . . . whoops! Did you just say, cackling girls?' he asked, leaning forward and peering deeply into her eyes. She nodded seriously. 'Dinah, my hearing is very special compared to humans. I hardly heard that sound from here . . . you see? You take your gifts much too lightly.'

'And you,' she rounded on him, all mirth banished, 'don't choose to put yours to work. You said, if there was no news from my father and my brilliant cousins in one month, you would help me find them. Well?'

Bubbi looked down, avoiding her eyes. His square little bare feet, each with seven toes, squirmed unhappily. He sighed with deep sadness and regret, shrugging his shoulders. Quickly, he looked from left to right, as though the shoulders had disobeyed him. He lifted his hands and pressed on his shoulders, obviously telling them to behave. As his feet began to sink into the earth, Dinah reached down and snatched up the small casket resting near her leg.

'Oh, no, you don't,' she warned, opening the lid and rubbing the tiny wooden frog's head. 'When I called for you, you came willingly enough. I haven't dismissed you yet, so don't try to sneak off — I mean, down — on me.'

'Dinah, my wife is not feeling well. She needs me now.'

He looked up pleadingly, his descent arrested.

'Oh,' the girl asked archly, 'are you a physician now?'

'That reminds me,' Bubbi answered with a bit more animation, 'would you ask your grandfather if he can help Momo . . . my wife, that is?'

'Why didn't you ask sooner?' the girl wanted to know. 'Now you ask? Yesterday he went on a secret mission for the sultan, the good Lord alone knows when he shall return.' The gnome's face puckered sorrowfully; Dinah feared he was about to burst into tears. She put a tender, motherly arm about him. Squatting on her heels as she knelt, she was still a bit taller than he.

'What is wrong with her, Bubbi?' she asked, rocking his shoulders gently with her arm, trying to shake the sadness loose.

'She can't have a baby,' he moaned. 'We've been married for ages and still no signs.'

'And you have to leave . . . right now? In God's name, what can you do about that?'

'My, you're younger and more innocent than I thought.' The gnome regarded her with the hint of a superior sneer. 'Do you think she can make a baby all on her own?'

'Bubbi! I'm surprised at you. I summoned you here to help me with a life and death emergency . . . for all I know. And all you want to do is go home and . . . and . . . really, Bubbi!'

'Dinah, I'm an earth spirit — how many times have I told you? I can do lots and lots of things for you . . .' He closed his eyes, pressed one hand horizontally across his brow, the other opposing against his solar plexus. Dinah felt his body contract, the enormous reservoir of magnetic energy flowing up from the earth and into his small body was very real to her; sitting so near him and with her sensitivity, she was buffeted as with great charges of electricity from a lightning bolt. The air whirred near them and two matchless swords in handsomely tooled scabbards fell noiselessly on to the soft earth before the girl's knees.

She blinked, blinded by the silver chasing, the jewels

encrusted in the handles of the two perfect, matching weapons.

'Oh, Bubbi . . . they're beautiful!' she gasped, reaching down to lift one. She eased the blade halfway out. It was such splendid steel she could find no words to equal its perfection. 'For me?' she asked incredulously. He nodded, so obviously happy she was pleased with the gifts. 'But what shall I do with the sword . . . two swords, in fact.'

'As you seem determined to continue on this madness headlong, I feel you'll need one. Perhaps there will be someone to help you.' He smiled and pointed to the blade she was holding. 'You picked the right one,' he complimented her. 'The other is male oriented.'

'A man? One who will help me find my father?' She put the sword down and reached out to hug the gnome. He slid from under her arm and bent over, placing a forefinger on each of the swords. It was not so much that they sank down as the earth seemed to bubble up and cover them. Yet, when it stopped, there was no telltale outline; the ground was smooth as could be, a row of carrots on one side, another on the opposite.

'It would be a rare man who could help you find your father,' Bubbi mumbled, his attention divided. 'You see, as I have told you, and as I've just demonstrated, there is a lot I can do . . . here. The sort of travel you desire, the distances involved are just beyond my powers.' He pointed down. 'That great network of energy . . .' he poked at the earth with the extended finger . . . 'corresponds to the cosmic one . . .' his thumb jerked upwards. 'I am limited to right here. But there are others who can help . . . however, there is such a terrible price.'

She pressed him, refusing to be put off. Finally, he reminded her of the demon who had rescued her from something vastly worse. Musa, that demon, was neither good nor evil. The words meant nothing to him; he was indifferent to such limiting human notions. Yet, he had been born of woman, Bubbi whispered superstitiously, but his father is a Djinn. The woman who bears a demon son after being possessed by a Djinn is a lost and miserable human being for the rest of her life . . .

'Bubbi? Why are you telling me all about the reproduction of demons? What has that to do with finding my father and those two ridiculous cousins?'

'Musa's father — the Djinn — is the one who can find them in a flash of light. He can take you there as quickly. He can go anywhere in this world. He has tremendous powers . . .'

'Then why don't we simply ask him to find them and spirit them back here immediately?' she asked, thinking it perfectly reasonable.

'Hoooooo-oo-oo!' he stopped her with a foggy whistling sound made deep in his throat. 'He'd help us get there. He'd help us to do whatever was needed for your father and your cousins. He'd even get us back here . . . but not them. They'd have to travel as normal passengers . . . you know, camels, horses, ships.' He shrugged, looking extremely uncomfortable. 'You see, they don't wish to involve themselves too directly in human destiny . . . alter the course of things too much, as it were."

'I see,' she said brightly. 'All right, I'll accept the limited help. Find father, get me there and back, if necessary. Getting them free — if they are captive as I suspect — and getting them on the way home, that's up to me, right? How do you summon the Djinn?'

'Hoooooo-oo-oo!' he held up his hand. 'You didn't even *ask* about the *price*. We're not talking about some corner of a garden, even a splendid fertile one like this. In this case . . .' he was suddenly crestfallen and his body sagged, his head bowing with sorrow . . . 'in this case the garden . . . the garden . . . is you.'

'You mean . . .?' she gasped. He nodded slowly, miserably.

'Musa is bad enough.' Bubbi admitted 'I've heard rumours, but I have no proof. What they like to do with human girls is not to be spoken about . . . it is just too awful. But the Djinn? . . . oh, no. You, the mother of a-a-a demon?'

Dinah sat back on her heels as far as she could and began laughing. She tried, but she could not stop. Not until she heard the sound of the gnome's hysterical crying did she bite off the laughter.

'Bubbi, what is the matter?' She placed a hand on each of his shoulders and shook him gently.

'I love you, Dinah, how can you be so . . . so common? You'll give yourself to a demon, then a Djinn and you think it's fun?'

'Who said I was going to give myself to anyone? I read a very rare book by a liberated woman saint who lived in Arabia nearly four hundred years ago. She knew exactly how to handle demanding, dominating male animals.' She punched his arm playfully. 'What is this about loving me, by the way? I thought you loved your wife.'

'It's different, I don't know how to explain . . . well, she's so nice and comfortable, like an old slipper. We want to make a family together. I love you the way I love the roots of a beautiful tree . . . when you stand under it and look up.' He looked down at his feet and coughed.

'You mean, you don't want to make babies with me?' she asked sternly. He coughed again, then giggled and shook his head. 'You'd better not, it sounds like I'll have my hands full with a demon and his demon-making father.' She hugged her little friend again. 'Tell me, how do we arrange this?'

'Can you get back to your own house?' he asked. She thought about it, nodding assent but not with full conviction. 'Because of the vibrations created there, it is the right place to try. But this time you have to be extra careful . . . one more time with that fiend on the loose and none of us may ever be seen again, never mind your father and cousins.'

'Who is he, Bubbi? Why are you always refusing to tell me?'

'Do you think you can pick me up? Lift me quite clear of the ground?' he asked, startling her with the odd, disconnected question. 'I weigh a lot more than you think.'

Winking and cocking her head pensively, Dinah rose and

looked about her. She stepped away from the vegetable patch and walked back and forth. She entered the patch again and moved carefully among the rows of vegetables. When she reached the wall, she turned east and took three paces; she stopped abruptly, as though she had found something. She signalled to the gnome, motioning him toward her.

He fairly flew to her. 'Wonderful, Dinah, you found the place where the ancient straight lines of the earth cross. You are right above the most powerful place in Granada. Always remember where it is.'

She reached down, slid her hands under his arms and lifted with all her might. He was heavy, even heavier than she. But the power beneath flowed upwards and with trembling arms she lifted the gnome to the height of her shoulders.

'He is Azazel, Archduke of Hell, one of the angels who fell with Lucifer. Were I even to think it too clearly with my feet touching the earth, he'd know, he'd surely know.'

She set him down again and, hand in hand, they paced back to the spot they'd left. Silently, he pointed to where the swords were. There was no more laughter, no more bantering.

'It would be unsafe for you to try this working on your own,' he warned her. 'Once you conjure up the unsuspected, the unwanted, that spirit finds the path easier the next time, his strength increasing as yours lessens. More often than not, the magician who calls upon an evil spirit to do his bidding is enslaved and destroyed by that entity.'

'Do you have a suggestion?' she asked, surprise lighting her face.

'Your grandfather's other pupil ... do you know him? The black one from the unknown wilds of Africa?'

'Yes ... from a distance,' she said with a certain aloofness. 'Why him?'

'Because he has the skills. He is becoming quite adept. You may have occasion when you will need him and those two swords.' His finger flicked toward the ground and there was a slight movement of the surface soil. 'I suspect he has no match for speed and skill. Find an innocent package — perhaps a small carpet from Persia — to wrap them in. Remember, in spite of your grandfather's exalted office in the sultan's service, the law clearly prohibits Jews from carrying weapons.'

'Jews? Carrying weapons? You mean soldiers would stop me and . . .'

'Not you — him.'

'Him? The black? What are you talking about?' she gasped.

'He's Jewish . . . didn't you know?' She stood with her mouth open. 'Tomorrow? Can you get permission to gather things you need from your house? Tomorrow?' She nodded dully. 'I'm dismissed, please? Momo really does need me . . . it's coming up through the ground in irresistible waves . . . please?' She nodded again, like a stunned lamb. Bubbi sank down rapidly, the ground closing over him in no way disturbed after he'd gone.

CHAPTER 5

Solomon and the leader of the cavalry squadron dismounted behind the square fringe of trees near the edge of the ridge. Two other soldiers bounded out of their saddles to take the reins while the two men walked up behind the tree affording more cover than any other near by. Silently, they gazed down at the smoking ruins of Illora, a lovely town less than seven leagues northwest of Granada. Even from this altitude on such a clear and still day, they could hear the shouts of soldiers, the screams of women. This was the mindless, wanton horror of war.

'If we had but enough men,' the captain whispered, 'we might surprise them as they murder and rape, we might teach them . . .'

'I know how you feel, courageous sir,' Solomon soothed him. 'I wish to cry for those people. It is all so totally unnecessary. Even if we surprised them, even if, by some great stroke of fortune, we defeated them, would that bloodshed bring back the dead? Would it stop things or would it create even more fury, greater lust for blood?' He looked at his companion with great compassion.

'How can we just stand here?' the captain demanded.

'We shall not. There is nothing we can do. What is done will not be undone. We must see how they are faring at Alcalá. Come, we have no time to lose.'

Alcalá, when they arrived, was undergoing a similar fate. Pressing on, skirting the area well beyond the invaders' camp, the small band of riders went north to Jaen as swiftly as they could with prudence.

Late that night, they found adequate accommodation in a very small village in the hills just east of Jaen. Solomon knew the city was under ruthless siege and he was anxious to get there as quickly as possible. He must convince the Castilian that the butchery he had started was all out of proportion. Yes, they needed attacks on towns closer to Granada to arouse the anger of the Granadinos. They were largely Yemenites and, like the sultan, more interested in enhancing what they had than in going to war for more. Nothing really justifies even a small atrocity, he reminded himself, but a little bit was needed here to galvanise the population, to create the righteous solidarity and give purpose to their outrage. Ferdinand's men had gone much too far, they had taken the assignment as an open fiat to level the countryside.

By two hours after sunrise, Solomon was sitting some distance from the royal pavilion, waiting for the return of his messenger. He was surprised to see the king himself emerge from the large tent and stroll purposefully toward the waiting emissary. He wore boots, hose, a simple tunic and no armour, no casque upon his head, only a plain sort of bonnet. He did not even wear a sword.

'Most welcome, noble ambassador,' Fernando addressed him warmly; he extended his arms to embrace the tall representative of the Muslim sultan.

Startled by this extraordinary gesture on the part of a monarch — one he would certainly not expect from Ahmar, as friendly as they were, as much as that sultan respected his personal advisor — Solomon stepped forward sharply, bending to kiss the king's hand before being enfolded in his arms.

The king led Solomon back to his headquarters pavilion,

explaining as they went that he had judged the messenger to be weary and hungry: if Solomon objected, he was truly sorry, but he'd sent the man and the other soldiers off to be fed.

The interior of the campaign headquarters was simple to the degree of austerity. Behind one pair of curtains, the patriarch guessed, was a bed for the king. There was no sign that his consort had joined him here. In the forward chamber where they entered, tables and chairs were crowded, arms and armour in disordered piles on the oriental carpets; it seemed to the visitor that this king was in no way concerned with worldly grandeur, quite unlike his Arabic and North African peers. The king led him through another set of curtains to a small study with but one writing table and two plain wooden chairs without even the slightest indication of carving; again, lush Persian carpets were scattered about on the ground.

'Please be seated, learnèd rabbi — my informants are correct, are they not?' The question forced Solomon's eyebrows to rise. 'I have been told you are a physician, a highly honoured rabbinical leader of your people, a scientist in the ancient mysteries as well as an unequalled diplomat and financier. Would that you graced my court.' The king smiled broadly and cocked his head with a hint of anticipation; was that an offer? Solomon wondered.

'You majesty has one of Spain's greatest financial wizards in his service, I believe.' Solomon answered the king's smile with a mischievous one of his own. 'Naturally,' he added, 'he's Jewish.'

'Don Zulema is one of the ablest administrators I have. But then again, your excellency, I have yet to meet a Jew who was not a brilliant master of finance.'

'With all due respect to his majesty's encounters, he is unlikely to meet any others. There are many more who cannot even manage a wine shop without becoming bankrupts. Of course, my distant cousin on my mother's side — your Don Zulema — is one of the great geniuses. In my family's trading enterprises, we often enter joint ventures with his family. Always, I assure you, the results are satisfactory.'

'Good sir,' the king spoke softly, 'the Jews of Spain undoubtedly have amassed more wealth than all the Christian kings, to say nothing of vying with the Khalifs themselves. How do you do it? More important, what do you do with all that money?'

Solomon smiled, more to himself this time. A king engaged on the ambitious course of conquest this one pursued needs must be forever preoccupied with the means to finance it. Hordes of money would not lay bare a barbaric streak of covetousness here as it would with many lesser men; but, his need considered, it was bound to fascinate him.

'His majesty knows how we do it, I'm sure. Since the start of the Christian calendar, the Jews have been scattered over the world. Many things are denied them — kingships, nobility, vast estates, even simple land ownership for the most part. They've had to develop those skills they could usefully employ. As to what they do with it ... well, often they finance their monarchs' adventures. Sadly, because of men's greed, they are sometimes relieved of it through the application of convenient massacres.'

The king's face became troubled, almost stern. 'In Castile, good sir ...' he began.

'Will his majesty allow an explanation?' Ferdinand nodded with seemingly no annoyance. 'In the year 1066 of the Christian calendar, an ancestor of mine was prime minister to the sultan of Granada. He was an arrogant man and made many enemies. It was the excuse the nobility needed: they killed him and went on to massacre four thousand Jews ... and, of course, take their money. I cannot speak with any such authority for the lands outside this kingdom.'

'Yes, I do know that story. His name was Joseph ha-Levi?' Solomon nodded assent. 'An abomination in the sight of God.' Ferdinand shook his head with genuine sorrow and made the sign of the cross. 'That such things can happen among civilized humans — all of whom claim to worship the same God — is beyond reason and all understanding.'

The king's mood changed drastically when Solomon described the scenes he'd witnessed in Illora and Alcalá de ibn Said. It was not so much blind rage — such an emotion would be out of character as Solomon read the man — as frantic bewilderment. Yes, they had been told to create a scorched earth effect, but to do so selectively . . . there was no intention to create a tragic famine. But rape, murder of non-combatants — in the name of God, women and children? The aged? Either the commanders had gone mad or had lost control of their troops. With an almost humble apology, the king excused himself. Not long after, he returned looking dejected and weary. There was a large contingent on its way to relieve both towns — and both commanders. There would be, he assured the envoy from Granada, very serious disciplinary actions taken.

'Will your majesty continue now with the siege of Jaen?'

'I must, your excellency. How shall I make you understand that my life is dedicated to the service of Our Lord, Jesus Christ? In the performance of that duty — a performance which must consider the most minute factors even in my everyday life — I am guided by heaven above to relieve this embattled land of all foreign invaders — all those who deny the ascendancy of Christ, the Son of God.'

'His majesty does not have to try, his simple servant here is keenly aware of his divinely inspired mission. But may I take it that his majesty does differentiate between the overall general concept of infidelism and — here and there — particular individuals who may well be as concerned about mankind's suffering as is the saintly king of Castile?'

'You speak, no doubt, of al-Ahmar your liege?' the king asked. Solomon bowed affirmation. 'I hear such intriguing stories about him. He is not warlike, though renowned as a great and courageous soldier. He is more concerned with the wellbeing of his people than aggrandisement, more dedicated to prosperity for all than to conquest . . . tell me truthfully, learned rabbi, is all of this myth?'

'By no means, sire. I think I may say this with no fear of contradiction: only rarely in the history of any great era a truly noble king walks out upon the world's stage. When two stand there simultaneously, it must be considered a miraculous happening — one that must bode good for mankind. Working hand-in-hand, as it were, my lord, you and the sultan could make those miracles realities for all our sorely distressed people.'

'But tell me, dear Solomon,' the king fairly pleaded on a much less formal note, 'how can I become the ally of the man destiny has decreed I must drive from these shores?'

'If I may be so bold, great sovereign, by defining exactly who that enemy is and is not. And who that enemy definitely is not is he who is my king. Why, two men more like brothers in every noble concern for this land you could not find were you to search from here to the far reaches of Cathay. But what might you do *together* to rid this country of your mutual enemy if you will only join hands!'

Appealing to the monarch's saintly nature, Solomon painted a picture of Ahmar the Castilian began to admire more intensely than that of any other legendary figure. He quickly saw the unbridgeable gap between the cruel and savage Almohades of the North African Mahgrib and the enlightened and civilized Yemenites who had been resident in Spain for more than five hundred years. How much nobler it would be to drive these Africans back across the straits and thus bring peace and prosperity to the lands where their cruelty, barbarity and financial and racial madness had created panic, poverty and chaos. In the end, one great king would rule over all ... would it not be a splendid jewel in his crown to have the kingdom of Granada willingly accepting his overlordship, contributing knowledge, industry, prosperous agriculture and world-wide trade to the other glories of Ferdinand's reign ... to say nothing of the considerable monetary tribute such thriving prosperity would produce, particularly with peace coming to all parts of the country?

'When may I meet this unique sovereign of yours? If his presence matches your description, how can I not offer him my friendship?' Fernando drew a sheet of paper from a box on the writing table. 'I shall send an offer of amnesty here and now. But he must understand, I cannot lift the siege of Jaen. My army is at its peak of fitness . . . to demoralise it so . . .' he left the thought hanging for his guest to complete.

'Majesty, have you considered the bloodshed that can be averted with Ahmar as your willing ally?' At these words, the king put down the quill he'd selected from the box.

Solomon predicted that city after city would respond to the sultan's appeals. So many of them boasted a population overwhelmingly Yemenite: a subject people under the heel of the Berber invaders. And in most of these cities, the Berber presence was limited to the military garrison alone. Doors would open as if by magic. The common citizen would aid the deliverers in so many subtle ways the Almohades would not stand a chance. Driven forth, the Berbers would flee and there would be no unnecessary bloodshed.

This pledge struck the note — if indeed an additional, compelling note was needed — that fixed the king on his humanitarian course. As his quill flourished, he listened intently to his new unofficial advisor, the plume rising frequently, pausing as the writer pondered what was being said.

The monarchs could not meet just yet. It would be a serious strategic error. In a more disciplined fashion, the outrage to the countryside must continue . . . until it almost impinged upon Granada itself. The sultan would be 'forced' to raise an army of farmers, artisans and tradesmen . . . there was no large professional standing army. And, to be sure, that army would be overwhelmed and forced to sue for peace. The mass of Granadinos would see the hopelessness of their position. There would then be no rabid outcry when their king sued for peace, when he offered this great land to the overlordship of Castile. The sultan would be honoured more than ever when it was proved how right his judgment had been: the man called San Fernando by his people was every bit as merciful and charitable as his legend claimed. Granada would be not only intact, but more prosperous than ever.

In the excitement of his subtle oratory, Solomon had gripped the edge of the escritoire; smiling, Fernando reached over and covered the envoy's hand with his own.

'Would that I had such a one as you to represent me in such delicate manoeuvring, dear Solomon. You are a master at the art of communication.' Solomon opened his mouth to protest but the king held up a dissuading hand. 'Tell me, noble envoy, of all these cities which are to hark unto the call of Muhammad ibn Nasr al-Ansari,' he proposed, nodding his head sagely, 'how do you calculate the response of Seville? Will they throw open the gates of those formidable, impenetrable walls and welcome me into the Alcázar?' The king had not missed the look of surprise in his guest's eyes when he reeled off the sultan's full and proper name.

'Ibn Hud professes sovereignty over Seville ... and yes, the defences of Seville are mighty. He is the one atypical Yemenite, is ibn Hud. He relies heavily upon the Almohade legions, particularly the toughened members of the frontier patrol. Your combined numerical superiority will avail little there. The only real bridge across the Guadalquivir is in Córdoba, as you well know. But the doughty bridge of boats linked together makes a most difficult task of starving them out. The Ajarafe plain on the west bank will be very difficult to conquer; thus supplies will cross the river on that bridge of boats. But, your majesty, there are ways and ways of skinning cats and walled cities. To apply them means you will need to have great faith in me personally. Even when it seems I consort with the enemy.'

Fernando powdered the letter and blew the powder away. He folded the fine paper — Solomon noted it was obviously from Jativa, an Islamic manufacture — and handed it unsealed to the envoy.

'I give you this unsealed, Solomon, for to seal it would be an insult. As it is in Castilian, not Latin, you will undoubtedly have to read it to the great sultan. I trust you, indeed. I trust you would pluck the eyes of our enemies from their heads as you would lay down your life for our friends.'

Solomon bent his tall, lean figure forward to kiss the king's hand. 'You do me great honour, malik akbar.'

'What, pray, does that mean?'

'A simple expression in Arabic, really. It means great king.'

'How vain a man would have to be to employ it referring to himself,' the king opined with barely visible mirth. As they neared the closed curtains he took Solomon's elbow, drawing him nearer. 'Emissary akbar,' he pronounced carefully, 'will you make all haste, please. The sooner we have this engagement in the field, the sooner we can meet and arrange our real campaign together, your king and I.'

'All haste possible, majesty . . . short of jeopardising either of your royal selves. It must all appear totally natural. I know you appreciate that.'

Nodding solemnly and reflectively, the king ushered his guest from the pavilion.

'Where are my manners?' he declared, stopping abruptly. 'You've not rested, you haven't broken your fast . . . this is unforgivable, Don Solomon, unforgivable.'

'Not at all, sire, I must hasten back. Surely there will be some provision left over from my escort's meal. I'll devour that on the way. As long as it is not meat, of course.'

'Ah, yes . . . the very logical dietary laws of Moses . . .' Fernando signalled one of his officers and gave him precise instructions for his guest's provisioning. And embraced Solomon once more before they parted.

CHAPTER 6

'Momo, why are you being so stubborn? I wouldn't say I had a lot of gardening to attend to if I didn't, why would I do that?' Bubbi's hat was lying on the small table in the centre of the room; without it, he looked hopelessly young, his wife always thought, particularly with that short straight hair standing up like the needles on a porcupine. She adored his merry brown eyes and the stubby little nose which became noticeably red whenever he was excited.

His wife looked up from the homespun woollen jerkin she was embroidering for him with threads of gold and silver. Although it was by no means overly warm, she had removed her short blouse and sat in the small chair wearing only her ample pajama trousers. Uncomfortably, Bubbi noticed the precarious tilt of her slender, flirtatious nipples. They would swell, entasis was not far off, he whimpered silently to himself. Why else would she have removed her blouse? Sheer provocation, he concluded.

'Why would you do that?' she repeated at last. 'To run away from your proper duties, that's why. You want to get back to that spoilt brat, that's why. You think she's prettier than I.'

'Dinah?' he gasped, visibly shocked by the accusation. Immediately, as though hearing an echo, he was shocked by his shock. Would she see through him, through his indignant protests? 'Momo, she's a little girl, may the Lord forgive you for such terrible thoughts.'

'Ah-ha!' the female gnome exploded, slamming the sewing down on a small table next to her chair. 'She's a *little girl* huh? May the Lord forgive *you*,' she mimicked. 'May I remind my fine upstanding scholar of a husband that also Abishag the Shunammite was a little girl. A young virgin. Do you remember who Abishag was, Don Scholar?'

Bubbi brushed a bit of dried mud from his leather britches which came to just below his knees. More caked mud was scattered along his legs. Unthinkingly, he picked up his hat — a gesture of habit.

'Put down that hat while I'm talking to you, Don Gardener!' she fairly shouted at him. The hat hit the table and his hand drew back as from a serpent's fangs. 'Well, who was she?'

'Who was who?' he asked miserably, scratching disconsolately through what his wife described as porcupine spikes.

'Abishag the Shunammite, that's who! We were talking about someone else maybe, Don Memory King?' She vaulted out of the chair and stood face to face with him. 'Abishag the Shunammite!'

Bubbi cupped a protective hand over his offended ear. What was all this about Shunammites, he wondered? What was she trying to prove? He shrugged, holding his hands up at shoulder level, the palms uppermost.

'They brought her to King David in his old age, that's what,' Momo chortled, wagging an accusing finger under her husband's nose. 'You know what for?' she demanded. He shook his head vigorously, denying all knowledge of such biblical carryings on. 'To put the fire back in his old chest, that's what for; but remember, the scriptures are often misleading about anatomy. To bring back the fire of youth to an old man . . . you understand, Don Puzzled Face?'

'What's the matter with you, since when am I an old

man?' Bubbi was showing the first signs of a temper wearing thin. Momo was a sound strategist.

'You're supposed to know your Torah? You study the Talmud, do you, Don Scholar? No old man, no good student would forget who was Abishag. But you're getting old because you neglect your duty, understand? I'm a sad person, can't you see that? I'm the only gnome lady my age who has no children yet. Do you know what that makes me? A freak, that's what. How long must I live with this shame?'

'Why do you always make out it's *my* fault?' he demanded. His nose was turning red, slowly but surely, she noticed over the finger brushing the tears from her eyes. 'Look around you. Only a good husband would provide you with such a fine house.' His hand swept the room in a grandiose gesture.

The earthen floor was packed hard and painstakingly levelled. The corners square and true, the overhead beams firm and solid. The stone fireplace, tables, chairs, cabinets and dressers all carefully crafted. The garden, a mirror image of the one in the palace, was carefully tended. There was even an extra bedroom . . . waiting for the 'little stranger' when he or she finally arrived.

'Somebody said you were a bad husband?' Her eyebrows rose, daring him to say such words had ever passed her lips. 'Your Jewish Andalusian Princess gave us a splendid garden plot that is mirrored in our dimension . . . please don't think I'm ungrateful. You built us a dream house here, our neighbors come for miles to eat their hearts out. But charity begins at home . . . remember? Your gardening chores for the princess can wait a little!'

She grabbed his hand before he could protest or escape and started dragging him toward the door leading to the bedroom. He nearly lost his balance reaching back for his old conical hat.

Still holding his hand, Momo practically somersaulted him up, and over and flat on his back on his side of the small, sturdy wooden bed. With an inaudible sigh, he slipped out of his leather jerkin and stretched out, his left arm raised over his head. Momo slid in next to him, her head in the opposite direction, her face wreathed in smiles. When she had stretched out comfortably, she pulled up her knees and squiggled down next to him until her left shoulder almost touched his. She squinted, judging the distance and angle, then raised an eyebrow, questioning him for accuracy. He nodded assent. She raised her arm and they inched close together until the two raised arms formed united pillars; a moment went by, each gnome looking tense, backs arched slightly. Then the arms moved down, intertwined; when the arms touched their respective bodies, each made one more effort toward each other, locking the armpits in an airight embrace.

'Oh, Bubbi,' Momo's voice whispered with tremulous delight, 'it's so wonderful, you do it so nicely, I'm in heaven already . . . is it good for you?'

'Perfect,' he answered, a slight purring in his voice; he was trying to keep his thoughts gathered in the here and now. Dinah, the swords, the garden, young Joseph, the secret room in Solomon's house, the difficulty of reaching Musa the demon . . . maybe even his father the Djinn . . . it all went spinning on and on, distracting him.

'Bubbi, Bubbi, do you feel how intense, this is going to be the most fantastic ever, it's going to be together, Bubbi, I know it, it's going to be together, this is the one, I know this one is going to take, this one was made in heaven . . .' her voice trailed off on a low, quavering moan. 'Oh, this is the Biggy, Bubbi, my splendid lover.'

'I'm not *Don* Lover now?' he quipped, nearly biting his tongue off for being so careless with his impish humour.

She had no chance to admonish him. Directly overhead a burst of bright light appeared. As quickly, it vanished and was replaced by the image of a huge frog. Brilliant red wine was pouring into that gaping mouth and a thunderous drumbeat of sound repeated the gnome's name with every splash of wine.

'She's summoning me,' Bubbi shouted, levitating to his feet in one motion, ignoring the sickening sound of the broken suction from their torn apart armpits. His knees flexed and he went straight up, clamping the hat on his head before he reached the beamed ceiling; his body shot through it like the blade of a plough and he heard Momo's faint, wailing voice following him even as the ceiling resealed itself after his prenatural passage.

'Bubbi, Bubbi, don't leave me now, this is *it*, I'm almost *there.*' The words haunted him even as he reached the surface of the garden.

'Are you all right?' Dinah asked, carefully closing the lid of the tiny casket containing the frog and the minute vial of wine. 'Did I wake you from a sound sleep?'

'Not quite,' he answered evasively. 'Ah . . . hmmmn . . . next time, maybe one *tiny* drop of wine . . . very tiny, then wait a little bit? I nearly forgot my hat in the rush.'

Dinah laughed, despite the serious intensity of her mood. 'It's so warm and you're worried about your hat?'

'It's not the weather,' he explained, rather nervously, looking about him. 'It has to do with getting here.' He cast another glance about, giving the impression there might be invisible eavesdroppers. 'Uhh . . . where do you think I just came from?' he asked.

'You just appeared,' she assured him. 'One second you weren't here, the next you were. I'm not too good about the small details of magic just yet, you see. Where did you come from?'

He stepped closer, inspecting the fine silk carpet she had spread on the ground to sit on, and to wrap the swords in. He pointed to bits of earth that still marked his naked shoulders . . . naked shoulders! He jumped back to the spot among the carrots where he'd appeared. There was his jerkin, just poking up through the earth. He remembered grabbing his hat but not the garment. In her anger, did Momo fling it after him?

'Bubbi, are you trying to tell me something?' Dinah asked, rising and stepping off the carpet. He looked at her, then touched a spot on the ground with his bare toes. The two fabulous swords suddenly appeared, lying on the soft earth, gleaming in the sparkling evening sunlight.

'Just like that,' he said. He snapped his fingers. 'Boom!'

'You came through the ground?' she asked, her face revealing great surprise. 'Are you trying to tell me you live down there? Under the garden?' His face screwed up, his head trying to nod and shake at the same time. 'In . . . in a hole?' she whispered, shocked.

'In a house,' he snorted, very close to burbling and burping. 'A very nice house, even my wife thinks so.'

'How do you breathe?' she demanded. He puffed his chest up and exhaled noisily. 'That's not what I mean . . . you know what I mean . . . down there!' She pointed her finger at the garden, as though accusing it of some misdemeanour.

'You're being too literal,' he answered unhappily. 'It is down,' he poked his finger rhythmically toward the earth, 'as far as you're concerned, because humans need up, down and don't mess around. To you it will seem so . . . that my house is down there, under the garden. Actually, it is another dimension . . . and there is no way you can say exactly which direction it's in.'

She watched him place the two swords on the carpet and roll it up tightly; he extended his hand expectantly. She blinked, then took the half dozen leather thongs she had tied around her waist and handed them to him.

'You mean, even if you came straight up from there, if I started digging straight down there I wouldn't find your house, I wouldn't meet your wife?' Poor Dinah looked and sounded flustered.

'If you did keep it up for years and years — maybe hundreds of them — you'd reach Cathay. Most humans don't know this, but the earth is round, just like a ball.' He stepped up to an orange tree and reached for a small orange, plucking it from a lower limb. He pointed to one side. 'Here, right, Andalucia?' She nodded. He turned the orange and poked it on the opposite side. 'Cathay. Take my word.' He laughed, shook his head and jumped up and down a few times. 'But I go straight down there and I'm home. Understand?'

'Absolutely not!' she protested, about to jump up and down herself with frustration. 'Are you deliberately trying to confuse me so I can never find your house?' He shook his head, his expression so hurt she thought he would cry. 'Oh, Bubbi, I didn't mean it to sound that way.' His face brightened somewhat. 'Oh ... why did you call me princess before?'

'My wife thinks you're a princess ... you know, like a fairy princess.' He was about to illustrate the statement with a reference to the frog she used to summon him, comparing it to the frog in the story of the princess who lost her golden ball in the pond; he quickly decided Dinah would not believe that outlandish story — but he didn't want to mention Momo's 'Jewish Andalusian Princess' to her.

Bubbi placed the rolled carpet on his head, tilting the hat to one side first in order not to crush the conical point. He told Dinah to hold the middle thong and start walking toward where the guards were waiting to escort her to her grandfather's house. They walked toward the setting sun, in the direction of the Alcazaba, threading their way through narrow paths among great expanses of glorious flowers the sultana's staff kept in ordered perfection. Everywhere workmen were pounding away on the great palace the sultan was constructing. Already named Alhambra because of its dominantly red walls, it was clear even in the early stages that it would be a place of splendour. No one paid particular attention to the young girl wending her way casually through the gardens, carrying a rolled up carpet. She carried it so lightly it caused no curiosity; no one would have suspected it of containing a latter day Cleopatra. Nor did any one of the onlookers see the small gnome who bore the weight of it on his head. Seeing Bubbi was a privilege unique to his mistress, Dinah.

'Where is Joseph?' Bubbi whispered. 'I mean, did you send him on ahead or is he waiting with the palace guards?'

'You mean that Blackamoor?' she asked with languid superiority.

'My dear princess, small errors in the definition of terms

inevitably lead to larger ones,' he answered pedantically.

His Hebrew was so flowery and convoluted she was not sure she understood exactly what he meant. 'Could you repeat that in the local language, Bubbi, you sound like one of the exalted propounders of the Babylonian Talmud.'

'I most certainly do not,' he huffed at her. '*They* used Aramaic. If you understand that better, what I was trying to say is that Blackamoor is a misnomer. Moors are from the Mahgrib, an Arabic term for the western area of North Africa. Joseph is a Nubian from far, far south of Egypt.'

'By the beard of the Prophet,' she breathed with heavy resignation, 'Africa is Africa, is it not? Your *glorious* Joseph was dispatched to our house an hour ago with a chest full of my things.'

The street door was ajar when they arrived, an uncommon occurrence lest someone was on the point of leaving or arriving. Not fully opened, Dinah ascertained for the second time. The half-dozen mounted men alighted, one handing the reins of his mount to another so he could hold Dinah's gentle and elderly mare. When he'd helped her alight, he reached up for the carpet balanced over the pommel. Before his hand touched it, the rug slipped off on the opposite side. When the soldier dashed under the mare's head to retrieve it, he was suddenly aware he had not heard its impact on the hard earth. He saw a pair of muscular legs ... very black. Looking up, he stared into an equally black and very handsome face grinning down at him. The carpet was slung over the youth's shoulder and the door was opened fully. The soldier did not see Bubbi standing there, pressing the door back with one hand, doffing his strange hat and bowing ceremoniously in Dinah's direction. With a more regal carriage, the girl drifted toward the open entry.

'When shall you return, Mistress?' the squadron's commander asked self-consciously. 'Shall we wait here?'

'No, no, Captain,' she answered grandly, 'there is no necessity. When I am ready to return, I will despatch our slave to summon you. Thank you so much for your kind offices.'

'But, Mistress,' he pleaded, seeing himself facing the

tribunal, or the sultan himself, trying to explain why he had left the minister's daughter alone where she had been attacked by Almohade raiders once already.

'Do not worry, Captain,' she reassured him, 'once this door is secured, no one on this earth will dare enter here unbidden. But, if you are that worried, post two men atop the hill to the east. From there they will be able to observe almost the whole of this house. Will that be agreeable?'

The poor man had little choice. The offer was strategically acceptable. He calculated rapidly. One man on the road to intercept the slave ... they could not fail to see him leaving. The balance in reserve behind the two sentinels. He could obey her and *just* keep his robes clean. He bowed politely and nodded assent.

Inside Solomon's secret laboratory, Dinah pointed to the dead centre of the floor, exactly in the middle of the last chalk circles she had drawn. Head cocked with a slight show of annoyance at her imperious manner, Joseph dropped the burden disdainfully. The loud clank reverberated off the stone walls.

'Be careful!' the girl ordered.

'Listen, child, I may be your grandfather's apprentice — that does *not* mean I'm your slave — understood?' She glared at him in utter disbelief, her eyes so round they appeared to be crossing the room to attack him.

'Just who do you think you are?' she demanded coldly, her lips compressing the words.

'A nearly recognized physician, an about-to-be-master magician, an already lightning swift swordsman and ... and ... how old are you?'

'What?' she asked, stamping her small slipper on the floor.

'How old are you?' he repeated in somewhat hesitant Hebrew.

'I shall be thirteen on my next birthday, not that it's any of your business.' She turned away and stared at a spot on the floor a few feet away. 'Bubbi, will you teach this unruly slave a lesson, please?'

Before the words were fully out of her mouth, Joseph leapt forwards, squatted on his heels, bent forward from his hips, placed a hand on either side of his face and exhaled a great breath of air. In that cool room at the base of the stoutly built house his breath congealed just enough to create a slight vapour. He had no trouble defining the outline of the gnome. In that brief part of a second he studied it so thoroughly it was transformed into a constant image in his mind.

'Greetings, Bubbi,' the exuberant young Nubian laughed happily with his unexpected discovery. 'Come on over and be real.'

As though saying it made it so, the gnome took visible form for the youth as the small figure moved toward him. When he reached Joseph, the lad held out his hand in friendly greeting.

'Can he see you?' Dinah asked, her voice choked with disappointment. Bubbi nodded, still shaking hands with Joseph and wondering why his mistress asked such an obvious, self-answering question — he was shaking hands, wasn't he? 'How did he do it?' she demanded, as though Joseph had stolen a personal possession.

'By a supreme effort of will. Not many humans can do that.' Without another word, the gnome stepped up to the carpet bundle and undid the thong fastenings. He rolled the carpet out, exposing the matchless swords. Joseph shouted, rose up into the air and dropped back on his heels, hovering over the gleaming weapons. He stroked one, cocking his head as though to listen to a tone it would sound. He merely laid a finger on the other and withdrew it immediately. He rose slowly, the first sword balanced on the palm of his right hand. He raised the hand as high above his head as he could, offering the weapon to heaven. His eyes closed and his lips moved rapidly, forming a reverent incantation in a language neither of his listeners had ever heard. The hand lowered slowly until it was at eye level. With no apparent movement of the hand, sword and scabbard flew up, separating. The hilt of the sword landed in the waiting right hand, the scabbard in the left. The sword flashed in so many cut and thrust movements, neither Dinah nor the preternaturally alert gnome could follow the pattern. The boy's laugh when the blade came to rest was one of glorious triumph.

'You like it, then?' Bubbi asked in a hushed tone.

'Like it? In my country the elder doctors of magic would claim it was made by the great spirits of the mountains, in the secret places where the precious metals dwell.' He dropped to his knees. 'Is it mine?' he asked Bubbi tremulously, as though his heart would burst if the answer were no. 'Please, I will treasure it with my life.'

'Yours?' Bubbi exploded with great agitation. 'The owner of that sword is probably now sending search parties far and wide to recover it. It came from the heavily guarded treasury in Bagdad, slipped from under the unsuspecting eyes of its very guards. The Khalif will have the thief torn limb from limb . . . even if he is a small gnome. Be satisfied to hold it and wield it as long as your personal powers rise and remain supreme against all opposition.'

'And the other sword' Joseph asked, rising as he sheathed the splendid blade, 'that with the female nature? What will you do with it, Little One?'

Bubbi whipped the hat from his head and dashed it on the ground. He was about to jump up and down on it but he actually bounded over it, making a leap much greater than might have been expected from someone his size; glowering, he stood toe to toe with the tall lad, shaking his fist.

'Don't you ever call me Little One, Black One. That sword is for Dinah. Her nature is female too, in case you hadn't noticed.'

'Hadn't noticed?' Joseph answered, his feelings hurt, 'I've hardly noticed anything else for months and months. I also notice you're prejudiced against black people.'

'Not unless they're prejudiced against small people first — you started it!' Bubbi's fist was clenched and shaking again.

'You're right,' Joseph admitted, bowing at the waist and offering his hand in apology and friendship. Bubbi stared at it, finding the anger draining away in spite of himself. He opened the fist and shook hands, grinning bashfully.

'Good thing *you're* not prejudiced, Dinah,' Joseph beamed at her adoringly.

'The consummate nerve!' She stamped her slipper with unbridled fury. 'You will address me properly and you can rest assured I'm totally prejudiced as far as *you're* concerned.'

'It's a good thing you're not a man!' the lad declared, his voice shaking with rage or hurt, Dinah could not determine exactly which; perhaps both, she concluded.

'Why? Would you split me in two with your glorious sword? Or just knock me to the ground and kick me about a bit? That's the usual treatment we expect from you bigoted servants of false prophets.'

'Dinah, what are you talking about?' Bubbi leapt to her side and tugged at her hand. She shook free, her eyes glaring at the Nubian. 'Don't you remember what I told you before. . . .'

Joseph laughed, the sword in its scabbard caught under one arm as both hands fashioned an intricate harness of the leather thongs to fix the scabbard to his waist.

'I love you too much for that,' he answered softly. 'No I'm happy you're not a man for quite different reasons . . . and not just because I love you either. You're such a bad-tempered little girl, think what sort of rabbi you'd grow up to be? One who hated a fellow Jew just because he was a different colour?'

Bubbi's last remark about telling her something struck as Joseph's words found their mark. She blushed deeply and hung her head.

'Bubbi, what is our real purpose here? I brought the chest I was ordered to bring, but I suspect that was a mere subterfuge . . .' Joseph patted the gleaming weapon now suspended from his waist.

Before Bubbi could answer the young man, Dinah produced a piece of chalk from a pocket of the voluminous trousers of fine deep blue silk and began making the traditional chalk circles. She had learnt a good deal from her grandfather since the last attempt. As she worked, she quietly breathed a prayer that her knowledge and technique would be faultless this time. She didn't even harken to the buzzing of conversation between the two males.

Remember, she warned herself when the devout prayer was finished, a ritual invocation is like baking in an oven — one slight mistake and you must start all over again. The powers you summon are most likely watching for just such an error ... and Whoof! You haven't them at your command, they've got you and nobody ever sees you again.

She felt a strong hand close over hers; looking down, she saw Joseph break the chalk in half, slipping one half back into her hand.

'What do you think you're doing?' she gasped.

'It will save time if I do the other part of the circle. Don't you think I know the correct letters and symbols, that I can write YHWH as legibly as you? You're not the only student of Qabala in this area, Lady Stuckup.' He patted her hand and she yanked it away, huffing as she did.

'Yesod,' Bubbi whispered to Dinah. 'Yesod the Foundation ... we shall need all the power we can muster on the astral plane,' he advised her.

'Good,' she agreed, 'I tend to favour that. Grandfather says it is important to stand against a tree with the feeling of its great power coming through to you. And then visualise the Tree of Life itself behind you, imprinting everything associated with each sephiroth on your own aura, allowing each to penetrate the parallel psychic centres of the body. I always feel Yesod the most strongly.'

She made a cross in the centre of the circle, squaring it with four triangles of different coloured silk, the appropriate ones for Yesod. The small charcoal brazier they had lighted on arrival she moved inside the circle and set a vial of incense close by. At the exact northern point outside the circle, about three feet distance from the outer ring, she drew a triangle in chalk and aligned the apex with north, the base toward the circle.

Bubbi leapt straight up into the air, reaching the high ceiling and pressing it with his fingertips; for a moment, he seemed to cling there like a fly, then he floated down to land in the middle of the triangle on the tips of his toes.

'How did you do that?' Joseph gurgled with the delight of a child, belying his powerful, manly physique.

'Oh, it's easy, really, I just throw away almost all my weight for a second or two.'

'But where does it go . . . the weight?' Joseph was totally fascinated with this supernatural power. 'Do the spirits take it away?'

'Don't be childish, Joseph,' Bubbi scoffed, coming down hard on his heels when the weight overtook him. He dropped on his bottom and massaged his heels with his hands, a rueful expression on his face. 'Spirits! You just hook the weight into the vast magnetic field beneath this house . . . and jump away from it, that's all.'

'And there's always a magnetic field just below . . .'

'Joseph, you are hopelessly naive,' the gnome rebuked him. 'The master of this house selected the site with great cunning and knowledge. It's a veritable powerhouse . . . and we're going to need all of it.' The mannikin bounded back to his feet. 'Are you nearly ready, Dinah.'

'Yes . . . you!' she addressed Joseph imperiously. 'Step inside here.' Bubbi winced, hating to see this sort of behaviour from one he adored so. He looked up at Joseph, offering him unspoken comfort.

'Yes, my beloved princess,' the Nubian answered with a huge smile, as though she had called him her precious dream prince. Without seeming to be busy at anything, he had created another sword harness for the girl. He bounded inside the magic ring with somewhat less weightlessness than Bubbi; landing by her side, he began fixing the harness over her shoulder and about her waist. She slapped his hands twice, indicating he was becoming much too familiar with her person, more so than the simple operation required.

'Yiiiiii!' Bubbi's howl hurt their ears; astounded, they watched him rise to the ceiling once again, suspend himself there, whirl so rapidly in the air that, like a top, he seemed to become a blur; almost too fast for the eye to see, he dropped back into the triangle.

'What's the matter?' Dinah cried, her hands fluttering with excitement.

'You ... that's what the matter.' Bubbi struck his forehead over and over, buffeting himself with chastisement. 'You're a *girl*!'

'You never noticed before?' Joseph asked with guileless ease. 'I know she's only a little twelve-year-old, but ... hmmmn, you didn't notice?' The lad made a suggestive sculpture in the air with his hands. 'I've never noticed *any*thing else ... and you call *me* naive ...?'

'I didn't mean *that*!' Bubbi shouted back, waving his arms furiously over his head. 'I mean, can you imagine facing what we may have to cope with on this journey ... with a *girl* ... a *lovely* girl? You and that sword will be busy full time protecting her from all the villains, bandits, soldiers, sheikhs, sharifs, kings, khalifs, clerics and beggars and all the other assorted rapists who will vie for the privilege and honour of introducing her to the delights of life.'

'You are not leaving me here!' Dinah stormed. She was just about to stamp her foot when she noticed that Joseph was watching that foot expectantly; with a shrug and a turning up of her nose, she refused to do what was expected.

'I didn't suggest leaving you, I was going to suggest that we transform you into a man ... a male, sort of — well, you know, make you look masculine, disguise your beauty.' Bubbi waved his hands in a helpless search for the right phrases.

'You want me to dress like a man, is that it?' she drew herself up, trying to stand as tall as she could. 'Preposterous!'

'Beloved princess,' Joseph asked reasonably, 'just where do we plan to go, what do we plan to do?'

Briefly, Dinah explained about her father and the two booby cousins. They were somewhere between Bactria and Bagdad, to the best of anyone's knowledge, based on the last communication which had reached Granada months earlier. Undoubtedly now held captive for ransom, they had been returning from the negotiation of a huge and very rich trading mission. In most parts of the world, they had international financing facilities, credits that could be exchanged instead of ferrying gold and silver back with them. This caravan had crossed India and continued to the frontiers beyond. Whatever they were bringing back, it had immense value.

'Are you sure they are alive?' Joseph asked, his voice gentle with concern. 'Whole cities have been massacred and plundered for less.'

'That is a possibility we have to face.' The girl's stature sagged slightly and she bowed her head. Tenderly, for one so broad and strong, he lifted her chin and smiled into her eyes.

'They live . . . I feel it in my heart,' he assured her. 'Now, please take Bubbi's advice. Go change your clothes. Unfasten the harness and leave it here.'

Bubbi was jumping up and own with agitation again. 'If anyone sees that face, all the male robes in the world won't hide her identity . . .'

'What do you wish me to do?' Dinah demanded. 'Grow a beard?'

'Exactly! That's it! Clever girl!' Dismay became delight in an eye blink. 'You see, Joseph doesn't have a beard yet, but no one with two eyes in his head would mistake *him* for a girl, now would they?' He nodded in agreement with his own excellent logic. 'That's it, the very thing, a beard!'

'By the beard of the Prophet . . .' Joseph began.

'Did you hear that?' the girl accused, pointing at the lad. 'Did you hear him . . . and you called him a Jew?'

'Oh . . . I'm a relatively new convert,' the Nubian declared, winking covertly at Bubbi. 'Did Moses not have a beard?'

'Of course he did. Now the important thing is that Dinah must have one . . .' the gnome began.

'Just how do you propose to accomplish that? Do you

know a sheep somewhere about that has red hair, like mine?' Dinah's fists were planted on her hips, her legs akimbo, her attention riveted on the gnome. He signalled her to step out of the magic ring. He took her hand, led her to the door and opened it as though it were not locked, the key still lying on the heavy wooden table against the opposite wall. In the hall, he beckoned her to bend over, bring her ear close to his lips. He whispered but a very few words and the girl straightened so violently she nearly lost her balance. Involuntarily, the young man's sword flew halfway from its sheath, he not even aware that his hand was on the pommel.

'How dare you!' she fairly screeched. 'What an out*rage*ous suggestion! I'm having nothing more to . . .'

He gestured her back down to his lips with great urgency. His fevered gesture communicated itself and, to her own surprise, she obeyed. She listened, nodded once or twice and shot erect again.

'They do?' she asked, her face a picture of utter disbelief. He nodded solemnly. '*All* of them? *Every* single one?' He nodded again. 'In the name of the Lord, tell me why that should be?'

'It's the law of Islam. For eating pigs, the law is "Thou shalt not." For the law in this case, "Thou shalt."'

'You are seriously asking me to believe you? You are seriously asking me to do what you suggest?'

'Not only that, but as fast as you can. Do you want your grandfather to get back from his mission to Jaen before we get back from our mission to the Lord knows where? Can you imagine the result? A great magician like Solomon could blast me into a strange universe from which I could never return . . . without Momo . . .' he began to sob softly. Dinah softened but she didn't move.

'What does he want you to do?' Joseph asked, pacing about the inner circle as though he'd been forbidden to leave it.

'Don't you dare ask such questions!' She turned back to Bubbi. 'If you so much as whisper a word . . .'

'Yiiiiii! I'm not whispering. Will you go ask that fat girl of yours . . . what's her name?'

'Farida? Please don't call her fat. She's been tormenting herself for so many days now I can't recall. She's lost so much weight. I think she's hopelessly in love with someone who can't stand fat. What shall I ask her?'

'First, if what I've told you is true — she's worked in Muslim households. Then, get her to help you. She'll know what to do.'

'How? She's a Mozarab, a Christian, how would she . . .'

'Because she has fancied a Muslim man here and there, that's why . . . do you think a serious Muslim would . . .'

'Don't say another word, I don't want to hear about *that.*' Tossing her hair with vexation, she stormed down the corridor.

Bubbi bounced back into the room and sat down in the middle of the chalk triangle. 'If her grandpa gets back here before we do . . . and what about the sultana, she'll notice Dinah is missing . . . and those guards . . . Dinah?' He looked up to the ceiling, his hands clasped in supplication. 'Will you *please* hurry?'

'Won't you tell me what she's up to?' Joseph asked, seating himself at the edge of the circle nearest the gnome. The mannikin shook his head violently. 'Is it *that* awful?' Bubbi nodded with the same vigour. 'Is it . . . naughty?'

'Is that what's on your mind all the time?' the gnome growled disapprovingly.

'Not until you started that strange conversation,' he pointed out resentfully, 'out there where I couldn't hear.'

'You're too young to hear that sort of thing,' Bubbi offered absently.

'Well! I'm older than she is — and you told *her.*'

'Yes, but you're not a girl, don't you see?' To the gnome, that was so obvious he shook his head at the youth with bewilderment.

'Well? Neither are you!' Now Joseph was shaking his head in a copy of Bubbi, considering the other end of the conversation ridiculous.

'Yes, and that's neither here nor there . . . so there! Or here . . . if you prefer.'

'Bubbi, what in the name of heaven are you talking about?'

'Not about me, I hope.' Dinah stood in the doorway tapping her foot. Bubbi's head whipped about, perfectly synchronised with the youth's. They both bounded to their feet. Next to Dinah, Farida stood simpering like a silly little girl half her age. Dinah was wearing a short-cropped, squarish beard on her chin, a thin, matching moustache above. Somehow, to Joseph, it seemed a bit more bristling than a new beard should.

'Yiiiiii!' Lad and gnome sounded their surprise simultaneously and on the same note. Dinah whirled round on her toes, facing away from them, leaning forward as if about to run off.

'It's beautiful,' Joseph sang out. 'Perfect. Just the right colour, a couple of shades darker than your hair, just as it should be. How did . . .' Bubbi's fierce hiss cut him short.

'Well?' She turned, glaring at the gnome.

He lifted his arms, moved his hands palms up, describing perfection with the gesture.

'Do you like it?' she insisted.

He shrugged. 'It suits you . . . what more can I say?'

For the first time she addressed the youth. 'Do I look like a man? . . . tell the truth.'

'You look wonderful, beloved princess . . .' she took one threatening step towards him . . . 'you don't look like a girl, that's certain.' He had been so startled by the beard he now noticed her robe and boots for the first time, the dark brown tailesan covering her head and wrapped about her neck, trailing down behind her. One tress of that brilliant red hair had escaped the woollen prison.

'Dinah, in the name of God the Merciful, let's go!' the mannikin wailed.

'Now, do you remember what I told you?' Dinah asked the girl; it was quite true, Joseph observed, she had lost a great deal of weight. He tried to picture the young man she had her passions fixed on.

'Yes,' Farida lisped, fighting very hard not to look at the indescribably handsome Nubian. Was it possibly true what they said about Nubians, that 'it' was almost frightening . . . 'Oh!' Dinah had slapped her arm as though to wake her up.

'I'll repeat it,' Dinah scolded, shaking the girl's shoulders to force her concentration. 'If my grandfather returns before I do, you tell him we are gone and will be back shortly . . . we hope. That I beg him not to enter here until we do return . . .'

'. . . and if you return before he does, I am to say nothing.' Farida finished, pleased with herself. 'Where are you going?'

Dinah turned the girl and pushed her gently toward the long corridor. Before the confused Farida could turn and ask another question, the door was closed and locked without making a sound. Dinah was inside.

When Joseph had attached her sword under the robe and let the garment fall back into place, he smiled down at her, his eyes fixed on the thick growth of strong, shiny red hair on her chin and upper lip. His eyes were full of mischief. She brought her booted foot down hard on his bare one, eliciting a sharp yelp of pain.

'You know the first stage?' she asked, her voice warning him to be serious.

'Visualise the four hexagrams — north-east-south-west. Join them with a ring of fire while you pronounce the banishing ceremony . . .'

'Well, are you ready?' she interrupted.

'Ready whenever you are, Princess ha-Levi,' he grinned.

She drew her sword and handed it to him. He drew his own and stood directly behind her, his arms encircling her at her own shoulder level, the blades crossed.

The atmosphere in the room changed radically. As Dinah finished the banishing rite and began the invocation to bring them out onto the astral plane, Joseph felt his perceptions expand with the speed of light in every direction. He saw Bubbi clearly, standing on the very tips of his two big toes, his eyes closed, his hands folded over his chest, almost as a reflection of Joseph and the two crossed swords.

All three began to feel the pull, as of some great force drawing them upwards and outwards. Joseph felt his feet holding him down, his head pulling him up; in less than a second he had the sensation that his body had been elongated by a league or more. Then, a new and distinctly terrifying shift occurred. A terrible moan broke from Bubbi's throat. Lad and girl saw a horrid brown footlike appendage take form in the triangle. Three large toes became more solid, each tipped with a long curved talon like an eagle's. The member clamped down, the talons forcing one of Bubbi's feet flat on the ground. The talons began to enter the little foot when Joseph's body swung sideways, his right arm rising and whipping forward with incredible speed. Even before the sword reached the ugly target, Musa the demon materialised in a flash of blue light, kicking the offending monstrous foot out of existence. For all his speed, Joseph's sword arced with the slow deliberation of a stately dance. It decapitated at least a dozen blades of strange purple grass.

Demon, gnome, Dinah and Joseph were standing in the middle of a strange land that seemed to extend to infinity in all directions. The sky above was a soft lavender hue, a pale reflection of the purple carpet at their feet. In the distance, Dinah could see, here and there, brilliant jewelled fountains spraying sparkling showers in graceful arcs. Further in the distance, trees grew tall with a similar bejeweled aspect. Even as she watched, trees and fountains seemed to multiply themselves; a strangeness she could hardly comprehend yet was ... nothing seemed to end. All these beautiful objects did run as far as the eye could see because there were no earthly limits ... she gasped; everything went on forever.

'No time for dreaming, little girl,' Musa ordered. She looked up, surprised. Not only did the light have an extraordinary quality that intensified colour, sharpened vision, but sound had altered too, or her ears had become unusually acute. The green demon had little Bubbi locked tightly in his arms; the gnome was grimacing vilely, growling deep in his throat. Dinah saw his fingers clawing at Musa's arms, his feet thrashing impotently at the demon's groin. The marks on one foot, when it appeared momentarily, were swollen, ugly and turning a nasty shade of dark green.

'Yes,' Musa apparently read her mind, 'he was infected by that arch-fiend. I hope, young one, you will keep in mind how that happened originally. Azazel got one foot back into your world through your ineptitude. And because of that, your grandfather has had an unpleasant encounter with him.'

'But . . . but . . .' she was so upset, furious and ashamed at the same time, her normally fluid speech got caught in her throat. She felt Joseph's hand press her shoulder encouragingly; he had slipped her sword into its scabbard without her being aware of it.

'Joseph, run to the nearest fountain,' Musa tossed his unruly deep red locks in the direction of the most vivid one to his left. 'Let the shower fall on the tip of your sword, but do not let it touch you, whatever you do.'

Before the words were finished the Nubian shot up in a huge bound and went off in the indicated direction with the speed of a gazelle, his feet hardly touching the ground. Fascinated, they watched the brilliant cascade of multi-coloured sparks as the substance from the fountain struck the blade. At the first flaring, Bubbi redoubled his struggles, howling like a wild beast.

'What would happen if the shower struck — uh — him-er — Joseph?' Dinah asked, her breath caught up in involuntary gasps.

Musa raised one thick, brick-red eyebrow and the corner of his mouth formed a sneer. Did it really hurt her to voice the lad's name? Momentarily, he wondered if only black skin did this to her . . . did she dislike green skin too?

'He would be evaporated totally, as though he had landed on the sun. That cascade is used by the Djinni, the natural inhabitants of this plane. It replenishes their powers.'

Dinah had no way of knowing, but Musa had become

incredibly tolerant and 'human' over the past few centuries. He still had a great capacity for capricious mischief, but he was sober beyond his years. Bubbi was the only one who would have suspected the real reason: Musa had been deeply affected by the death of his saintly mother four hundred years earlier.

Joseph flew back, if possible, more swiftly than he had departed. Musa dumped the hysterically enraged Bubbi on the ground and kneeled on his chest, holding the hands pinned together in one of his, the legs pinned down with the other. He didn't have to say a word to the precocious young apprentice-physician. Using the blade of the sword near the tip as he would have a white hot cauterising iron, he wiped the wounds clean. There was a stench of burning flesh, a scream from the captive gnome, a bright flash from the point where sword touched foot and then . . . nothing.

'The wounds have disappeared!' Dinah exclaimed. Joseph stood back, Musa was erect without having visibly moved and Bubbi bounded to his feet with that weird weightless knack of his.

'Are we ready to go?' the gnome demanded. 'You people waste more time . . .'

'Hush,' Musa ordered, 'we must speak very softly here and only when absolutely necessary. I will not cause much stir, but mortals appearing here in such solid form can be detected from great distances.'

'Why were you kneeling on me?' Bubbi demanded. He turned on Joseph whose sword had leapt into its sheath the second the cauterisation had been performed. 'And what was he doing? I thought I saw something flash through the air.'

Musa picked him up, dropped him on his shoulders, one leg on either side of his powerful neck.

'Hold on tight to my hair. Whatever you do, don't let go.' Bubbi began pounding the demon's head with his tightly clenched fists, demanding answers. 'You had a tummy-ache,' Musa explained patiently. 'I held you down, the good physician administered to you. Instead of beating on my head, I think you would show greater courtesy if you thanked us both. Don't you feel better now?'

Bubbi desisted, a puzzled look on his face. He felt his tummy, rubbed it a few times and looked at Joseph, then Dinah. Sheepishly, he said thank you in a very quiet voice.

Extending his arms, Musa beckoned the other two, telling each to stand on one of his feet and grasp him tightly about the waist. As they did, he circled their shoulders with his enfolding arms.

'Hold on tight!' Their eyes burnt so with the rush of the wind they hardly perceived more than the sensation of shooting upwards then forwards, whatever direction that might be. To Dinah, the speed increased constantly, doubling itself every few seconds . . . or that, at least, was how it felt. Speech was impossible.

Her mind was tormented, in spite of the indescribable voyage they were making. That fiend, the one Musa had named as Azazel . . . she had been responsible for giving him substance and access the first time she had done a magical exercise to summon an earth spirit. It was no accident that those huge talons had sunk into the poor gnome's foot. Her fault! And it had infected the gnome, had been a way of possessing him . . . yes, that was it; Azazel was trying to use Bubbi as a medium to gain full manifestation . . . and then what? Was Bubbi cured by that application of the sword?

To Dinah, it seemed like a large, tender hand entered her mind and patted it soothingly. Bubbi would be all right for the time being. Yes, it was dangerous; each time a gap is bridged, it is bridged more easily, more forcibly the next time. They would have to be more careful. Azazel would not be so foolish again. He wouldn't allow his ephemeral presence to announce itself as broadly in taking over Bubbi as they had just seen. Back on the earth plane, it would be so subtle that insight and sensitivity such as her grandfather's would be necessary to discern the evil spirit's presence.

As it began to dawn on Dinah that Musa was actually communicating directly with her mind, her whole insides tried to climb up into her mouth. The vertigo was overpowering. It took a moment to realise they were plummeting downwards like a fiery meteor.

CHAPTER 7

Solomon arched his back painfully, shifting his sparsely padded hams on the saddle, searching for relief from the stiffness and irritation. Much too old for this travelling life, he upbraided himself. On the way back, they had stopped briefly at Alcalá and Illora: neither town was as badly damaged as they had originally feared. But there had been mindless, indiscriminate killing, to be sure. Sickening, sickening what people do in the names of their gods and godlets. Mohammad is a redeemer, he brings the message of love. Get out there and kill all those who refuse the message ... it's a holy war. Jesus is the Prince of Peace, he is the Saviour, get out there and slaughter the infidel in the name of Jesus. And the Chosen People? Slay, slay, slay the enemies of the Lord — from Moses to Herod. Has anyone killed in Buddha's name? If people must convert, why not in a logical, humane direction? Because Buddhists don't threaten you with the sword, that's why.

The sultan was pleased. Solomon smiled at last, his heart lightening as the outline of his own house appeared limned against the night sky. The brightness of the evening star, the sharp outline of the moon's crescent reminded him of his youthful travels through the Near East and Central Asia. A desert moon, a sky for harsh and silent lands. The sultan had looked at the many significant gifts sent by the Christian king. Looked and nodded: the gifts of a thoughtful rather than a lavish man with no taste. As Ahmar knew, all Christians were by no means barbarians, any more than all Africans. He had been elated when Solomon had described Fernando's reaction to the razing of Illora and Alcalá de ibn Said ... as with the immediate corrective measures, the unreserved disciplinary means applied. A very tired old rabbi left the king still fuming unhappily about the time it would take to create an authentic engagement between his own inexperienced civilian troops and Ferdinand's professional, hardened soldiers. That the civilian militia would be no match for the king's fighting men was not in doubt; that to be meaningful, the engagement could not be too far from the walls of Granada itself was obvious. But to a man with Ahmar's honourable family and personal history as warriors and able generals, the potion was a bitter one indeed.

'Poor Ahmar,' he uttered aloud, unaware he had voiced his thought.

'Pardon, your worship?' the leader of the escort asked nearby. This was not the group he had travelled with over the last days. That captain's voice rang with sincerity and respect — this one could hardly disguise his contempt: assigned to escort an old Jew home? He thought about the massacre of Jews here less than two hundred years earlier ... when the king does go, will my son retain his offices? Moses is not arrogant or willful, but he is not very smart, either. If a treaty is forged soon, will Ferdinand's son honour it? Who then will punish my people with abominations because I lifted my head too high, I rose above my station? Would they say: 'Ha, he would not be satisfied with lucrative cesspool cleaning contracts, with the wealth of world-wide trade pouring into his coffers ... no, he had to seek high office, honours and dignities that belonged only to the great and noble tribes of Arabia.' And after that fine speech? 'All right, to those coffers, men!'

He felt the household guard drawing near. 'Nothing, kind sir,' Solomon answered courteously, 'just a tired old man talking to himself.' He turned in the saddle to face the man. 'Why come further? You can wait here until I reach my own gates ... it is so near, really, and so late for men who have been on duty so long.'

The guard answered with an affirmative salute and drew his men up. A few minutes later, Solomon and one of the royal mules were safely inside and the gates bolted again.

Seated in darkness, his elbows on the high table, feet drawn up on a rung of the stool, the patriarch rested his chin on the knuckles of his clasped hands. The star's course was marked through the window. The moon's acceleration almost absurd by comparison.

'There's eternity,' he pronounced softly. 'Is it?' he asked without a pause. 'Why should I assume the moon, the stars ... this earth, for that matter, are eternal? That a cosmos such as this — or unimaginably different — is created every few billion years ... that such a process had no beginning and will have no end ... is that not more like eternity? We are forever trying to capture God inside the confines of our limitations.' He laughed softly, but respectfully. 'God will simply not have it, and who could blame Him? But the important thing to think about, one that lends itself to some solution, is the aches, the pains, the weariness of my bones, the smell of my skin and these clothes.' Maybe he should have taken the sultan's kind offer to join him in the palace baths. Heat, steam, the lovely scented balms and unguents. Young girls to apply them, to shampoo one's skin until it glowed, till fiery darts seemed to rise from it. Then lolling in the large pool, soaking in that very hot water ... it would have been too long, too formal. When a king is so courteous and generous to his servant, that servant must know how to demur.

He closed his eyes and visualised himself standing inside the two chalk circles. He summoned Serafina and she stood before him in the triangle, waiting obediently for his command. It wasn't much, just a hot tub of water, one handmaiden to scrub him and annoint him with perfumed oils. To stretch his weary body out on a freshly made bed and massage all the soreness away ... just possibly, if she would not find it loathsome of course, he had no wish to force the young thing as most cruel potentates would ...

'You stop that, you lascivious old man!' he scolded himself aloud. Just before the vision faded, he saw a horrible, claw-like foot materialise in the triangle. The fearful talons imbedded themselves in the smooth, reptilian skin of Serafina's hind paw.

Solomon bolted off the stool, tore the door open and ran to the stairs. Moments later, he pressed his ear against the wood of the laboratory door having forgotten the key in his headlong dash. Silence. He felt no unwholesome emanations. Had Azazel been there and not properly banished ... but who would summon *anyone* in there? Dinah was in the palace ... were she not, surely they would have told him before he left. Maybe Joseph? He had been assigned to the palace, to do surgical services in his master's absence. Only partially satisfied, Solomon backed away from the door, his eyes still fixed on the dark, forbidding wood. Something would not let his guard down, but he simply could not find it. He turned and paced slowly down the corridor. An hour or so of meditation and prayer could prepare me ... rising through the Tree of Life, my other eye would see what these two cannot, it would penetrate many barriers and veils ... you'd fall asleep, you old fool, you can hardly stand up as it is!

'Ah, my lord, you're home,' Hepzie, the cook, touched his sleeve gently, urging him into the large kitchen. 'God is merciful, God is great, God be praised, you're safe and sound.' A candelabrum with four flaming candles threw light up into his face. 'Safe, but you look terrible, so weary, a good thing I had a vision, an inspiration, revered sir, a genuine revelation. I saw, I looked up at the moon and saw you trudging home, weak and weary. See!' She pointed triumphantly to a large wooden tub belching a cloud of steam. 'I heated the water ... I knew, I just knew. And hungry, you must be ravenous, you must have starved rather than touch any of that Gentile food, it would poison you . . .'

He held up a hand, arresting the monologue. Hepzie was rather ageless so his son and granddaughter always said. Forty-five, fifty? A widow for twenty years . . . no doubt a reborn virgin for all of it. No children. Funny little woman, the top of her head below his shoulder, thin little legs and narrow hips, but those ponderous breasts . . . as though placed there to nurse the earth and she's barren . . . his school teacher self pulled him in sharply. She came here after losing her husband . . . what do you know about why or why not she had or didn't have or couldn't or wouldn't have children, Most Illuminated Rabbi? He stole a quick look at the breast swinging to the right a split second after she began turning her torso to move toward the charcoal fire. Ponderous, not pendulous, he observed with scientific interest . . . what engineering feat is this? The air about her person is as buoyant as water? Is she a witch of sorts and I never detected it? As he pondered, a big bowl was set before him on the kitchen table: a large and heavy slab of oak on legs as thick as tree trunks. A huge chunk of dark bread followed and that in turn chased by a wooden spoon.

'I made the soup just this evening. I got plenty of extra chicken feet, it's strong and nourishing . . . lots of vegetables too. Eat, then I will bathe you.'

'You will *what*?' he choked on the first hasty spoonful. 'Since when do you give me . . .'

'Shhh . . . eat.' She whisked a fly away. 'You can't eat and talk, look, you're choking already. It was part of my vision,' she informed him with the same adamant determination of an emperor making an unalterable proclamation. 'You were so weary, so in need of kind treatment, I was washing you, scrubbing away the dust and weariness, forgetting totally my own modesty, the shame this very act might cause any decent woman who was doing it for a man who's not her husband. It was like a prophecy of old,' she intoned, clasping her hands, closing her eyes and tilting her head blindly toward the ceiling.

Solomon shook his head with bewildered concern. If she gets violent, he figured, I will have to tie her down, wake the other servants and plunge her into a bath of *cold* water. Perhaps she is reaching that age when most women lose their reason, become temporarily insane . . . what a pity, she is such a good cook . . . nobody makes soup like this, she was so right. Starved, starved for a proper meal. Well, then, maybe you should just sit in the hot bath, close your eyes, concentrate on other things and allow her to do what you are already too tired to do for yourself.

This time, the school teacher and the Most Illuminated Rabbi left him alone. With a satisfied burp, he lowered his lanky, hard body into the comforting, enfolding bliss and warmth. Hepzie was still facing the wall, her hands covering her eyes as he had instructed her. God alone would know what a such sight could do to a woman in her uncertain, fragile state. Unhinge her totally, no doubt. He called her and then closed *his* eyes.

She scrubbed and scrubbed with a rough cloth, humming a tuneless ditty to herself as she worked. Her patient had almost fallen asleep when she yanked one of his legs up to wash it. When he opened his eyes slightly, his head snapped up. She was leaning over the tub, her head bent to one side, scrubbing under his thigh. Her two huge breasts were floating on the surface, her robe pulled down from her shoulders and the sleeves tied about her slim waist.

'Hepzie, what do you think you're doing? What would anyone say, walking in here . . . what would young Dinah say, in the name of heaven?'

'Don't have bad thoughts, bad thoughts are very bad for you,' she advised him, dropping that leg and capturing the other. 'Do you want me to get my robe all splashed? I'm being practical.'

'I can finish the rest by myself, thank you,' he coughed, grabbing the cloth when she got too close, her arms immersed nearly to the shoulders, those inexplicable breasts still rising like inflated bladders. She had a lost, delirious look on her face, her eyes rolling upwards, her lips moist and parted slightly.

'You're such a wonderful looking man, my lord, you would make any woman's heart proud, it doesn't matter how old you are.' Her arms were still in the water, those magnetic orbs bobbing. He backed up as far as he could.

'Hepzie, it is time to adjust your clothing. I'm serious, others simply would not understand your practical streak. Besides, I want to stand up and get out . . . and dry myself. You'll have to go back to the table and face the door.'

When she stood up straight, her anatomy defied nature. Those huge things stuck straight out in front of her, refusing to answer the earth's pull. She smiled demurely and walked over to the table; she faced the door and began humming again. From the tilt of her head, he knew she was listening for his descent on to the floor. She had laid a small clean cloth there for his feet. And she must have had laundry ready, for a long white shirt-like garment was draped over the nearest chair. On the floor were his old pointed camel-skin slippers.

'My lord,' she sighed over her shoulder, 'do you recall the story of Abram and Hagar, the handmaiden of Sarai?'

'That is a strange question to ask a teacher and Talmudic scholar, is it not? Of course I recall the story.' He dropped the towel and slid into the light cotton robe, jamming his feet into the slippers as he pulled the robe down fully.

The woman turned, causing his mouth to open involuntarily; she was still naked to the waist. And her nakedness was beginning to have an effect on him. Before she could open her mouth, he snapped his fingers and gruffly ordered her to cover herself up. She looked down with surprise, as if to say, fancy that . . . I forgot.

'I was thinking, your excellency, about how Hagar's son Ishmael went out in the wilderness and all, how he was apart from men, how all men's hands were turned against him. But the Arabs claim they are all descended from him and look what they've achieved. Now, you are still a very fine figure of a man, you would undoubtedly still be able to sire a healthy son . . . why, with your background, with all your fabulous abilities, he would be bound to turn into another Ishmael . . .'

'Hepzie, what in God's name are you suggesting?' Solomon was so thunderstruck, his voice came out as a restricted whisper.

'Well,' she bumbled on, clapping then clasping her hands; she had done the robe up so loosely, one of the ripe melons nearly broke free, 'if Ishmael could start off tribes who conquered the world for *their* God . . .'

'Hepzibah, *their* God is *our* God . . .' he began, but she took no notice.

'Yes, but they know nothing about Torah, you know that and there is no Mohammad in Torah and I know that . . . but what I'm trying to tell you is your son could be the one to father a mighty race that would stamp out all our oppressors, the Christians and the Muslims, they would usher in a new glorious era for Israel . . . we could have the Promised Land back . . . once again, we would *actually* be The Chosen People . . .'

'We *are* The Chosen People,' he corrected her.

'Yes, but we're the only ones who know. But with a new Ishmael, a genuine Jewish Ishmael who is not interested in starting off a whole race of Arabs . . .'

'Hepzie, what makes you think such a man would be so fantastic he could actually influence the Lord?'

'Your Excellency, Abram practically helped God make the right choice when He was choosing The Chosen People . . .'

Solomon sat down and rocked with laughter. Hepzie drew herself up, a look of resentful injury crossing her normally happy features.

'Hepzie, how are you suggesting I create this . . . this . . . you know, you are talking about a messiah, do you realise that?'

She nodded, her face beaming again. 'You forgot already?' she asked. 'It's been so long since your wife died, may the Lord have mercy on her? I'll show you, I haven't forgotten.'

'Hepzibah, this is ridiculous ... besides, I already have a son,' he tried to effect a severe growl of disapproval, but the movement of her breasts as she turned away aborted the harsh sound.

'No offence, your honour, but your son is hardly the type,' she sniffed deferentially, but stood her ground.

'I suppose I would have to agree with you there ...' he began as the door flew open. Farida stood there, her eyes wide and wild looking, darting from one to the other.

'Hepzie, off to bed with you, you won't be able to rise early enough in the morning ...' dismissing the older woman with a careless gesture of her hand, she drew close to Solomon and sighed with agreeable modesty. 'Oh, good sir, I am so happy you have returned to us safely. I know your bones must ache after such a journey. I have prepared scented unguents with camphor, myrrh and sandalwood to rub into you so that you may ease those stiffnesses and enjoy a long, refreshing sleep.'

Hepzibah sniffed to herself and charged out the door in a great huff. Solomon hardly recognized his granddaughter's handmaiden. Half of her had disappeared, and what was left had a shape, a very pleasant shape, he had to admit.

'My dear, it is very kind of you to stay up to administer to me, but a hot bath has worked wonders ... now, I will just repair to my chamber ...'

'But sir, that is where I have set up the charcoal brazier, to warm the towels and unguents ... all you have to do is climb up on your bed, allow me to massage you deeply and you will drift off to sleep. In the morning, you will never guess I had been there.'

Lying on his stomach, only his brief loincloth covering him, he drifted happily as the girl's nimble but strong fingers kneaded his muscles; the unguents were truly penetrating and the scents were more than pleasant, suggesting an eastern potentate's harem. Once more we have a hummer, he observed dreamily. But this one hums with an understanding of tonal structure. With the loss of all that fat, she has become quite a comely girl. If she were not a Christian, if I were a few years younger, she might easily please my last westering years. They say celibacy is good for the body and the soul . . . well, the Sufi ascetics claim this, so do many of the Hindu yogis, even the Christian hermits . . . but I'm not so sure. What has twenty years of it done for me? The Lord said be fruitful and multiply. You can't do that if . . .

'Sir?' the girl called, pitching her voice a note or two below its usual level, suggesting something with a quavering throatiness. 'Sir, do you remember the story of King David in his last years, how he could never feel warm and they went all over the land to find a comely young virgin, to place upon his breast that he might take her unto him and know warmth?'

'Yi!' he whispered to himself. 'You mean Abishag the Shunammite, of course,' he suggested pleasantly.

CHAPTER 8

One moment, it seemed to Dinah, she was whirling down so fast she lost consciousness, now, here she was standing, no, crouching, a naked sword in her hand, Bubbi pressing his back against the damp, seeping wall and — she gasped, turning her head slightly. Joseph was beside her, his sword flicking the air before him menacingly. Where was the demon, Musa? Where were *they*? The guards running toward them gave her little time for further reflection.

'Remember what I told you,' Joseph whispered, 'watch their eyes. I will engage them, but you crack their shins or ankles with the back of your blade. No unnecessary bloodshed.'

'*Told* me?' she whimpered, confused. But it was too late, the first two guards were rushing them. Bubbi turned his back, braced his hands against the wall and thrust his foot out behind him. The nearest guard tripped, the sword went clattering along the ground as the man's momentum caused him to make an involuntary tumblesault. There was a loud ringing sound as the flat of the Nubian's blade put him to sleep. Even as his sword leapt up to engage the second attacker, Dinah's sword echoed the ringing tone with a severe crack on that man's ankle. He dropped his sword, howled in pain, lifted the afflicted leg, hopping in circles on the other until Joseph's singing blade put him to sleep alongside his companion.

Four more guards rounded the bend in the passageway, swords in hand; the man in the lead hesitated only momentarily, then sliced the air over his head.

'There they are . . . get them! Don't let them get away. The Kadi will reward us for this night's work.' He howled with joy and raced toward the two invaders. They did not notice Bubbi tying the fallen guards' hands and feet with their own turbans. To the eyes of the running guards, two of their companions lay stretched out on the stone floor, their arms and legs twitching erratically.

With a frightful roar, the heavy wooden door of a dungeon was blown off its hinges and sailed along the passageway floor, nearly tripping up the oncoming guards. From the gaping doorway, an object like a thick pole with spiral stripes shot across the passage, just above where the door shuddered. It struck the opposite wall, forming a barrier against the oncoming guards. The leader raised his sword high over his head; the pole lashed around the group of men like a circling whip. Less than a second later, they were jerked off their feet and yanked back through the open doorway. The three companions down the passage gasped in unison. This sound was followed by a louder one, a mingling of fear, surprise and all the wind being knocked out of the bodies of the five captured guards.

'What was that?' Joseph gritted, his knees flexed, poised for the next attack.

'Musa,' Dinah answered. 'He blew the door open, but don't ask me how. He just gathered those guards up like faggots of twigs . . . from the sound of it, they are now unconscious too.'

'But what was that weapon he used?' the Nubian lad persisted, 'did you not see it? It had spiral silver stripes painted on it, over some darker vermilion . . . it seemed to have a life of its own, a flexibility no sword . . .'

'Please, Joseph, that's enough,' Dinah snapped demurely.

'I don't understand,' he protested, 'what are you talking about?' She scowled at him, her lips compressed.

'I don't think we'll need these any longer,' she announced brightly, sheathing her sword.

'Bubbi, did you see that?' Joseph turned to the gnome who was standing upright, dusting his hands.

'Don't you have one?' the mannikin asked roguishly, inclining his head toward the Nubian's groin. 'We always heard that Nubians have the biggest . . .'

'Bubbi!' Dinah cried with great indignation. 'Stop that right now! Can't you see what this impudent slave is up to?'

'I am not a slave, I'm an apprentice,' Joseph shot back, sliding his sword into its scabbard.

Before anyone could utter another word, a sudden blaze of light filled the doorway of the dungeon. A magnificent apparition stepped lightly into the passageway, legs spread wide and head bent in order not to touch the damp ceiling which was more than eight feet above the floor. A long wail issued from Bubbi and he darted behind Dinah, wrapping both arms about her legs and holding on with sheer terror.

'It's a Djinn,' he moaned, the word dying in a gurgle.

'Djinni do not eat earth-devouring gnomes, pitiful worm. You are an undignified sight hiding behind a woman's trousers.' The Djinn bowed even further and smiled at Dinah. 'My name is Hutti, young lady,' he introduced himself, ignoring Joseph as though he were not there.

'I am Dinah ha-Levi,' she replied with dignity which suffered from the way she pulled at her leg, trying to dislodge the terrified gnome.

'Jewish, I presume?' the Djinn inquired with evident delight, his handsome face beaming. She nodded, ending the gesture with a proud flick of her head. Just as she did this, a terrible question presented itself. Surreptitiously, she brushed the back of her hand across her mouth. The beard and moustache were securely in place.

'Not only that,' the Djinn continued, 'but a very young virgin to boot . . . yes?'

'I beg your pardon!' Dinah's hand flashed to the hilt of her sword, the gesture shadowed by Joseph's.

'Twelve, possibly thirteen?' the Djinn cooed, his eyes eating her up, reminding her of a lion contemplating a tasty young gazelle.

'See here, whoever you are,' Joseph shouted, 'touch but one hair and you will answer to . . .'

'I was not talking to you,' the Djinn pointed out. 'Whoever I am? Do your ears fail to function? I just introduced myself . . . what did I say my name was?' The huge presence gestured in the lad's direction. Joseph's hands flew to cover his ears. He winced with terrible pain and his body rocked as though stricken by shock wave after shock wave. Dinah became aware of a high-pitched tone that seemed more sensed than heard. As she listened, she began to feel some of the same pain and an intense nausea as well. Suddenly, it stopped.

'Do you hear that rhythmic shuffling sound to your left?' the great entity asked in a congenial tone. 'Just over there, see that tiny hole at the base of the wall?' He pointed into the deep gloom.

'I hear the sound but I cannot see the hole . . . it is very dark in here,' the Nubian answered, his temper calmed. There was but one torch near the bend in the passageway and it was nearing its end.

Hutti gestured once and then a second time, as though it were an afterthought. Joseph's hand clapped itself over his eyes, a second later, the other hand covered his nose. It seemed to Dinah that the distant torch flamed brightly, and an unpleasant odour struck her nostrils.

'Now look,' Hutti ordered. Joseph uncovered his eyes. The light was considerably increased and, as the giant had said, there was a tiny hole in the wall. The shuffling was quite distinct. Even Dinah cocked her head, although the sound was so faint to her it hardly could be credited.

'You're listening to two mice mating,' the Djinn informed them. 'Do you smell it?' Joseph's nostrils wrinkled and his upper lip rose in a very positive expression of disgust. 'Now, you can see where it is, you can hear it clearly and, in fact, smell how unpleasant it is. Are you not suddenly and almost painlessly better equipped to protect this precious princess of yours?' Stunned, the lad nodded. 'Oh, don't bother to say thank you . . . I don't think I could stand the shock of a grateful human.'

Joseph, speechless, stood with his mouth gaping. The Djinn pointed to the unconscious guards and flicked his head in the direction of the open dungeon. Still without a word, the lad lifted one easily and slung him over his right shoulder. With help from Bubbi and Dinah, he bent his knees deeply and shouldered the other. The girl and the gnome followed him as he in turn followed the Djinn.

The dungeon was pitch black, none of the dying torch's light penetrating at all. Joseph dropped his burdens and turned to fetch the torch. Hutti snapped his fingers, arresting him. The lad never saw the next gesture, but suddenly there was a ring of bright lights on the wall, high up as though they joined the wall to the ceiling in fiery fashion. Dinah gasped. The seven guards made a heap in the centre of the large cell that had no window, no source of light or air. Up against the far wall, each of them chained to a ring in that wall, were her father and two cousins. When she reached them, she cried out in desperation. They were emaciated, their tongues were bluish and lolling from their mouths for lack of water. Before she even turned, the Djinn thrust an earthenware jug and a wooden dipper into her hands.

'Slowly,' he warned, 'or they'll get sick. They don't look strong enough to withstand such an attack.'

For the next quarter of an hour, Dinah was in such a state that things happened around her and she seemed unable to keep up with them. Her father and cousins had been stripped, washed, fed with some rice and vegetables, fruits and nuts and refreshed with a clear, sparkling wine. They effected a recovery in amazingly quick time. Next, they were dressed in the clothing of the three guards who matched them most closely in size and stature . . . not that there was much meat left on the former prisoners. Dressed in the prisoners' rags, three guards were propped against the wall and chained securely. She had tried to see how Hutti had managed all this, but his hands moved too fast. He reached for locks and they leapt into his hand . . . opened. She had not helped . . . certainly, there was little the others had done.

Dinah's father Moses seemed to recognize her, yet he was showing no emotion, no delight. Seated on a wooden bench fixed to the wall and near the door, he leaned his head against her shoulder in weariness, she presumed, but would not answer her questions, if he even heard them.

When she looked up, Joseph and Bubbi were gone. The splendid Djinn was standing in the centre of the large cell, his body in part profile, one arm across his midriff, elbow cupped in palm, his chin resting in the supported hand. He was looking intentely at the sleeping guards, contemplating them . . . or . . . communicating with someone who wasn't here. She wondered where that flash of intuition had come from. When the Djinn had sharpened their other senses, did he do anything else? Stealthily, her hand ran across her thighs, then upward. No, nothing seemed to have approached her while she was partially delirious.

As she watched, unable to take her eyes from the magnificent denizen of another world, she could not help the emotions he evoked in her. His body and face were without a sign of hair, but dark, burnished coppery ringlets fell from his head to his shoulders. Two small golden horns protruded from either side of his lofty brow; his body actually emitted light, a very pale emerald glow and she could see a fine tracery of gold lines coursing just under the translucent skin. Everywhere she looked, bright points of silver twinkled on those golden lines. Most extraordinary of all was that which she tried to force her eyes away from. Even as she fought with those rebellious, traitorous eyes, the Djinn's body turned slightly toward her, bringing this fabulous, forbidden member more prominently into her line of vision . . . her heightened vision, she reminded herself miserably. Not that her experience, visually or otherwise, with this particular appendage was wide and detailed . . . she stopped, suddenly remembering a rampant stallion she had seen as a small girl . . . yes, that was it, like a stallion . . . she shuddered to think what an appalling sight it would be if . . . and then she blocked that thought, but her eyes were still fixed on that ruddy-gold and copper-hued member, almost exactly the colour of his hair. The tip, the colour and translucency of a ruby, actually sparkled in the firelight from above . . . it must be circumcised, she assured herself, though the thought offered no comfort. And there was one enormous sphere the likeness of a pearl . . . just one and it did not seem attached to his body, though it followed every slight movement perfectly. She was about to swoon when her head was drawn mysteriously toward the door. Across the passageway a tall, lean figure stood, back braced against the wall and entirely hidden in the folds of a copious robe; even the head was lost inside a very full cowl. From a sleeve, one slender finger beckoned her.

Hutti's contemplation never wavered; it seemed his consciousness was millions of miles away. She stood and headed toward the doorway, walking slowly and softly, stealing away. She turned her head once to look back at that . . . that . . . thing. Obscene! As she thought it, the member coiled and swung in her direction, the tip poised over the coil like a cobra. It was looking at her! It was quivering with rage . . . it had 'heard' her thought!

She hadn't realised she'd run the last few feet. A pair of strong arms caught her up. Without the sensation of footfalls, she was swept away from the doorway and landed in another part of the passageway. She looked up. The cowl fell away and she was staring into the most inspiring face she had ever seen. A beautiful face with a long, blanched auburn beard, a beard that appeared to have been bleached by the suns of countless years. Such a sublime, such a serene face, would not any human being kneel to bask in the light of that countenance? she asked herself. This magical, almost divine man was holding her hands clasped between his.

'I am Isa ben Maryam,' he whispered. 'I have come here to help you . . . you will need that help very soon.'

'Isa ben Maryam?' she breathed, hardly able to make her vocal chords respond, 'he who is the messiah of the Christians, the one they say is the son of . . .?'

'No, no,' he smiled, his mouth not actually seeming to form the words, 'the one you mean is Yehoshua ha-Mashiah . . . in Arabic he is known as Isa ben Maryam. I am a different Isa and my spiritual mother a different Maryam.'

'You are a Muslim, then?' she squeaked.

'I am a believer in God, as you are, Dinah, nothing separates us. A great saint, my godfather, is very interested in your well-being. You remind him so much of his granddaughter when she was your age. You see, she was ravished by a Djinn and, as a result, she produced Musa and her life was destroyed. My godfather Anwar does not wish that this fate be yours.'

'Was it *that* Djinn . . .?' not trusting her voice further, she pointed down the passageway, her eyebrows arched questioningly. He nodded affirmation. 'Ohhhh . . .' the breath left her body and she would have sagged to the floor had Isa not supported her.

'Here,' he whispered, placing a small object in her hand. She looked down. She saw four tiny hexagrams joined point to point to form the sides of a square. The fifth and sixth hexagram made a perfect box. Something ephemeral shimmered inside, as though held captive. She felt it was a sphere of sorts, faintly suggesting opalescence . . . like . . . like that . . .

'Similar in substance, quite different in nature,' he informed her, having captured her worried thought about the Djinn's pearly sphere. 'And that is exactly what we hope will protect you when the crucial moments come.'

'Moments?' she queried nervously. 'There will be more than one?'

'Musa, who has been very good so far, considering he is a demon, found that what would be needed to free your family was a bit over his head. So, he called in Hutti, his father.

Normally, they don't get along very well, but ever since Hutti had a proper Djinn son a few centuries ago, he has become uncommonly mellow. He agreed to help his demon son. That means, they will both want the price of a young virgin's favours . . . namely, yours.'

'Oooohhh.' She shook for a moment like a distempered dog. 'What do I do with this?' she held up the amulet.

'When you need it, place it under your tongue until it warms and then clench it between your teeth and compress your lips until air can escape only through the front hexagram.'

'What does that do?' she asked, bewildered.

'When you leave here, you will cross a large part of the astral plane . . . do you know where you are now?' he asked suddenly. She shook her head. 'In the dungeons of the Khalif's palace in Baghdad. You must cross the astral plane to get back to Granada as quickly as you got here. On that journey, you will be met and spirited away briefly. Neither Hutti nor Musa will realise you are, in a sense, absent.'

'Who will I meet . . . I mean, who will spirit me away?'

'Anwar, with the help of Aysha . . . she is the mother of Hutti's Djinn son . . . among many other things. All of this you will learn as you progress in your chosen path. That path will become more the Sufi path as you go . . .'

'I am not converting!' she maintained forcibly. 'I shall never desert Israel.'

'Of course not,' Isa ben Maryam assured her. 'No more than your grandfather did when he studied as a young man with the revered ibn al-Arabi, one of the greatest Sufis of this age.'

'Tell me, Isa, how did Hutti know immediately I was a girl?'

'For a Djinn, it was very easy.' He reached out and touched the bright red beard on her chin. 'Do you not recall that when he sent his powers into young Joseph, that same Joseph could smell the coupling of the mice?'

Appalled, her hand came up to cover the beard, to hide it as if it offended the whole world. 'Is it . . . is it . . . that bad?' she cried.

He leaned forward and kissed her brow tenderly. She felt a strange and wonderful power touch every part of her, filling her with hitherto unknown strength. She lifted up on her toes and then she was no longer touching the ground.

'No, dear Dinah, it is that wonderful. Now, put your talisman in a safe place on your person, a place where you can reach it with ease.'

Before she could answer, Isa faded away and she was sitting once more on the bench against the cell wall. It seemed Hutti hadn't moved ... no ... that thing was no longer coiled to strike out at her. That thought made her squeeze her hand ... the hexagram was still clamped tightly in her hand, her hand in a small pocket sewed to the inside of her robe, just over her left breast.

A noise outside turned her head. Bubbi and Joseph walked in, royal raiment of all sorts piled high on their extended arms.

'Enough here to clothe a small army,' Joseph declared, settling the huge pile on the bench next to the stunned Dinah.

'All right, let's get these three clothed royally first ... in the pick of the lot ... they will be the delegation from Egypt and North Africa. The rest can be from Mecca, Spain, Persia and Turkey.'

Once again Moses and his nephews were stripped down to their fresh, new loincloths and dressed in splendid robes, brilliant turbans, bejewelled daggers. They did look like princes. The unconscious guards were dressed much the same way; however they did not offer the minimum cooperation of the ha-Levi group.

'What is the matter?' Dinah demanded, glaring at Hutti. 'Why don't they say anything, why are they like sleepwalkers?'

'Because getting them out of here safely and without suspicion requires that nothing goes wrong, that's why. Once they are safely on their way, they will snap out of it.' Hutti placed his hands on his hips and laughed down at her mockingly. 'You want them to finish the journey, don't you?

Complete with all the wealth they're bringing back to Spain?'

'Of course I do, that's why I'm here, isn't it?' she retorted. 'I doubt if my father even recognises me . . . surely, my cousins don't.'

'Look, little princess, can you imagine what would happen if either of those dummies opened his foolish mouth when I get the "next Khalif" wrapped around this finger?' the Djinn held up the little finger of his left hand. She saw the insult implied . . . no Muslim would use his left hand for wrapping people around.

'What are you going to do?' she asked. 'Can't we just spirit them out and take them back with us?'

'Only those who came that way can return that way . . . if you understood those mystical practices of yours a little better, you would not ask such questions. If we just got them free, there would be no recovering the household treasure. Oh, yes, we could take it by force, but since Musa asked me to do this for him, I prefer to do it with style, to create a wonderful triumph of brilliant illusions . . . now, do you mind if we get on with it? If you just watch with no advance knowledge of what takes place, you'll enjoy it more.'

Paying her no more attention, Hutti tore one of the iron chains from the wall with simple ease, opening the attached collar with the same ease. He slipped it around his neck and closed it again. With the loose end dangling from one hand, he stared at Moses and his two nephews. Idly, he lowered the end of the chain and allowed it coil on the floor. Dinah actually saw his terrifying appendage bend sideways, the tip rising defensively; it glowered at the snake-like coil of chain.

'Fully understood?' the Djinn asked, as though he had been giving a lecture to the three men. They nodded assent. 'Right then, on your feet, look lively there.' He yanked the chain free of the floor. His appendage flew back, coiling behind his far leg in horror. Hutti snapped his fingers three times, once in front of each of the vacant faces. They became animated immediately.

With an imperious gesture, Moses took the end of the

chain and yanked it severely. Hutti stooped comically and played the part of an obsequious slave, bounding forward to do his master's bidding. The three men marched out of the cell, the Djinn bounding up and down behind them like a buffoon. Dinah was deeply disturbed because her father and cousins seemed totally unaware of her presence.

When she turned back into the cell, as though she'd been told to wait there, Joseph was standing so close she nearly bumped into him. Bubbi was a few paces behind the Nubian, hopping from one foot to the other and wringing his hands.

'Why are you fretting so?' she asked, stepping closer to the gnome and sitting on her heels. He crept under her arm and leaned against her flexed knee.

'I didn't know Musa was going to do this,' he whined. 'I felt I could talk to Musa . . . he owes me a few favours, do you see? Some very difficult things *he* couldn't do. It was my call for help he answered that first time . . . remember? When you — er — ah — forget a little something in your grandfather's private temple and that fiend arrived? In his own realm, Azazel would grind Musa's bones to dust, but Musa banished him that time. Musa's been worried somewhat since then. Azazel is no one's friend, but he's the last person in any world you'd want for an enemy . . .'

'Yes,' Joseph agreed, 'he broke into a working of ours in the prison of Alhambra. He was frightful — and very powerful. It was he who got the prisoner to talk . . . and that man died of fright just the same. But my master banished him successfully,' the lad added proudly.

'No doubt he did, but not before his helper Serafina was badly wounded,' Bubbi retorted.

'Why are you so worried, what did Musa do?' Dinah asked.

'He called in his father . . . that big, powerful Djinn . . . that's what. I'm sure I could have talked Musa out of any foolish notions about exacting a price . . .' he stopped talking and looked away from the couple, too embarrassed to hold their eyes.

Dinah rose and patted his shoulder to comfort him. She passed a conspiratorial smile to Joseph before speaking. She also slid her hand inside her robe to make sure her new talisman was still there.

'Bubbi, what sort of price are you afraid the Djinn will demand?' she asked with beguiling innocence.

'Oh, Dinah, it will be terrible,' the gnome started wringing his hands and hopping from foot to foot again. 'And you being so young and innocent and all,' he fairly wailed. 'It isn't fair.'

'If he means what I think he means,' Joseph growled, slapping the handle of his sword for emphasis, 'that Djinn will have to tear me apart first.'

'With what we've seen so far,' Dinah warned him, 'tearing people apart should present no problem . . .'

A tumult of voices, the clash of weapons, the clatter of boots and slippers carried deafeningly down the passageway, halting the girl's comments. A few moments later, Dinah and Joseph were seated next to the dressed-up guards, affecting the same stiff, staring-straight-ahead attitudes. Bubbi was under the bench, hunkered up behind the folds of Dinah's robe.

'So, you see . . .' Moses entered the cavernous room, his hand moving in a sweeping gesture. 'Now, if you are willing to assume the Khalif's throne as our committee instructed us to offer you, then there is nothing in the world to prevent you from starting your glorious rule with a gesture of charitable benevolence.'

The attendants bustled forward, making room for a small, quite portly man. More men rushed in, bringing chairs and cushions, small tables laden with sweetmeats and dates. The two cousins, Abraham and Ichabod, entered triumphantly, Hutti in tow on the end of his chain.

Moses ha-Levi was a man of similar height and build as his father, his long black beard but lightly touched with silver. In the princely raiments, he looked every inch a king of old. He pointed to the wall at the end of the chamber.

'As you may remember, early in the Christian development in Jerusalem, the Temple was sacked. There had been accrued there over many years of prosperity a treasury, the like of which had never been known before, nor has it come to pass since. If you, good Kadi, will accept the throne and free these poor merchants with all their goods and chattels, that treasure can be yours.'

The portly man addressed as the Kadi stepped forward hesitantly, glancing quickly over his shoulder at the overpowering sight of the Djinn. He licked his lips nervously and cleared his throat.

'There is no question but that the Khalif was tried and condemned for heresy?' he asked.

'As I told you,' Moses intoned with great authority, 'he was returning from Mecca. When his boat docked, he was seized and immediately brought to Basra. We have very little time, good sir, we must be on our way this night. Will you accept? Say yes and the treasure is yours.'

Once again the perspiring, uncomfortable judge in the Khalif's service licked his lips; there was an urgent murmur from the attendants surrounding him. He looked at Moses and nodded.

Moses took the end of the chain from his nephews and feigned dragging the Djinn to the centre of the chamber.

'You, bold creature whom I have bound over with the power of Solomon, yield up that which I have demanded of you and freedom will once again be yours. I demand it!'

Hutti hobbled forward, half bent toward the floor and rolled his head from side to side, his tongue lolling out grotesquely. Dinah and Joseph nudged each other, finding it difficult to hold back their laughter. Hutti raised his wobbling head and glared at the wall at the far end of the chamber. He started to permeate his lungs. With gasps and cries, the entourage fell back as the Djinn's expanding body began to fill the large cavern-like room. Soon, none of them could see the far wall as the Djinn's body had expanded from one side wall to the other. By now, the least intrepid of retainers, even soldiers, had retired hastily to the passageway. There was a roar, like the explosion of thunder cracking a blackened sky and the far wall was blown out of existence.

Greatly deflated, the simpering, fawning Djinn fell back on his haunches, a picture of exhaustion. A cry of wonder went up from every throat. Spilling into the chamber from the recess beyond, a vast treasure trove glittered in the lights from above. Even after the chamber was half-filled with riches, the recess beyond was still choked to the ceiling. A gorgeous bracelet of thick yellow gold studded with enormous emeralds rolled across the floor and came to rest at the tip of Dinah's boot. Even before he moved to fetch it for her, sensing how she admired it, the toe of her boot kicked it out of Joseph's reach. She reached beside her and patted his hand to show her gesture was not against his generous thought.

Hutti roared again, stood as straight as he could and snapped the heavy iron collar with the muscles of his neck. He caught it in his hands and crushed it, pulverising the metal. He snapped his fingers and there was a bright flash of blue light, so brilliant the witnesses had to cover their eyes. When they looked again, the Djinn was gone.

'If there is any deception, any effort to renege on the arrangements we have concluded under the watchful eye of that supernatural monster,' Moses announced solemnly, 'he will return and destroy those who betray our agreement . . . as easily as he did that iron collar.'

Everything seemed to rush blindingly from then on. The three stupified guards playing the prisoners' rôles were bustled out. The Kadi — now proclaimed Khalif — sat on a pile of cushions at the edge of the horde. He fondled a jewel-emblazoned crown resting on his knees.

Dinah and Joseph ran from the room, hot on the heels of Moses and the nephews. Bubbi was seated on the Nubian's shoulder, totally invisible to the rest. Camels seemed to appear from nowhere, and in no time were loaded with all the goods confiscated from the traders months earlier. No sooner were they all mounted when the new Khalif's men ran back through the large gates to the south of the city and the riders heard them clanging shut.

Hutti was grinning at Dinah like a cat savouring a canary. Even mounted on a camel, she hardly seemed taller. Without seeing how it happened, she discovered he was suddenly a head taller, now looking down into her eyes.

'Has all that treasure disappeared by now?' she asked him accusingly, remembering what her father had said about keeping the agreement.

'Of course not, silly girl, do you wish them to come tearing out on horseback to cut you down before your voyage has even begun? No, the treasure will stay there until late tomorrow morning ... until al-Abbasi, the real Khalif, arrives. Then Musa will pick it up and put it back where it belongs.'

'Oh, that poor little man, what will happen to him?' Dinah asked, picturing horrible tortures and worse.

'Not a thing. He'll be warned, and he will be sure to climb down off the throne and change his clothes in time. As it was his own personal militia who captured your father and cousins, it will teach the greedy little man a lesson. Goodbye, Dinah, I will be seeing you soon.'

'Are we going to stay with my father? I thought you said we would be going back with ...'

'You will,' the Djinn assured her, his outline becoming a bit vague, almost transparent. 'That is, all except your young African admirer ... he will stay with the caravan to protect it with that amazing sword of his.' He shook a finger at Bubbi who was seated in front of Joseph on his camel. 'When the Khalif discovers those two special swords are gone, I would not wish to be in your earth-burrower's skin. Al-Abbasi has a reputation for conjuring up the likes of you and cooking them in boiling oil. It won't take him long to figure out the only way those swords could have been — ahem — liberated, shall we say?'

'What if I don't choose to leave my mistress? I came here with her and wish to return with her.' Joseph tried to sound authoritative, but it came across rather hollowly.

'You take that up with my son, Musa. He will be meeting

you where the three guards will be deposited. Farewell.' Hutti was no longer there and the camels set up a pace that the riders could not believe. The stride was so long and so rapid the night flew past them with the reckless speed of a nightmare. Something had been done to them, Dinah was sure, and that something would probably not wear out until the riders were so far away no pursuit would catch them up.

Moses edged his she-camel closer to his daughter's so they could talk across to each other against the whistle of the passing wind. As quickly as she could, she informed him of everything that had transpired during his absence. He was particularly concerned about the intrigues of the Castilian king, as he called them. Then he asked her how she got here, and how was it that she'd brought her grandfather's young medical apprentice, to say nothing of her outrageous impersonation of a man. She was trying to piece together an answer when her cousins moved in; with her father on one side, the cousins crowding the other, it impressed her as potentially very dangerous ... if one camel fouled another, they would all be dumped ...

The camels came to a screeching halt as though they had run into a giant hand. Both cousins flew over their camels' heads but, amazingly, they seemed to float down to the ground and then bounce right back up into their saddles. Mouth agape, Dinah stared at her father to observe his reaction. The cousins' camels shuffled a few paces off and stood still. Moses and the boys were sitting erect, their expressions like fixed images on Greek pottery.

'They've been captured in that magical forgetfulness once more,' Joseph whispered, his lips close to her ear. 'They undoubtedly remember nothing of the scene in the palace ... when they continue on, they probably won't remember coming this far. For all we know, they may assume they never broke their original journey at all.'

'Quite right, my quick-thinking young Blackamoor,' a disembodied voice rang out. One by one, the three stupefied guards flew out of their saddles to land atop a huge boulder at the roadside. Like mechanical toys, they sat forming a back-to-back triangle. They linked arms jerkily, crossed forearms over abdomens and linked fingers together tightly. They were so rigid, it seemed improbable that this statue could be knocked over or pulled apart.

'Whoever you are, invisible magus, I am not a Blackamoor . . . there is no such thing. I am a Nubian . . . in fact, a Nubian prince of royal birth,' Joseph added with fierce pride. Young Dinah looked up at his handsome face and smiled with reflected pride. She reached out and touched his sleeve shyly.

'Just a fashionable term one hears in the best courts of Europe these days. They dress the likes of you up in fancy, wildly colourful and exotic outfits, put boots on your feet and gloves . . . white ones, mind you . . . on your hands and have you walk about leading monkeys on golden chains or waving huge feather fans about to stir the torrid, humid air. I could probably get you a job in Venice, if you'd like.'

Musa appeared in a bright flash of blue-green light. He was standing on the boulder looking down at the three entranced travellers, the girl, the Nubian and the gnome.

'Hop down, Dinah, and take your pet mole with you. Your camel will lead the other three back. That will confuse any pursuit party.' Joseph leapt to the ground, held his camel with one hand while he tapped Dinah's to couch it. He held out his hand and helped her alight. When he turned to fetch Bubbi down, the gnome was already leaning against Dinah's leg.

'Say goodbye, bold Nubian prince,' Musa suggested pleasantly. Joseph bowed, then impulsively lifted her hand and kissed it; he stepped back, confused and surprised with himself. Dinah bit her lip and reached down for Bubbi's hand.

'Listen carefully,' Musa called out. 'Go straight on, the beasts will not tire nor will they need forage and water for a long while. Cross the river at a point just below Hit, no further south. Press on to the oasis of Ghadir as-Sufi. Rest there just long enough to refresh yourselves and the camels. Bir Sejri Oasis is your next halt. Skirt Damascus to the south and you will find a ship at Tyre. Do as I tell you and you will avoid trouble — and arrive much sooner than you think. Wait five minutes after we leave . . . your companions will awaken then.' He pointed down. 'These three will stay like this until the sun is well up into the sky.'

The Djinn landed next to Dinah in one bound, lifted her and Bubbi off the ground and there was another bluish flash. Joseph was alone with three mounted somnambulists and the entranced guards.

CHAPTER 9

The scene exploded before her eyes with such brilliant splendour, Dinah was momentarily blinded. The beauty of the dazzling, bejewelled trees, the purple carpet of strange grass underfoot, the vault a paler lilac-lavender above . . . it was too stunning to take in all at once. She knew it was the same enchanted land they had passed through on the way to Baghdad, but they had been moving so swiftly each individual item vanished as it appeared, leaving but a blurred visual memory, and that none too certain. Now, the landscape and the girl were standing still. Then she heard Bubbi's rebellious scream.

With his arms wrapped tightly about the struggling, frantic gnome, Musa leapt free of the soft ground; it was as though there were an invisible slit in the atmosphere a few feet above his head: he went through it, his head disappearing, his body and feet vanishing a split second later. She ran forward, jumping as high as she could to catch the feet which were no longer there. Hutti appeared from behind the nearest tree, diamonds, rubies, emeralds and sapphires of enormous size filling his large right hand. He was popping them into his mouth, one and two at a time. She expected to hear a loud, ear-splitting crunch as his teeth bit into the stones. There was no sound.

'Where is he taking Bubbi ... I want him back here immediately, I'm ... I'm ... well, responsible for him.'

'You'll see him soon enough, Musa will not harm him. He's just taking him home while you stop off and do all the wonderful things you're about to do ... just to please me.'

'While I do *what?*' she choked, stepping back and drawing the sword part of the way free of its scabbard.

The Djinn's hand stopped halfway to his mouth with the last gem. He looked at the girl, then at the hand gripping the richly chased hilt of the fabulous weapon. An irrepressible giggle rose up and he had a difficult time controlling it. With a roar of laughter, he threw the last gem over his shoulder and slapped his thighs over and over with glee.

'Do you plan to split me down the middle with that?' he chortled, bending almost double with mirth. 'Or just ... just ... cleave my head from my shoulders with one blow, O mighty warrior?' He shook his head, sparkling tears rolling down his beautiful, smooth cheeks. 'Don't be difficult, my dear, you owe me that pleasure.'

'What do you mean ... *owe* you? Whose rule is that?' she cried, stepping back a pace and drawing the blade fully, levelling the point at his groin. His bizarre appendage whipped between his legs, dragging the opalescent sphere with it. A moment later, she saw the ruby tip glowering at her over the Djinn's shoulder.

'You have just frightened my ranji,' Hutti rebuked her severely.

'I've what ... your what?' she stuttered with confusion, the tip of the sword rising to point at his heart.

'My *ranji,*' he repeated, pointing over his shoulder. The ruby lashed out viciously with lightning speed, striking the back of his hand so forcibly she thought the bones were cracked. Hutti yelped, cleared the ground and jammed the back of his hand into his mouth.

Dinah could not help herself. She momentarily lost her fear and confusion; she laughed.

'It's not funny!' he bellowed with the force of thunder, deafening her. 'Because of your attitude, he's blaming me. Now, just what is wrong with you, little girl? I've demanded payment . . . you got good service, your father, your cousins and all their goods are well on their way safely home. What more do you want? I've kept my end of the bargain.'

'What bargain?' she cried, thrusting the sword before her defensively.

'What bargain?' he repeated, slapping his brow with the heel of his hand. 'For services rendered. Once upon a time, we could have captured your soul just for such services. But some years ago, a meddlesome old man you humans thought was a saint . . . well, it's a long story and we don't have much time . . . let's just say, our females warned us if we ever took another human soul they would take us apart and never would we be able to put ourselves together again.'

'Take you apart . . . ?' she whimpered, shaking her head, obviously on the point of tears.

'It's all too complicated . . . I'm sure your famous conjuror grandfather could tell you about it, ask him when you get home. For now, all you need know is we get bodies, not souls . . . all right? Take off your clothes . . . yes, and get rid of that silly beard.' He pointed and began laughing again, in spite of his attempts to maintain a stern attitude.

'I'll do no such thing . . . you take one step toward me and I'll die fighting for my honour . . .' she looked about and cried out plaintively: 'O, Joseph, why didn't you come with me? I need you more than they do.'

The long cloth wound about her head unwound itself so fast the air about her ears made a singing noise. The tail end of cloth passed over her chin and mouth, yanking the glued-on hair free, the other end wrapping itself about the scabbard, working up through the leather thongs undoing them and, in the next instant, the traitorous cloth slammed the scabbard home on the naked blade, tore the sword from her grasp and flew to the topmost branch of the tree directly behind the laughing Djinn.

She had not seen him gesture with his hand the first time;

now she did. Her robe blew up so furiously she could not detain it with her hands. She caught hold of the end just as it too sailed toward the tree. Just as her feet left the ground, the loincloth began unravelling. Her hands shot down to prevent that even more embarrassing loss, but the magical powers of the Djinn were just too much for her. Crying out with shame, one arm stretched across her chest, her other hand splayed out as widely as possible over her shorn treasure, she started to sink to the ground helplessly.

'By the invisible sun above, I don't understand you human females. The most delicious pleasures known this side of paradise and you create such a fuss . . . why?'

She looked up, her body folded at knees and hips as though falling in on herself would prevent the terrible desecration she feared was about to threaten her. She saw the Djinn as a wavering blur through her tears. She shook her head to dislodge them, fearing to move her hands lest she expose herself. Her vision cleared. Directly above the Djinn, on a branch, a very shadowy figure appeared. An indescribably ancient man with silvery hair and beard of a shining purity she had never encountered before. Her mouth began to fall agape and the ancient personage raised a warning finger. Reaching behind him, he revealed a small ewer; he held it over the Djinn's head and allowed the few drops it contained to fall on the coppery locks.

'You know, you're a very lucky, young woman,' Hutti confided. 'Had you not made that false beard of yours, you would not have been permitted to indulge me in all those pleasures we are about to enjoy. The law specifically states that women must be shorn . . . there . . .' he pointed and Dinah bent even further forward, having to strain her neck now to look up.

A slender, ethereal arm reached out of sheer nothingness behind the ancient saintly figure in the tree; it was the reverse of Musa's strange disappearance. The hand grasped the ewer and vanished. Two seconds later it returned, slipping the ewer back into the old man's waiting hand. This time, a greater quantity of sparkling drops descended on the unsuspecting head below.

'Hmmmn!' Hutti's hand went up to massage his head. He looked at the damp palm as he withdrew the hand. 'Rain? Here?' He looked up, but not directly overhead. 'Absolutely ridiculous! We never have rain here, we don't need . . .'

The tall, noble and awe-inspiring body began to collapse, the limbs becoming jelly-like, the head sagging to the point where chin touched breastbone; like a bird pierced on the wing, he struck the purple carpet under the tree without a sound. His deep breathing alone assured Dinah that he was not dead. The back of her hand across her mouth, she looked up at the venerable man with the flowing silver mane. Coming from behind him, two arms like the one she had just seen materialised as from the other side of an invisible curtain. They stretched endlessly until the hands caught the surprised Dinah under the arms. Before she could gasp, she found herself sitting next to the kindly, smiling patriarch.

'The blessings of God upon you, dear child,' he said in a sweet melodic voice that quavered slightly. 'I believe you have already met my godson, have you not?'

'The one called Isa ben Maryam?' Dinah whispered, her small, exquisite young breasts reverberating visually the thunderous pounding of her heart. The ancient one smiled assent. 'Who is he really? Please tell me . . . and you, who are you?'

He told her he was Anwar ibn Muhammad al-Hazza. She smiled at the description, al-Hazza, and wondered why he was designated the shoemaker. He answered her smile and told her precisely because that is what he had done for all the early years of his earthly life. Before he had devoted his life totally to God and the Brotherhood of Love. He knew about her and her quest for knowledge, about her grandfather who would be remembered as one of the great scholars and wise men of his age. He was here now to help and guide her. When she asked again about Isa . . . how he seemed so . . . so like everyone on the earth but here . . .

well, Anwar seemed different, more like a spirit. Well, he told her, Isa's rôle is to help those who need it . . . in a sense, he was the apprentice of a great saint known only as al-Khidr. Some say he was originally the unnamed companion of the Prophet. Others believed he had been in this world in one form or another from the beginning . . . if such a thing as beginning could be conceived. And yes, Isa did seem a solid form on earth. Anwar was now a resident of an entirely different world. Fortunately, when it was necessary, he could visit this plane . . . admittedly with the help of a loving friend.

When he said that a vision of such loveliness took form — and solidity of a sort — right next to Dinah. She gasped. If she could believe her eyes, she was looking at the female version of what men described as an angel. The long, powerful wings were folded tightly behind her, just the joints thrusting above the vision's shoulders.

'And this, my dear,' Anwar introduced her, 'is my dear friend Aysha. She doesn't always wear this guise. She is either trying to conform to what you would imagine her to be or once more she wants to convince me she is my guardian angel. Well, I must admit she is — I don't know what I'd do without her.'

'Hello, Dinah,' the sweet voice reached her as though it had crossed many great mountains to find her. 'Now, we must start with your lessons. My erstwhile mate below will not dream forever. The few drops from the Fountain of Forgetfulness will last just long enough to prepare you. When he wakens, he will remember nothing from the point when he extended a rude finger in the direction of your sweet young secrets.'

Only when the angel said that did Dinah remember she was unclothed. Her eyes shot skyward, searching for the branch where her clothes had been spirited to. Aysha pointed to the ground. Everything was neatly folded in a pile. She could see no trace of the "red beard" that had been whisked away with her head cloth.

'You won't need that just now.' Aysha assured her. 'By the time you do, nature will have replaced the . . .

well, you understand, don't you?'

'I shall leave you now to Aysha's expert care,' Anwar murmured as he leaned over to kiss her brow gently. 'Your instructions are really not for men's ears, my dear.' He held his hand over her head for a few moments, then touched the top of her head lightly.

The strangest sensation began to invade every part of her body at once. Her mind began to expand and her heart and soul felt as if they were about to soar up to the lavender sky. She perceived so many things at once that she could define none of them. Then she realised that Anwar had imbued her with something mysterious and wonderful. She reached both arms out to him in gratitude, only then discovering her eyes were closed. When she opened them, Anwar was no longer there.

When Aysha stroked her arm a few times, the touch no heavier than a feather, the girl was able to relate to her surroundings again.

'Anwar has blessed you, my child, he has poured his grace into you. One day soon, you will learn about the giving of baraka from a great master to a disciple. You are most fortunate, believe me.'

Aysha produced a small sphere carefully bound in a luminous cloth. She explained how it was to be placed inside the girl's most secret entrance and kept there at all times save during the cycle of the moon when she was indisposed. Aysha told Dinah the story of Anwar's sorrow ... about how his granddaughter had been enticed by the Djinn sleeping below. Musa was the result of this encounter and it had doomed that much-beloved granddaughter. Just in case Hutti proved too wily for all of them, the small object she had just been given would protect her from that fate.

Dinah blushed and stammered, protested and pleaded but Aysha would not be budged. It had to be placed inside now; waiting could be fatal. Finally, sense overcoming embarrassment, Dinah submitted. She was amazed at how gently Aysha was able to accomplish the feat, and how painless it was.

Next, the angelic image asked her to hold out her hand. In the open hand, Aysha placed the hexagram cage the girl had received from Isa ben Maryam. Her look of astonishment was so comical Aysha could not hold back a tinkling, musical laugh. Of course she'd extracted it before placing the clothes on the ground.

Aysha struck a strange, quavering note deep in her throat. It affected Dinah's skin and nerves more than her ears; in fact, she suspected the note was hardly audible, perhaps not at all to humans who had not had the benefit of Hutti's preternatural heightening of the senses. Over and over, the angelic female coaxed Dinah to reproduce the sound. The unhappy girl was nearly in tears with her dismal failure before she finally got close enough to gain new hope. Even then she realised that, as simply an earth mortal, she never in a lifetime could have accomplished it without the help of Aysha's otherworldly skills and Anwar's grace or baraka. Once the tone was perfected, Aysha whisked the girl up in her arms and a fraction later they were on the ground, but seemingly miles away from the tree where Hutti slumbered on.

'Now you must learn to dance,' Aysha winked provocatively at her young companion. 'Men talk about paradise being filled with houris — a sort of heavenly dancing girl, you might say — because all such descriptions are couched in terms of their limited experience. In the time before history, higher life forms mingled more readily with mortals, particularly those of the high civilisation that existed in a great island kingdom long vanished from the earth. Those mortals knew many of the secrets of nature now lost to men. The great magical power in transcendental music, dance and extraordinary vibrations included. I shall now teach you this esoteric form . . . with Hutti you will use that tone you have just learned. When you project it through the hexagram box held between your teeth and dance the dance I am about to teach you, you will create an experience for Hutti that will border on ecstatic madness . . . an experience he will never be able to forget, one he will give anything to know again.

He will be repaid for his services and you will remain intact, a pure and innocent virgin.'

'What is it called?' Dinah asked in a hushed, awe-stricken voice. 'I mean the dance, the music . . . what he will experience?'

'The Ultimate,' Aysha answered blandly, her voice indicating it could hardly be called anything else.

'The Ultimate?' Dinah puzzled innocently. 'The Ultimate . . . what?' A stubborn, pragmatic streak was announcing itself.

'Just . . . The Ultimate,' Aysha explained patiently. 'There are no words to describe exactly what.' The glorious creature took the girl's arm and turned her slightly, gazing reflectively at the clean-shaven area at the base of her abdomen.

'That is very professionally accomplished, considering you are not Muslim,' Aysha commented, nodding in agreement with her own statement. 'Is that the . . . first time?'

Dinah blushed and admitted her serving girl Farida had been the expert . . . though she was not Muslim either. The blush prompted a strong lecture on the comeliness of modesty . . . at the right time, in the proper place. When it came to what she was about to perform with — or on — Hutti . . . well that would be neither the time nor the place for girlish modesty. Her dancing had to be wild, abandoned and wanton, expressing the most delicious depravity . . . but, with heavenly grace. It had to be as erotic, as debauched as the debased mind of the male could imagine, yet it must always reflect regal, practically divine, spirit.

Aysha's 'divine' presentation was electrifying. In what would have equalled five earth plane minutes at the most, Dinah had mastered a fabulous art, considered by men to be rightfully practised only by the legendary houris of paradise.

Back under the tree again, Dinah trembled on the brink of her trial by fire. She glanced longingly toward the pile of clothes. As she did, she felt a stern, rebuking slap on her bare buttock. Aysha may have disappeared, but her spirit — if one could actually think of a spiritual entity as having a spirit — was still watching over Dinah. That thought renewed her courage and determination not to fail. Stepping closer to the somnolent Djinn, she placed the small talisman behind her lips. During the lesson, Aysha had revealed that its powers were many. For example, she could sound a different note and even heavy objects would fly through the air to do her bidding. She breathed a short quaver of allure through the hexagrams.

Dinah leaped straight up into the air when that amazing appendage — ranji, had he called it? — flew up like a ship's mast and quivered wildly, vibrating too fast to see while swaying madly from side to side; suddenly it stretched horrendously to wrap itself about the limb of the tree overhead. With a fearful contraction, it yanked the unconscious Djinn to his feet. Hutti opened his eyes and yelped with pain. The ranji released the limb and fell back into its proper place, but it swayed provocatively as though appraising the nubile young girl with hair so vividly red it made Hutti's look mahogany by comparison. He pointed to Dinah's shorn secrets and repeated the words he'd used a few moments before passing out.

'Are you ready, Hutti?' Dinah breathed through her talisman, her hips swaying from side to side, creating a counterpoint to the ranji's rhythm. She drew closer, making her small, hard, perfect breasts quiver like light shimmering on water. 'Lie down here, you great big gorgeous brute and let me get my hands on you. When I'm finished, you are going to be so exhausted you'll think you'd created the entire universe with your bare hands.'

She skipped over to the pile of clothing and patted it suggestively. 'Put your ravishing head on here where my lips can find yours . . . place your body here where my hands and lips and body can find all of you . . . now, lover.'

Hutti flung himself into the air with a triumphant whoop of delight and made a perfect landing on his back, his head cushioned on her clothing. Without a second's hesitation, Dinah began dancing around his prone form. To the fascinated Djinn, her movements were beyond his wildest experience. She was humming louder and louder, creating a crescendo of divine music that made his head swim. The louder and faster the song, the more her dance movements quickened, becoming so abandoned even the hitherto unshockable Djinn was visibly shaken. The ranji was sweeping around in circles, flying up and down, swaying and shaking, curling up into a huge coil, then springing up like the rigid mast of a ship. The right moment! she concluded.

The note that now came through the hexagram box made the ephemeral sphere in its centre vibrate with something like the speed of light. The sheer power was so great the light and shadow in the area altered noticeably. With her next increase in volume, flashes of light shot up from the ground and down from the sky simultaneously, striking bolt rising by bolt descending, creating a pattern of explosions that filled the sky with enormous rainbow patterns which, in turn, ignited a whole new display of heavenly lights.

Hutti's body rose straight up off the ground, his ranji now so rigid it could practically smash boulders. He quivered for two seconds about five feet above the purple grass then shot straight up to the sky, crashing down and going to all four points of the compass at the same time. To Dinah, she watched one Djinn become two, then multiply the number by the number so rapidly there seemed to be thousands of him filling every space there was to fill. The roars and screams, the pleadings for more and more and more filled all the air at once; a moment later and it seemed sky and plane would be torn to shreds or implode.

With a loud thud, the Djinn's body struck the ground exactly where it had last lain. Limbs and torso were twisted terribly, so much so that Dinah nearly swallowed her talisman with fear and concern. The look of divine bliss on his shining face belied her suspicions. Looking ridiculously shrunken and harmless, the ranji was collapsed on his abdomen, tied in a very complex knot. The pearl sphere looked dull and half its normal size.

A very dim outline of Aysha's face appeared close to her own. 'Slip your clothing from under his silly head and tuck it all under your arm. I'll speed you off to your next destination. Musa is waiting impatiently.'

'Do I really have to do *that* all over again?' Dinah pleaded breathlessly, removing the silver box from her mouth and wiping her glowing brow with the back of the other hand.

'Do as I say . . . by the time we get there, a few seconds from now, you will be thoroughly refreshed.' Dinah felt the heavenly scented kiss on her cheek. 'There, don't you feel absolutely bursting with female power? Just look at the happy fool . . . he won't be able to move for hours.'

As soon as the girl had slipped her clothing under her arm, she felt Aysha's arms about her. The whole scene vanished. She blinked once, it seemed, and she was standing in a huge hall. It was a palace certainly, from the size of it. She looked at the walls and began walking slowly toward the far end. Such exquisite mosaics, she remarked to herself, and the intricate pattern of sculptured plaster vied with anything in the new palace being erected in Granada.

'Well, well, you finally got here . . . what took you so long? Was my father as insatiable as ever?' She looked up and a cry escaped her. Musa was lying on the ceiling easily twenty feet above her, his legs and arms spread out like a huge bird. His fearsome appendage was now covered in spirals of gold and silver and it pointed straight at her. Before even thinking, she popped the talisman in her mouth and dropped the clothes.

'Come on down here where I can get my hungry, greedy hands on you, you delicious green brute of a lover,' she intoned, matching her body rhythm to her words.

* * *

Aysha landed the girl lightly in the central, flower filled court of her family's house.

'Dear, dear, I hope I don't have to do *that* again in a hurry. Aysha, feel me, I'm shaking like a leaf. I can't remember the end . . . what happened to Musa?'

Aysha laughed softly, becoming quite corporeal in the darkened court. She was standing solidly next to the young girl, holding her in her arms. Her very presence, the contact with the angelic skin sent tremors of excitement all through the half-exhausted, half-impassioned girl.

'When last seen, Musa was hanging from a fixture in the ceiling, that striped affair of his tied around it in a glorious series of rather fancy and terribly witty knots. He won't forget The Ultimate in a hurry either. I must say, young Dinah, you are a unique student. All that and not yet thirteen. My, think of what you'll be able to do in just a few short years.'

'Whatever *that* is, I hope it won't be so tiring . . . still, my nerves are so jangled I don't think I'll be able to sleep the entire night . . . or whatever is left of it.'

'Come, I'll see that you relax. Take me to your bed-chamber.' To Dinah, it didn't seem she was walking or, indeed, taking Aysha anywhere. It had the feeling of that effortless, motionless travel they had been doing all along. The next thing she knew, her clothes were again neatly folded on a low table, she was stretched out on her sleeping couch and Aysha was lying next to her.

'Remember, dear one, you must never forget the ritual of that sphere Anwar gave you . . . hmmmn?' Dinah agreed sleepily. 'And wherever you go, that talisman must be with you, on your person. You never know when you may need it . . .'

'Does it work with normal . . . I mean with our men?' Dinah asked, suddenly awake again, her nerves singing, her skin tingling.

'Oh yes . . . but in the name of the Most Holy, do not apply as much of it as you did with Musa and Hutti. Just a small amount will derange a man for months. Enough talk, put your arms about me.'

Dinah obeyed before she even thought about what she was doing. When she did, when she was about to pull away and bound out of the bed, Aysha's hands had done something which caused her to simulate turning inside out in her own mind. It was so delicious she had to hold her breath and couldn't exhale. Arms and legs entwined themselves with hers, lips found places she never knew about and made them vibrate with unendurable pleasure. Wave after wave of ecstasy washed over her before she began to explore the beautiful creature who was literally transporting her to paradise.

Dinah was not aware of Aysha's presence evaporating. Suddenly she was alone and it was just like waking from a blissful dream. Only the extreme langour of her limbs, the wetness of her body from head to toe informed her that that shudderingly delightful memory was more than a dream.

'Grandpa!' Dinah leapt up and started pulling her clothes on. How terrible! How long had she been home? How worried her poor grandfather must be . . . had that silly fool Farida told him . . . there you go, you don't even know if he's back yet, do you?

As she slipped silent and barefooted along the hallway she blushed deeply. Her thighs felt as though they'd been buttered. Something inside was throbbing so badly it hurt . . . no, it was just waves of pleasure washing over her. By the time she reached her grandfather's study, she had herself under control again. He wasn't there. He usually worked there until all hours of the night. He must not be home then, she told herself. She hesitated for a few breaths, wondering about checking his bedchamber. Make sure! she ordered.

Her hand was on the latch when she heard the hushed voice — Farida's! What did *that* mean? If Bubbi were here . . . she stopped in her mental tracks, thrusting her hand to her mouth to stifle the cry. Then she remembered . . . they had brought Bubbi back with them. Yes, he dropped out of Aysha's grasp just over the garden patch. They'd seen him plough straight through the ground.

A hand touched Dinah's elbow and she rose straight up, releasing the door latch. A very tenuous outline of Aysha stood there beckoning her to follow. The apparition entered Solomon's study and waited until Dinah was inside, then shut the door.

'I suspected Hutti was up to something,' Aysha confided, pointing to a heavy, large black cloth bag standing on the work table; Dinah saw a square of paper fixed to one side.

'What is it?' Dinah asked in hushed tones, fearful of waking someone in the sleeping household.

'Some mysterious powder your father and cousins received with that last caravan out of Cathay,' the wraith answered just as softly. 'It must have some devastating magical properties or Hutti would not have been tempted to steal it. I found where he'd hidden it and brought it here. Rightfully, it belongs to your family with all the rest.'

While Hutti was still wandering out among the stars of a large variety of universes in the spiritual sense, Aysha had been able to read his mind. Isa ben Maryam's amazing talisman was something to be reckoned with. Hutti was possessed, captivated, possibly madly in love, if such were feasible for Djinni with a human female. And that made him very dangerous. She could not caution young Dinah enough. Essentially, as with all Djinni, Hutti was not evil. Simply amoral. He did not see the world about him in terms of good and evil. But, when in a state of total derangement like this, he would do practically anything to possess the object of his desire.

In a practical sense, it meant he could create an evil manifestation. Though that form would no longer represent or resemble the basic Hutti, the harm would be the same. For example, he could change himself into a zar . . . a zar al-Auf . . . she knew what that meant, did she not? Only then did Dinah realise that Aysha had been speaking Hebrew to her all along. A zar in Arabic was an evil spirit that would enter a human and turn her into an energumen . . . and zar al-Auf meant a really bad spirit.

'Be on your guard at all times,' Aysha warned. 'Be ready to pop that talisman in your mouth faster than a humming-bird can move its wings one-quarter of an inch. But don't give him The Ultimate — for that's what he will want again. You must tell him that it was done on the eve of the summer solstice on the first day of the new moon. Only on exactly such a day will you have the magic to repeat the performance, understand? And should he try to molest you physically, you must warn him the magic depends on the unquestioned sanctity of your special state as a magical virgin. Even a profane touch upon your secret places could destroy the magic forever. That will stop our greedy Hutti in his tracks, I guarantee you. But he must never catch you offguard or it will all be over before you can raise a talisman to prevent it.'

'I will be careful,' the girl protested, her feelings piqued by the suggestion implied: she was a careless girl.

'You have not been so far,' Aysha announced flatly. She pointed down toward the floor, in the direction of Solomon's magical laboratory. 'You completely forgot to close the ritual and pronounce the banishing ceremony. Were Hutti up and about, he could invade this house in very material form. You are not quite the master magician yet, my dear.'

Aysha was gone before the girl could answer. But a fiery kiss burned her lips and sent little darts of delirium through her veins. She sped downstairs and, once in the chalk circles again, composed herself so that she would not rush and make a careless error. Aysha was right, her accusation so strong it seemed to burn itself into her mind. Five minutes later she stood before her grandfather's door again, anxious to tell him about the mysterious black bag. A giggle carried through the door and she pressed her ear closer.

'My dear girl,' she heard her grandfather say, laughing softly as though something was tickling him, 'you are obsessed with this notion of Abishag the Shunammite, don't you see?' There was a snort of objection from Farida. 'In the Torah, Abishag is described as a fair young virgin . . . really, my girl . . .'

'That's not just . . . I may be a little fat still, but why do you think I'm not fair?' Farida sounded more irate than wounded.

'All right,' the patriarch conceded, 'let us call you fair . . . but really, the virgin part?'

'Well . . . I'm practically a virgin . . . almost . . .' Farida's voice ran down, impaling itself on the contradiction. She sobbed.

'Now, now, don't cry. I can't stand to hear a woman . . .'

The door burst open and Dinah ran across the room, jostling Farida to one side as she vaulted to her knees beside Solomon on the large bed.

'Grandpa . . . you're back!' She kissed him a number of times loudly, hoping Farida would leave before it was necessary to thrust her out of the room. Abishag, indeed . . . with *her* grandfather!

'Easy, my child, easy,' he protested, sitting up and throwing a robe around his shoulders. 'I've not been back long.' He fussed with covering his legs as well, sounding quite embarrassed. 'Hepzie made a delicious hot bath to soak my weary, saddle-damaged bones and now Farida has been massaging soothing unguents into my aching muscles . . .'

'So I notice,' the girl sniffed, shooting Farida a venomous look. 'You may collect all that and go, Farida, I have some things to discuss with my grandfather.'

Farida's look as she left the room was just as venomous but Dinah had already turned her back, disdaining to notice the poor girl any longer.

Solomon ranted and raved, swore she needed a thorough thrashing, despite his lifelong aversion to corporal punishment and any disrespect to the human body. She had taken such chances! Why, did she know what could have happened to her? Was she aware of what a clever Djinn could do to her? Her life would have been ruined if she bore a demon . . .

Gently she calmed him down, assuring him that she had been very careful and now she had some extremely powerful allies. She showed him her new magical talisman and described the bewitching of Hutti and Musa, interspersed with many giggles and chuckles. By the time she ended that story with the word picture of Musa, entranced and enchanted, hanging from the ceiling, even Solomon relented and began laughing. When she mentioned Aysha and Isa ben Maryam, he sat up and stopped laughing. When the old shoemaker's name was pronounced, there was a definite look of awe on the man's face.

'Are you aware that he was one of the most revered saints of his age?' he asked. 'He lived in Arabia over four hundred years ago and people throughout the world speak of him still with enormous reverence. If his spirit came to protect you, you are blessed indeed.'

When she told him Anwar had blessed her in a very real sense, imparting his baraka or grace, the patriarch blinked. Handing her the bedside candle, he directed her steps to the far wall and told her to place the holder on the floor near her. He watched the light play about her for a minute or two and called her back.

'It is true,' he agreed quietly. 'Your aura has grown as a tiny chick becomes an eagle. Dinah, have you any idea how fortunate you are . . . and how right your angelic mentor is? Like every young genius, you are slipshod and careless in your rush to the rainbow.'

'Please, darling Grandpa, lecture me no more. I've had so much from Aysha already. She's worried sick about me. I promise to be ever so careful from now on, and I'll study twice as hard.'

He patted her cheek and drew her close to him; when he'd kissed the top of her head, he suggested they could all use some sleep or no one would be able to rise in the morning.

'Oh! The big black bag! Come, I have to show you what Daddy and the cousins were bringing home. The Djinn thought it was so important he tried to steal it.'

She led him to the study and he opened the bag. It was filled with a slightly coarse black powder. Solomon took a palmful, sniffed it, touched it with the very tip of his tongue and spat it out immediately. He emptied his hand into an unused candle holder. With a bored shrug, he tied up the sack again.

'What is it? Aren't you going to read the letter? Grandpa, what's wrong?'

'Nothing's wrong, my dear. *You* read the letter,' he suggested. 'It will tell you that combining charcoal and saltpetre creates a very flammable substance.' He moved the candle holder with the remnants of powder to the far end of the table, as far from the bag as he could. Taking the candle from Dinah, he lit one of the short tapers kept in a vase on the table and stuck the other end under the loose powder. She watched it burn until it reached just less than an inch away from the powder. The bright flash made her jump back.

'Why, that's wonderful,' she exclaimed. 'What practical use can be made of it?'

'The scientists in the southern part of Cathay pack it tightly in rolled up paper and insert a wick, such as we use for lamps, into one end . . . but the wick is made in such a way that a small amount of the powder is blended in. If you light that, the wick burns down rapidly and the paper cylinder explodes violently, making a terrible racket. The more you confine the powder, the more volatile the reaction when ignited.'

'Can we make some of those?' She clapped her hands with the excited enthusiasm of a young child. 'Think of the screams in the harem when I set them off.'

'First thing in the morning, I must remember to get rid of all this. Undoubtedly, this was the brainchild of those great scholars, Ichabod and Abraham. I wonder did your Aunt Rebecca have a suspicion when she named that one Ichabod . . .'

'In the Torah, the naming of Ichabod was stated as "the glory is departed from Israel".' Dinah looked up into his eyes. 'Isn't that unkind — they're your grandchildren too.'

'Perhaps you are right. But what they brought back could make more mischief than you would ever dare to imagine. If you think about compressing that powder into confined spaces and exploding it violently, then it likens itself to the pent-up energy in the steel of a crossbow, does it not? They should have left this devil-powder where they found it.'

'Please don't throw it away, Grandpa. I have the

strangest feeling we're going to need it for something some day.'

'We'll talk about that in the morning,' he soothed her, ushering her towards the door. 'I repeat, let us all get some sleep now.' Once more he kissed the top of her head and held the candle high as she raced down the hallway to her own room.

Solomon yawned, scratched his stomach and chest and climbed into bed. He blew the candle out and sighed, leaning back and hesitating about drawing up the coverlet. It was such a warm night. He heard the door ease open ... his hearing for his age was unusually acute. The next thing he knew, naked flesh pressed into his, the bulk of two large, firm breasts squeezing his chest.

'I forgot the part about warming your breast, I was so busy massaging you,' Farida whispered huskily. The insides of her legs gathered the outsides of his possessively.

'Adonai, Adonai, Adonai protect and defend me,' he chanted softly, girding up his mental loins, gathering his strength to remove the noticeably heavy body and deposit it unceremoniously on the floor. Unfortunately, his hands found their first grip on the firm, full buttocks. Traitorous fingers created small circles, smoothing and kneading the soft flesh. He sighed, a sound of defeat, of the acceptance of fate. The probing fingers stopped suddenly, registering surprise.

'Farida!' he sounded shocked. 'You've shaved yourself. A Christian girl in a Jewish house ... and you follow the Muslim rules? Why?'

'In this crazy place you have to be prepared to be all things to all people,' she confided ingenuously for an almost-virgin.

'Well,' he admonished sternly without releasing his grip, 'I do hope you haven't been too many things to too many people recently, my dear. There are some diseases even I can't cure.'

* * *

A tall, elegant Djinn, slightly thinner than Hutti and, if such things can be measured, somewhat younger, strolled across the limitless plane of purple grass. When he saw the fountain he was searching for, his pace increased, bringing him to his goal in mere seconds. With a look of delight, he stood under the brilliant shower that cascaded down over his body. Muscles swelled, his chest expanded, his ranji and the large pearl sphere filled out and the silver points on his network of golden vein-like lines began flashing brightly. Hawwaz, who was like a younger brother to Hutti, had just replenished his supernatural powers. Now, all he needed was some of the abundant fruit from the nearby trees — the delicious varieties unknown on the earth plane that always looked like huge gems to human eyes.

Munching quietly and pensively, Hawwaz arrived under his and Hutti's favourite tree. He jumped back and began rocking with contained, silent laughter when he saw his ludicrously contorted companion on the ground. The ridiculously knotted ranji was the funniest part. What could have happened to old know-it-all Hutti? He must have met his match in some form or other.

Hawwaz's ranji did not take the same uncharitable view as its master. Swinging into action and ignoring all authoritative efforts on the Djinn's part, it curled, coiled, wiggled, squeezed between tight loops until it had its opposite number unknotted and free. Hutti's ranji sank to the ground, exhausted; and Hutti vaulted straight up to a sitting position, rubbing his eyes.

'What happened to you?' Hawwaz asked with sly undertones.

'Wha ... where ... oh!' Hutti was on his feet, his head rotating searching every part of the horizon. 'Oh, no! She's gone! Never in the history of all the ages has there been ...' He turned toward Hawwaz and crouched low, his hands resembling the tensed claws of a roc. 'Did you take her?' he hissed threateningly. 'Where did you take her?'

Hawwaz stepped back, shocked. 'What are you talking about, you idiot? I just arrived, seconds ago. Your ranji was tied up in some rather painful-looking knots. My ranji untied them . . . but do we hear one word of thanks? Oh, no. Where is she? he asks. Who?'

'You didn't see her then,' Hutti answered listlessly, his hands falling to his sides. He looked on the verge of a new collapse. He glared down at his ranji, seeing all the wrinkles and creases for the first time. He groaned. 'How can I go anywhere looking like this?' he asked, addressing himself more than his friend.

'Will you please tell me what happened?' Hawwaz was beginning to lose his patience and good humour.

When the whole story was told, Hawwaz was caught between laughter and awe. The description of what the little earth girl had done to world-weary Hutti, the experienced dean of Djinni . . . it was so hard to believe!

'How did you find her? How did you get mixed up in this to begin with?' Hawwaz wanted to know.

'I told you. The first time she created a magical ceremony, she was looking for an earth spirit, one of those grubby little gnomes, but she somehow — and don't ask me how — made an error.' He shuddered. 'That Azazel nearly materialised fully.'

'Don't you start telling fibs, now. King Solomon bound him below for all eternity.'

'Yes, so long as nobody interfered. Weren't you listening when I told you about what Azazel did with the prisoner?'

'Of course. I thought you got him mixed up with some other archduke.'

'I don't get such things mixed up, if you don't mind,' Hutti snapped back.

'What's the story, then? The girl is a wizard and yet she's careless, is that it?'

'Careless?' Hutti drawled slowly, his mind working furiously, 'Yes, that's it . . . say, what an idea . . . I'll be right back!'

Before Hawwaz could open his mouth, there was a loud Pop! and Hutti was gone. The young Djinn shrugged his shoulders, throttled his curiosity and yawned. Taking one step backwards, he stiffened his body and rolled back on his heels. His body wafted to the purple carpet slowly, his head coming to rest against the bole of the tree. His eyes had been closed for a few minutes, the first delicious waves of sleep rolling over him, when an angry howl brought his head up with a snap.

'Ouch!' Hutti was squatting on his heels, both hands holding his head.

'What did you do this time, brilliant Big Brother?' Hawwaz asked with sleepy annoyance.

'I was so sure she had forgotten to close the ceremony and recite the banishing ritual, I crashed headlong into a stone wall, so to speak. I'll just bet that meddlesome Aysha has been nagging at her about caution . . . hmmmn . . . yes, I wouldn't put it past her.'

'Or Anwar?' Hawwaz looked up, staring at the branch overhead. The edges of his fine nostrils were quivering slightly. 'Even his spirit's aura leaves traces, it's so strong. Didn't you detect anything?'

Hutti looked at his younger 'adopted' brother and shook his head. Four hundred years later and the poor boy was still obsessed with the old saint.

'I have enough trouble with Aysha. Let's get some sleep now.'

BOOK
TWO

CHAPTER 1

The children laughed uproariously and rolled about on the hard-packed earthen floor. Momo looked up from her knitting with pursed lips of disapproval.

'Why do you always have to get them so excited just before bedtime?' she scolded, shaking the disengaged needle at poor Bubbi. 'And you two ... Poppy? Popo? Are you listening to me?'

The twins stopped rolling, giggling and laughing and sat up, endeavouring to fix serious expressions on their faces. Poppy, the girl, looked at Popo and nearly became apoplectic holding back her laughter.

'What silly bit of nonsense caused all this?' Momo's head went back and she sighted along her nose, the slitted eyes fixed on her beleaguered husband.

'There's nothing silly about passing through to the earth plane, they have to know how it's done ... why, before we know it they'll both be old enough to ...'

'Bubbi! Are you stark, raving mad? They're hardly walking and talking a year and you want to teach them how to pass through the dimensional layers? What's come over you?'

Bubbi's discomfort under fire became so agitated he bounded to his feet and began hopping from one foot to the other. Delighted with this display of unexpected activity, the twins stood and tried to imitate him. It was a clumsy performance as they were much too young to master the technique of throwing their weight to one side and latching on to a magnetic field.

Momo decided there was more here than met the eye and he needed a good talking to. Not, however, in front of the twins; they were like monkeys for mimicking and they had the memories of elephants.

'All right, children, we've had enough play for one day. Inside and get ready for bed. And I want to see clean nostrils and toe nails when you come back to say goodnight, do you hear me?'

'Come on, Popo,' Poppy bellowed, standing up and reaching down for her brother's hand; he didn't seem to understand how annoyed their mother was.

'Why were you so harsh with them, my dear?' Bubbi asked, a conciliatory tone in his voice.

'If you don't stop that silliness from going too far, they get sick. How many times do I have to tell you?' she asked, her own tone softening. She held out a hand to him. 'Come here and tell me what's bothering you. You must never keep anything from your loving wife. I am here to share your troubles.'

He held her hand, attempted to sit on the edge of the chair but he was back on his feet, hopping up and down in a few seconds.

'Do you realise how long it is since Dinah summoned me?' he blurted, the hurt spilling over into his words.

'I certainly do! I am not an ingrate. I say a little prayer every day . . .'

'Momo, what is wrong with you? All right, I admit, once upon a time she had me running myself ragged, but I can't help being worried. What if she is in desperate trouble?

What if she needs me and . . . and . . . well, what if she lost her little casket with the frog and couldn't . . .'

'Bubbi, what is the *matter* with you? You call it *good* luck to have a human's spell find you, force you to visit their plane and do all sorts of dirty jobs for them? You act as though that was what gnomes are for, are you losing your mustard seeds or something?'

'I didn't say that,' he protested. 'She's such a nice girl, a really good girl, nobody messes with her, I just want to know she's not in trouble.'

'Well, if it bothers you so much, why don't you do that special trip; you know, the one where you send your eyes and ears and find out everything.'

'You mean a scrying sensory teleport,' he informed her a trifle pompously.

'Oh, how nice, he even remembers the fancy names. Never mind the scholarly trimmings, Don Know-it-all, let's just send your eyes and ears and instead of worrying about what *might* be happening, you can come back with the right information.'

'Momo, you know we have to do . . . you know . . . in order to do a scrying sensor . . . to send my ears and eyes to see what's happening.' Bubbi looked stunned by his own suggestion.

'Oh? Oh-ho! Now you don't like what you used to call "Blissies", hmmmn? Now it's just "you know" — that's what you now call it?' Momo's body began to rise with the rising level of her indignation.

'You don't understand,' he tried to calm her. 'It's still "Blissies",' he insisted, 'I didn't want the children to overhear. You had so much trouble, you always say the twins are such a handful.'

'And you're *worried* for me, right?' she chimed in more cheerfully. 'Well, don't worry so much. It took the good Lord long enough to smile on us and when he did he smiled twice as hard. Even if he smiles again, it is not a disaster, understand? You don't spend years praying for children then become an ingrate the minute you . . .'

'We're all ready . . . look!' Poppy and Popo rushed in, both in matching long nightdresses made of soft, light blue wool. They held up their chins so Momo could inspect their nostrils, then their feet for her approval. She smiled and rewarded each with a kiss and a piece of wild honey cake.

A short while later, Momo and Bubbi were stretched out in their own nightshirts, but with the left arms free of the sleeves. A moment before they brought their armpits into the suction-tight grip of 'Blissies', Bubbi warned her about self-control. If she let herself go trekking off to the legendary Golden Caverns, she would spoil everything, she would break the telergic force pattern.

'Bubbi, stop the lectures and let's get started, huh?' She gave him a loving peck on the cheek. 'You do be so eldritch betimes,' she added dreamily, lapsing into her original country dialect, a thing she did only when very tired or secretly excited.

The words still caused a slight smile of amusement to play about his lips as he saw, behind closed eyelids, the large study of Solomon ha-Levi take form. And there was Dinah, sitting on the high stool, her shoulders bent and quivering slightly; Bubbi directed his vision forward until he could peek over her shoulder. She was writing in her diary. Diary? Since when did she . . . he cut the internal dialogue abruptly so he could concentrate on the words. Thank the Lord she was inscribing it in Hebrew. Arabic gave him a headache and, half the time, he got it all wrong. Naturally, you dumb-dumb, if she wrote it in Arabic, *everyone* could read it.

Through the entire autumn there has been such hectic activity. Father was sent to Carmona — we thought for making a few arrangements for the sultan and his new ally, the king of Castile. He came back once, but briefly, and now he is commissioned to supervise all the supply routes to north and east. His last letter tells us that he enjoys splendid accommodation in the palace — a palace he claims is as fine as the alcázar of Seville. It seems our two kings, the Muslim and the Christian, are benefitting from their careful teamwork, to say nothing of Grandfather's clever campaign organisation. He says now that Alcalá on the Guadaira River has been secured by the sultan with practically no bloodshed — and the same for Alcalá del Rio and many other towns — the siege of Seville will begin in earnest. Grandfather passed it off as simply as that, but Joseph had a good deal more to say. He is becoming quite famous, my bold Joseph, and his feats have both our kings vying to interest him in making the proper conversion. Fernando would have him as his first and only black knight — imagine that! Of course, Ahmar is not so insistent that a knight of his realm must convert to Islam. Joseph gave me the code for an Arabian knight. He must be liberal, courageous, a skilled horseman, have personal beauty and poetic talent (he has written me some lovely verses . . . some quite excitingly suggestive), eloquence, strength, a master of spear, sword and bow. Well, he is all of that, but they've never before seen one with his ability as a swordsman . . . and his skills with other weapons seem to come as easily. No one can match him now with the bow, even the crossbow. He tells me that the cuadrillos, those square bolts they are using now, will go through armour, the man and then bury themselves in the earth. He has seen it happen when they are fired upon from the ramparts of a fortress.

According to Joseph, the sultan is phenomenal in making the hosts of so many cities see the futility of resisting the generous terms of the Castilian king. Most of these towns have large Yemenite populations and merely a military garrison of Almohades. In no time, the Yemenites see the wisdom of Ahmar's proposals and they throw open the gates . . . the garrison force has no choice but to flee, thus saving countless thousands of lives. Only one life was lost in the taking of Alcalá de Guadaira, and that by the fast response of Joseph when some fanatic leapt from a wall, intent on assassinating the sultan. That capture alone is incredible. The fortress is admitted, since it was strengthened recently, to be impregnable. The old Roman aquaduct from there has been delivering water to Seville for centuries and it is vital to the city. Also, the flour mills are powered by the Guadaira and all Seville depends on Alcalá for bread. I like to think that Joseph captured the fortress single-handedly!

Joseph has been so busy in the court here that he hardly has time to breathe. I do think al-Ahmar made a good decision when he gave the talented Nubian to Grandfather as a slave — not that dear old Solomon thinks of anyone as a slave, not even that uppity Farida who has become intolerable since the poor dear gave in and allowed her free rein for her Abishag the Shunammite fantasies . . . and who can blame him, he's been so lonely for so long . . . yet, I must say, she has improved her mind a good deal and lost still more of that atrocious fat . . . stop right there: this record is for important *things. It was a good idea that Joseph came to us. Soon, I will be eighteen and I suspect Joseph will ask father about marriage then. What can poor Daddy say? Grandfather says the young man is an excellent physician now; two kings want him to be knighted and grace their courts; everyone admits he is so splendid and learned in synagogue . . . and so adorable sitting there in his prayer shawl . . . I look down and can't keep my eyes off him. His voice is so beautiful they want him to study to be the next hazzan. Must stop now, I hear the thunder of Grandfather's escort approaching the gates.*

Bubbi's teleported vision blinked; he had to read the last line again . . . had he been going to sleep? he chastised himself. He watched Dinah close the manuscript and put the brush back in its holder. Bubbi's senses sped down the hallway with her, followed her into her own chamber. She secreted the diary on a cabinet shelf behind her more intimate apparel; how clever, he thought, who would dare to look there? Another female, you dumb-dumb, hooooo-hoo-hoo . . . what about that Farida? He had no chance to pursue that because Dinah threw the robe on the bed, stripped out of her trousers and slipped the light bodice over her head.

Back in his own bedroom, Bubbi's body twitched so badly he nearly broke the precious suction with Momo. If Dinah had been beautiful when she was not yet thirteen, how gorgeous she was at not yet eighteen. There was no more puppy fat, just a perfect, sinewy body that moved with the nonchalant elegance of a leopard. Those breasts, how they mocked the moon for magnificence of form. And the same globe-like grandeur mirrored in the quivering buttocks. When she turned towards his projected eyes, he was dazzled by the fiery copper and gold of the triangle beneath her flat, well-muscled abdomen with its tiny, almost infantile navel. The skin glowed with the lustre of cream atop a bowl of fresh, rich milk. But that divine face, those sparkling green eyes . . . he made the inner voice stop; had it continued, *he* would be guilty of breaking the telergic force . . . he would be off to the star-splashed Golden Caverns. With a silent, internal sob, he closed his eyes until she finished dressing in raiment more suitable to meet her grandfather.

She had just opened her door when her grandfather strode by, calling her to follow. A few paces behind him, his headcloth whipped aside, the robe flowing open, the sword clanging and a fine crossbow over his shoulder, Joseph stepped lively to keep up; Dinah fell into step and he reached out surreptitiously to take her hand. As soon as he did, as though the very contact had done something to shift her psychic level, she spun about and stared at her own doorway, nearly tugged off her feet as a result by the hurrying Joseph.

'Somebody's been watching me,' she fairly hissed. 'Even as I dressed, someone was there . . . I don't mean physically, understand. Contact with you,' she confided to the Nubian, 'suddenly sharpened my awareness . . . how careless of me! After all the warnings . . . I wonder . . . now who would . . . Bubbi!' She stopped abruptly, nearly spilling Joseph over backwards. 'Bubbi? Are you here?'

Before Bubbi could even attempt to answer, Momo forgot herself and did what she was not supposed to. As she catapulted herself to the Golden Caverns, Bubbi's perceptions were dumped unceremoniously on the bed. He trembled with vertigo, the psychic shock hitting him so hard in the solar plexus he couldn't breathe for a few moments and controlling the nausea was quite difficult. He felt like he was stuffing miles upon miles of invisible silver cord down his throat. The suction broke and he moved away from Momo slightly. She would be in the land of 'Blissies' for quite a while yet.

'Daddy, I'm thirsty,' Poppy called out. 'Me too,' echoed from Popo before his sister's words were stilled. With a groan, Bubbi shot up and landed a few feet from the bed.

* * *

'I think you're stark, staring mad, the pair of you,' Dinah exclaimed, her hands on her hips and her eyes shooting fire. 'If Sultan Muhammad thought this up, I'm going to tell him what I think of him, even if it costs me my life . . .'

'Dinah, my dear child,' Solomon soothed, 'you're letting yourself get out of control. That is a dangerous thing for one with your . . .' before he could add a word, a large clay water jug on the table of Solomon's study lifted itself off the table and hurled itself out the open window.

'Temper, temper,' Joseph added mildly, trying to soothe her by patting her arm. She yanked the arm away and glared at him. He looked like a freak!

'Look at the pair of you. Is there nothing you wouldn't do for a pair of crazy kings who can't leave well enough alone?'

With his skills in a very advanced form of science — half chemistry and much more than half comprising alchemical principles and a good deal of esoterica — Solomon had prepared a thick paste and a ewer of a bitter-smelling solution. He had applied the paste to all of Joseph's body save what remained beneath his skimpy loincloth; then he'd washed the skin down a number of times with the bitter-almond solution. Joseph was the colour of mahogany, the colour of a desert warrior.

To Joseph's scanty, rather sparse new beard a good deal had been added; and added in the hard, squared style favoured by the Berber tribes of North Africa. With the new Almohade headcloth wound about his tightly curled locks, he was no longer a Nubian.

'We'll have to think more about the hair,' Solomon mused. 'You won't be able to keep that tailesan wrapped about your head all the time. Perhaps a kaffiyeh would be better . . . no, not for an Almohade.' The old man thought a moment longer. 'Ah. Ah-ha! Yes, I think I know something that will make it straight, lie flat . . . remind me when we get to Alcalá de Guadaira . . .'

'You are really serious about this farce?' Dinah demanded. Her grandfather's beard had been cut short and squared, a more luxurious version of the one Joseph wore. The hair was braided and both beard and hair were dyed jet black. The old man had used some of the formula on his own skin and it was many shades darker.

'You know who we are, my child,' Solomon soothed her. 'When we get to Seville, two obvious strangers of Berber background — don't forget, we have some authentic-looking documents concerning our skills in medicine — who will challenge us? They'll be so happy to have two physicians, both skilled as military surgeons, they will undoubtedly greet us with open arms.'

'Yes, and you'll just open up the gates and let the troops pour in . . . one more city taken bloodlessly?'

'No, that's not how it will work. We must prepare a whole section of the citizenry for their emancipation. Until this is done, they will continue to believe we, not their Almohade masters, are the enemy. Then, there is the all-important job of communications, keeping the brotherly kings aware of . . .'

'Grandfather, that is termed spying. And you are both going to be killed, I just know it . . . you're not going to leave me here and stick your necks . . .'

'Of course not,' Joseph pleaded, 'we are taking you with us . . . as far as Alcalá. You will have a very important role to play there.'

'What, seeing to it the mill and bakery work full time to supply the troops? I will not be left behind, you two need watching over. Anyone who allows a king to send him off on such a dangerous assignment, such a foolhardy errand, needs watching over.'

'We'll talk about that on the way,' Solomon promised. 'Besides, it was the sultana's idea.'

With the mention of the sultana, a complete change seemed to alter the room. The candles sputtered and Dinah began to sway; her eyes rolled, then began to rise until the whites only were visible. Joseph leapt forward and caught her, lifting her off the ground before she fell.

'Quick, here on the table.' Solomon pointed. Together, they stretched her out, placing Joseph's robe under her head.

'She's in a trance . . . something has suddenly warned her about the sultana,' Joseph guessed.

'It is amazing how in this last year her psychic powers have increased. However, I don't think it is the sultana so much. Ahmar insisted on leaving for Seville again before his full replacement troops were ready. He is going to give me a heart attack yet . . .'

Dinah's eyes fluttered. She struggled to sit up but the seer held her down until she recovered fully.

'It's the sultana's eunuch . . . you know, that terrible devil who hates us so . . .'

'My dear, Abu has always been a problem. There is not one Slav, as they call everyone from east of the Alps, who has not been a danger to his rulers — this one is no exception.'

'If it is simply court intrigue, why does he want you two away while the sultan is gone?' Dinah dropped to the floor lightly.

'You don't think . . . ?' her grandfather began.

'I am certain. I didn't visualise it, it was a smell more than anything. It smelled like ibn Yakub, ibn Hud's villain. With you and Joseph out of the way, with the sultan gone and most of the able-bodied men with him . . .'

'You know,' Joseph interrupted with a bright smile, 'if it were suddenly to appear that this eunuch was no eunuch at all, he'd be in very serious trouble, wouldn't he?'

Solomon laughed. 'He'd be lucky to leave the palace alive. The captain of the household guard would need no one's permission to carve him up for the stable dogs. How will you go about proving a eunuch is not a eunuch?'

'You're leaving at dawn tomorrow,' Joseph answered. 'You go with your escort and wait for us at Alcalá de Guadaira . . . two days at the most. If I succeed, I will tell you how it was done. If I do not, well, we'll be no worse off, but I'd rather not tell you then. May I have your permission, master?'

'As long as you promise you will not be careless in such a way that it all comes home to roost. It suits our purposes that ibn Hud's chancellor is not aware that we suspect anything.'

'Exactly!' Joseph agreed warmly. 'That is why I suggested letting Abu the eunuch be the author of his own undoing. No suspicion. But, sir . . . I'll need Dinah's help.'

Solomon rose from his seat and glowered down at the young athlete. 'You may don your clothing, Joseph, it is no longer necessary to expose yourself. I should think that application will last at least three to four months.' Solomon turned as though he had already dismissed the young man.

'Sir? You haven't answered my request. I need Dinah's help. Otherwise, it will not work.'

'Do you really expect me to leave my granddaughter here, with no supervision, no proper guardians, just you? Do you think I'm senile?'

'No sir, but you have Farida to watch over . . .'

'I wouldn't trust that nymphomaniac to guard a cat on heat! Besides, I plan to bring Farida to Seville with us. A Christian slave — and particularly a young, attractive female — lends great authenticity to our impersonation of Berber physicians . . . she will be very useful in assisting us with many of the less demanding chores . . .'

'He's not senile, the old goat,' Dinah whispered to herself.

'Well then, what about the cook, Hepzie?' Joseph's voice was losing its enthusiasm in his premonition of defeat.

'I wouldn't set her to watch over Farida! No less a hot cat.'

'Grandfather, do you not realise I am my own best protection . . . after Joseph? We shall travel alone and none will molest us. Any man foolish enough to try, will feel the wrath of that mighty sword. Besides, it is time I travelled incognito again. I shall go as a man.'

'And who protects you against Joseph's ardours?' Solomon wanted to know.

'I do. Ask him.' She slipped her talisman from her pocket and held it up. It glinted with an unearthly illumination. Solomon blinked, Joseph's eyes opened wider, the whites reflecting the strange, enigmatic light.

'She does indeed,' Joseph agreed cryptically, not caring to elaborate.

'Umm al-Ha'it will always protect me,' the girl intoned in a deep, invocational inflection, holding the silver box of hexagrams higher, then slipping it back under her robe.

'Mother of Life . . . why do you call it that?' Joseph asked impulsively.

'Never mind . . . boys just don't understand such things.'

'If I agree,' Solomon rounded on the youth, his eyes made even fiercer by his new harsh desert aspect, 'will you take a solemn oath that you will in no way . . .'

'Sirrrr?' The distress in Joseph's voice had Dinah holding the edge of the table with one hand, her aching side with the other, trying mightily to stifle the burst of laughter.

'What?' Solomon asked with as close to imperiousness as he ever came.

'You make me take an oath every time I escort Dinah from Alhambra to here. Won't the oath from two days ago, last week, the week before . . .'

'Take the oath!' The old man boomed.

CHAPTER 2

As they moved in single file, Dinah, in the rear, turned and looked behind her. Looking back eastward toward Granada, the land through which they had passed had a different aspect than when first approached. South of Archidona they had seen a great craggy rock formation which rose fantastically, forming the vision of a fortress. Looking back, she could not find it. And the clouds which had circled the mountain peaks formed crowns for Christian monarchs, turbans for Muslims. From here she noticed a huge, reclining woman, with a pointed chin, pointed breasts and a very pregnant belly. Very clever, those Christian and Muslim monarchs, wearing crowns and turbans. She breathed and turned back, hoping the track would widen soon so she could ride with Joseph. The smell, the endless stretches of dusty, furry grey-green olive trees, never out of sight, league after league.

The path narrowed rather than widened as they ascended a gentle hill; Dinah paid more attention to the thoroughbred mare who picked her way daintily among the sudden scattering of rocks and stones. Joseph halted and turned, waiting for her. He rose in his stirrups, his arm extended straight ahead. Drawing up to him she stopped and caught her breath; with a quick look behind to check on the two pack animals following, she then turned her full attention to the panorama unfolding before them. The river sparkled in the first warming sunshine of spring. In the distance, Alcalá de Guadaira stood like a sentinel, lowering over the water, the walls seeming to touch the stream. Joseph had described it as impregnable, with the river, the thick walls and the gates so contrived that narrow winding paths made any mass rush impossible; in fact, but a few well-armed men could hold off an army.

'We'll be there by sunset,' the Nubian-turned-Berber exclaimed, his voice vibrant in spite of the long hours in the saddle.

'I look forward to soaking in a bath for at least an hour. Bathing in cold rivers, never knowing if you are hiding in some convenient undergrowth . . .'

'That is unfair, my lady, quite unfair. I took yet another oath, if you will remember . . .' Her unbridled laughter stopped him short. Even through the mist of tears, she looked up at him, discovering for the thousandth time over the past few days that he made an extremely handsome Almohade, much more so than any she had seen in her young life. Certainly, he represented the Arabian ideal of a knight in every way. Surely, Grandfather would treat with the sultan to gain the youth's freedom. Then, quite possibly, both Ahmar and the Castilian king would knight Joseph. Still, he could not stay this way indefinitely, with that silly brown stain all over him . . . except under his . . . she stopped that thought and mentally reprimanded herself. Anyway, he was still more handsome in his normal state . . .

'What are you thinking about, now that you've stopped laughing at me for the chivalrous way I accept your grandfather's relentless, remorseless demands, countenance his insults to my piety, chastity and integrity where your precious immaculate condition is concerned; the most brilliant scholar, the wisest of men, yet he becomes an impossible, demented zealot when it comes to . . .'

'Stop! You'll knock me off my perch with all those words . . .' she could not go on for another fit of laughter; Joseph waited with feigned indignation. 'Oh, Joseph, I don't know which of you has the more comical role in this morality play, but I was actually thinking how handsome you look in your new medical-military role. Very handsome indeed.'

'You prefer the lighter colour, no doubt,' he observed, a hurt look about his eyes.

'Will you stop that, please? You know I love you, I've told you often enough . . .'

'You can never tell me too often,' he reminded her, 'so please don't stop.' He dismounted in one easy bound and, before she could move, he pulled her off her saddle. She gasped, struggled weakly, then submitted to his eager kisses.

'Joseph, be careful,' she gritted in stops and starts when she could free her mouth from his ardent attack. 'You'll ruin my beard and I cannot possibly replace . . .' Realising what she had said, she fought free and slapped him.

'It looks gorgeous,' he chided her, still holding her shoulders in his powerful hands. 'So much fuller, so much more luxurious than when you were a little girl of thirteen.' He ducked under her flailing arms, caught her up under her sword belt and tossed her up, catching her about the waist as she descended, her arms pinned to her sides. Before she knew what was happening, he tripped her with his heel, falling with her, one arm about her, the other hand extended to break their fall on the soft grass. Lying atop her, he pressed her body with his, all the youthful fire in him communicating itself to her, inflaming her own nerves and flesh; his mouth pressed down, pinning hers.

'Mmmmnmm-mrph-myimmmm-nooo-rrrhh.' Hard as she struggled, he held her, using her efforts to protest to insinuate his tongue inside her resisting mouth. At last he moved back, gazing down at her with a perfect combination of adoration and mischief.

'Not only does it look redder and fuller, it tastes better, the flavour is richer . . . hmmmn . . . shall we say, more mature?'

'I hate you!' She managed to free one hand to pummel his chest. 'Get off me, you big oaf, I'm going to tell my grandfather how you keep your oath.'

'I haven't so much as suggested doing what it takes to break that oath . . .' as he spoke he rolled his hips from side to side, thrusting his lions at her in the same rhythm; she could feel how frighteningly excited he was, the entasis creating a deep impression on her own tender, abdominal flesh. Perhaps not as terrifying as Hutti or Musa, but certainly formidable.

'You're a brute and a bully. I hope a squadron of Almohade soldiers ride up here and . . .'

'You'd better bite your tongue. They'd all line up behind me and *they* would have no oaths to honour.' He kissed her again and this time she responded warmly, her arms encircling his neck.

'Joseph, please,' she sighed at last, breaking free. 'Don't you think it's hard for me too? It's not that I don't wish to, I've told you that so many times . . .'

'Yes, if you lose that precious virginity, then all the fiends of hell will be able to undo you and your defences will no longer work. That reminds me . . .' he rolled to one side and helped her sit up, checking that the horses were quietly grazing nearby . . . 'what about that special thing you do — you know, the one you did to the Djinn and the demon that nearly drove them mad . . . why can't you do that for me?'

'I don't want to. When the time comes, I hope I shall prove to be *all* you ever want. Before that, I don't want you getting spoilt. Now, let's get going or we'll be stumbling about in the dark. Aren't you just dying to see the look on Grandfather's face when we tell him about Abu? And wait until ibn Yakub hears that his spy has been executed for impersonating a eunuch in the sultan's harem . . .'

'We're not sure about that yet,' he reminded her. 'The sultana seemed terribly partial to Abu for some unfathomable reason . . .'

'She's kind and gentle with everyone,' Dinah protested, 'it has nothing to do with him. Do you think Ahmar would listen to her about a crime like this?'

'Oh, no more than you'd expect me to listen to you ... and do exactly what you told me to,' he teased sarcastically.

'I'll ignore that,' she sniffed. 'And I will remind you that the queen is no fool. We spent many long hours together in serious studies. Not only does she read and have excellent skills in mathematics, but she is becoming an outstanding poet.'

'Just the skills needed to talk the sultan out of removing that villain's head.' He paused, squinted and checked the sky carefully. 'We may be in for a storm soon, we'd better get moving.'

When they were remounted and moving down toward the long plain ahead, Dinah reached out and held his hand.

'I think you're right, you know. She will talk him out of it just because she is soft-hearted and a very persuasive lady ... in her case soft heart belies strong personality.' She smiled a bit unhappily. She didn't like the idea of Abu free to do as much damage as he could. 'What will they do with him, imprison him?'

'Either that or banish him. Where would you go if you were banished from the kingdom of Granada?'

'Well, not back to Murcia, he'd be not much use to his evil master ibn Yakub there, would he? As we know, though they are both Yemenites and great soldiers, Yakub's master ibn Hud and our master al-Ahmar are enemies ... even if ibn Hud had to send troops to aid Don Fernando as a loyal vassal. One of Hud's own captains is the only governor in Seville now. This Sakkaf is an Almohade, but one loyal to Hud. There is little doubt that Hud wants Fernando's holy war to fail, Ahmar's arms to collapse so that he can regain Seville ... then Granada.'

Smiling as cheerfully as he could, Joseph raised her hand and kissed the palm tenderly. 'Well, my pretty fortune-teller, daughter and granddaughter to mighty sooth-sayers, your words lead me to expect Abu in Seville, working for Captain Sakkaf.'

* * *

'I'm not joking, a donkey . . . one of the biggest donkeys I ever saw . . . and it was painless, that Joseph is a wonder . . . well, almost painless, he brayed once or twice.'

'Bubbi,' his wife complained, 'I don't want to complain, but could you just start at the beginning? I'm not sure what Joseph cut off the donkey, but I'm *very* sure I don't know why. Please, darling, from the beginning and slowly. When I don't know a word, explain, huh?'

Bubbi described how they had slipped into the stable, knowing that this donkey was scheduled to be castrated the following day. Dinah stayed outside the stable. She had a wonderful talisman that could make people feel very, very peculiar . . . well, males, that is, and there would be only males about the stables. Something to do with their weird sexual practices, but he was not absolutely sure. If any stable boy got curious, she would aim this little box at him and he'd go off whirling about, doing the oddest things to himself and, likely as not, wouldn't be seen for days.

Then they had to make their way all around the new buildings that were going up and into the new harem. That's where Dinah was at her best. Not that Joseph couldn't enter the harem as the court physician's assistant, but they didn't want anyone to know they'd been there at all. It took them a long time to find the head eunuch, a bad man named Abu, all on his own. They had hidden here, climbed under furniture there, they had even nearly run into the sultana at one point, but finally, there he was, in a little room he used to prepare sweetmeats and delicacies for the queen. As often as he'd been there before, Joseph didn't know about that room. From behind a curtain some distance away, Dinah saw the sultana signal in a certain way, knew what she wanted and led them all to that obscure room. She beamed her talisman at Abu and he went straight up in the air and came down hard, landing flat on his back with a terrible thud. He didn't like it very much because he didn't have the things other men had to make them enjoy such sensations. It made other men delirious, but it just knocked Abu out. Momo protested again, repeating over and over: what things? First, the donkey, now the eunuch. As delicately as he could, fearful of upsetting her sensitive nature, Bubbi described the anatomical parts which had been removed from Abu so that he could qualify as a eunuch. Then, of course, the practical part of Momo's nature came to the fore and he had to find a way of telling her that men who can afford it, buy other men called eunuchs to watch over their wives. So that no one else but the owner does to the wives what only the owner is supposed to. Naturally, the one doing the minding must be incapable of doing what the owner doesn't want anyone else to . . . Momo asked him please to get on with his story, much more of that sort of talk was bound to make her ill.

Bubbi sat on the eunuch's face since absolute unconsciousness was required. Once again, Dinah stood guard just inside the door to the private pantry and then Joseph went to work. What a wizard that boy was with surgeon's tools! There was practically no bleeding because the incisions he made were so small and neat. In fact, Bubbi, as an observer, found it hard to realise how he could do such sculpturing, in such a miniature form, until he remembered what that big Djinn Hutti had done for his eyesight. In less than one-quarter of an hour, that sack and its rather large contents — the one Joseph had removed from the donkey — were not only invisibly attached to the eunuch's groin, but all the fine internal threads and tubes had been connected. Joseph deemed the whole system would be in perfect working order when the brute awakened.

All the while — working with a speed hardly compatible to the delicacy of the operation he was performing — the good-humoured Joseph had kept up a whispered monologue. He imagined that in a few days the eunuch's toe nails would expand and get tougher, forcing his toes to splay out like the struts in a fan. Yes, and there would be a very definite change in the quality of his laughter . . . if indeed he laughed at all. The noise would be deafening, even if he was simply raising his voice in anger with some of the younger eunuchs. In fact, Joseph giggled as he wiped one or two tiny drops of blood away from the completed operation and began packing his tools, it was quite possible Abu's ears might elongate a bit . . . with perhaps a profuse covering of hair. Bubbi was bouncing up and down with laughter by this time, actually paining himself each time he landed back on the prone man's nose.

Joseph signalled Dinah and gestured for Bubbi to move past her and stand inside the door. He explained that they did not know what possible effect Dinah's talisman might have on a gnome, so they were taking no chances. Joseph backed up too when she removed the talisman, placed it in her mouth and created a strange, haunting note that vibrated so violently it made Bubbi hop up and down. It lifted Abu off the floor and nearly to the ceiling. He stayed there for a few seconds, his body jerking furiously, his arms and legs waving about as though they had no bones, only thousands of spongy joints. When he settled down on the floor again, all those external organs seemed in a terrible state of arousal; the ones Joseph had just added, plus the thing which had been there all along, were fiercely agitated, slamming about wildly . . . and yet, the man snoozed on as though it were all happening to someone else.

As they worked their way to the exit carefully, again cautious that they should not be seen, Joseph explained why Dinah had created that unconscious madness in the eunuch. Deep in his memory he would retain the experience so vividly — an experience unlike anything the normal run of humans are ever lucky enough to know — that should anyone, even under Abu's instructions, come near him to remove once more that which had been miraculously returned to him, he would fight with the manic strength of a demon.

'Bubbi, that was a very interesting story,' Momo assured him regally. 'A very interesting story. First, and not for the first time, mind you, we are just on the threshold of

"Blissies" and Bang! she summons you.' Momo rubbed under her left arm ruefully, remembering the pain of it all. 'You shot up so fast, the noise of us tearing apart nearly broke my heart ... to say nothing of the pain in my "Blissatorium" ...'

'Momo ... are you going to ask me a question? I don't understand why you're ...'

'Listen ... what is all this impatience, please? Did I interrupt you?' Momo glared at him until he coughed uncomfortably, propped his ear on his palm, the elbow on the bed and made a small moue of apology. 'The question is: why did you do to that man what you did to him? You said before that he had an operation years ago to have those — whatever they're called — removed so he could get a job in a harem ... correct?' Bubbi nodded, dreading what was coming. 'Then you walk in because Dinah summons *you* and you help *them* put back on another pair from a donkey which he definitely did not order, if I heard the story correctly ... correct?' Again the miserable gnome nodded his head, mentally kicking himself: why hadn't he told her their swords needed sharpening, the garden needed weeding ... something?

'Are you listening to me, Bubbi dear?' It seemed to him his head was bobbing up and down continuously. 'What you did is going to make that man lose his job, that is if anybody discovers what you did. Is there anything you wish to tell me?' Bubbi looked at her, his eyes filled with marital terror. Lose his job? His head would roll across the central court. He'd be chopped into scraps for the stable dogs. Not so much in Yemenite Arabic courts, but in Moorish ones, as the gnome well knew, the stable dogs develop quite an addiction for those kinds of scraps.

'Well, darling, he's a very bad man. He works for the sultan's enemies, he's a threat to the kingdom, I guarantee you ... he was one of those planning to abduct poor Dinah ...'

'Bubbi, don't trifle with me, please. You're talking ifs, buts and maybes ... sand castles in the air ... I'm talking about a man losing his job . . . . *definitely* losing his job.' she leaned closer, checking his ears, his lips, the palms of hands, searching for those irrebuttable signs that, since time immemorial, have always told the female when the male is lying. 'Did you tell anyone?'

The shock on his face had every indication of the genuine . . . it had, not because he was shocked that she should think he would do such a thing, but because Joseph had already arranged to have an anonymous note handed to al-Ahmar denouncing the eunuch and saying if he went immediately to the small pantry, he could prove it to himself. How had Momo known!

'Darling, you know how upset you were when that summons came in? Well, I've been thinking . . . we should lose no more time trying for a brother or sister . . . I know Poppy is dying for a baby around the house . . . after all, most of her friends have new baby brothers or sisters . . . and Popo will get a lot of pleasure out of . . .'

'Bubbi, are you being evasive? You promise me you didn't say anything about that poor man and the donkey?'

'I promise.' He clasped his hands, falling back on the bed and staring up at the earthen ceiling overhead. 'Alohim, Adonai, strike me dumb if I said a word to anyone.'

Hardly had the words left his mouth than Momo pounced, slipping her left arm under his, levering the two arms up, interlocking them.

'Oh, lover,' she breathed huskily, 'do to me what you alone can do.'

CHAPTER 3

The last days of April brought with them heat more normal to the middle of summer. In the area of Tablada, where San Fernando had made his second camp outside the walls of Seville — the first one on the Prado de San Sebastian proving much too close and vulnerable — the scale of activity vied with that to be found inside any large city. Laid out much like a town with neat streets formed in a quadrant pattern, merchants of every description catered for the needs of the besieging troops. Butchers and fishmongers shouted wares, there were cloth merchants displaying textiles of every design, armourers and blacksmiths working hand in hand as well as taverns with a very permanent air about them despite the fact they were created from tents placed together.

Crowds of shoppers milled about in the late afternoon, and not all soldiers or administrators. Whole families had worked together to set up this town outside a town as the Castilian king had sworn when he invested the city he would not relinquish the siege until Seville fell. As the word of San Fernando was equal to gold coinage, merchants and labourers brought their families as no one could predict how many years this 'impregnable' city could hold out.

The camp city was, of course, by no means always a safe place. At regular intervals, knights and soldiers from the army of the Almohade defenders would slip out of the city gates, down to the only bridge across the River Guadaira, just before it joins the wide and deep Guadalquivir, and attack their enemies with determination and total contempt for the odds against them. Great numbers of these Moorish daredevils were slaughtered, yet they took a terrible toll of the hapless foraging parties which had to roam the area daily.

On the east bank of the Guadalquivir, the walls of this queen of Andalusian cities were formidable indeed. The Golden Tower stood out from the embankment, praised, like the Giralda tower at the great mosque to the east, as one of the masterpieces of Islamic architecture. On the west bank stood the Triana castle, itself every bit as impregnable as the city of Seville opposite. A daring soldier, known as the Master of the town Uclés, had taken less than three hundred knights and men across the river to attack Triana. Sorely pressed himself, his host under constant attack from the bold sallies of the castle defenders, his only salvation was the heavy reinforcement sent by Fernando — troops he could hardly afford. Yet, the Master of Uclés and his brave band stood on the threshold of the city's sustenance.

Between them, Fernando and Ahmar had managed to capture — more by diplomacy on Ahmar's part than sieges and battles — every strategic point above and below the city. Alcalá del Rio to the north was the gateway for supplies from the mountains. Alcalá de Guadaira to the southeast controlled the bread and water. Only the rich and fertile plain to the west was outside the Castilian's grasp. Known as the Ajarafe, this productive farmland stretched from Aznalfarache, just south of the city, to the town of Niebla on the Rio Tinto, then down all the way to Jerez de la Frontera. And from massive iron rings in the wall of Triana matching those on the opposite wall across the river, was chained a bridge of boats, the only bridge across the Guadalquivir south of Córdoba, nearly thirty leagues away.

Each time the Christian king saw this bridge he felt pained. In his heart, he knew that as long as that bridge was there, the chances of reducing Seville, bringing its commander to his knees, were very slim. Nightly, protected from the ramparts by hordes of archers, the porters went back and forth across the bridge to bring the needed supplies into the city. Niebla, at the northwestern end of the Ajarafe plain was yet another virtually impregnable town under Almohade domination. So was Jerez to the south. With the exception of the bold Master of Uclés, the marshalled forces of the two invading kings were impotent on the west bank, until that bridge was taken out.

Head down, the long headcloth wrapped about her head and neck to ward off a hot and fetid wind blowing across the encampment city, Dinah picked her way among the stalls. Her red beard was fuller once again and she moved with great assurance, confident that her disguise was impervious to any glance. Every now and again, she stopped at a stall, but bought nothing. Halting now at a large display of fine silks made in Seville, she whispered to the man in charge. He was a partner in one of the family enterprises and informed her about the fast turnover being done. He too believed the 'man' standing before him was David ben Immanuel ha-Kahan, the youngest son of her Aunt Rebecca who was married to a renowned rabbi in Alexandria. So far, no one in this part of the world had met young David — the real one — and that included Dinah.

She smiled and nodded as she moved on. Seville is under siege. Fernando has no hope of starving them out until he finds a way to destroy that bridge of ships. Every night the supplies across the river to feed the inhabitants of Seville. Every night the Almohades slip out and attack one part or another of the camp-city. Every night emissaries of Ahmar slip into the city for conferences with the leaderless majority of the citizens ... and to gather the news gleaned by an Almohade physician, his assistant and one young, silly Mozarab girl called Farida who was supposed to be helping them. As the Sultan had often said, had not ibn Hud had their leader assassinated, this whole war could have been avoided, like the Yemenite majority in so many other cities, they would have thrown open the gates and the Almohades would have had no choice but to leave. Yes, and with the same punctuality, every night loads of silken fabrics leave the city, along with leather goods, jewelry, pottery and glass for sale across these stalls . . . and not infrequently, some of the surplus supplies which crossed the bridge the night before! The ironies of war!

Having finished her enquiries, she gazed toward the setting sun. If there was any chance at all, she must hope that today she would see Joseph atop the wall. It had been two weeks now that he had been so busy night and day with his duties he could not chance slipping out for a few moments in the middle of the night. Moving with studied and casual haste, she drew as near as she could to the distant city wall with safety. In less than half an hour, her prayers were answered. Even from that distance, she recognised him immediately. She closed her eyes for a few moments, composing herself and willing herself to block all else save the view of Joseph when she opened her eyes. Over and over she repeated that she had been inadvertantly given a similar gift of preternatural eyesight by the Djinn. It was up to her to optimise that gift.

When she opened her eyes, there was a soft fog everywhere save the one tiny spot on top of the wall. Joseph began creating numbers with his hands. They were both now so well versed in Gematria, the numerical correspondence of the alphabet, they could send messages back and forth with ease. He loved her. He missed her. Her father was well . . . enough. No, not sick, just tired, run down. He was showing his age a bit, nothing more. Their worst fears were justified. Abu had been released . . . he was here and had convinced Sakkaf and his colleagues that he would be invaluable as a soldier and a smeller out of spies and infiltrators. There was a staff meeting called by Ahmar for tonight. She was to attend. He would wait below, just outside the

Jerez gate, close to midnight.

Keen as her eyesight was — more so, Joseph's — neither chanced to notice a silent observer across the river, well concealed behind the parapets of Triana Castle. Pale, thick-nosed, grossly heavy of jowl and neck, watery grey-blue eyes sunk deeply in his head . . . very little of those recognisable features showed; Abu, the ex-eunuch, managed to conceal nearly everything. The lad he had seen with the Berber doctor, a young Almohade, from the look of him. But his friend in the distance? And what were they up to? Spies, of course, what else? Although he had not been touched by the powers of a Djinn, Abu's eyes were extraordinarily sharp; much like an eagle's, they were particularly keen at great distances. Before the young man's companion below was lost in the crowd, a sudden shaft of strong sunlight struck head and shoulders just as a gust of wind lifted the end of the tailesan and exposed some hair and the beard. Abu clenched his teeth and the molars ground against each other frightfully. That specific colour of hair he had seen only once before in his entire life; but there had been no beard matching the hair then — who would expect to see a beard on the sultana's favourite, that arrogant, overbearing Jew's granddaughter?

When that impossible combination of thoughts struck home, Abu leapt to his feet, abandoning caution. The young military surgeon was no longer there . . . was it . . . could it be possible? he wondered, stroking his smooth cheek. The brazen young black slave turned over to the old necromancer as an apprentice? Was there some form of magic which could turn a black skin into one like a Berber's, merely weathered by the desert sun and wind? How? Of course! That Solomon fiend has control over Djinni, that's how. How else could they have managed to attach these obscene and horrendous big spheres to my body and make it seem they'd always been there? Black magic! How else can you do Satan's work? Ayiiii! There is an older Berber physician with whom the black youth works . . . of course! Black beard, black hair, skin like old dark leather . . . but it is

Solomon! They are spies! Spies for Ahmar and that Christian devil who wishes to conquer Islam . . .

By the time all this had sunk in, the shattered Abu was sprawled out on the path inside the wall. For the thousandth time, he saw the sultan's soldiers lifting him to his feet that day in Granada, beating him and pointing to the vile, huge testicles. In chains, thrown to the ground before the sultan, he heard the order: remove his head and place it on a pike, high on the wall nearest the harem, as a warning. The rest could be chopped up for the stable dogs. Then the Nightingale's voice. Abu had served her faithfully, she would pledge on her life that he had never molested any of the women. Ahmar spared him, but he was driven from the kingdom, never to return under pain of immediate, ignominious death.

Forehead to the stone, sobbing and nearly retching, his body caught up in a terrible paroxysm of hate, a desire for vengeance against those who had plotted and engineered his disgrace and downfall, he heard the muezzin call the faithful to prayer from the great tower inside the city. He thanked God fervently for revealing to him the authors of his tragic state.

Moving with purpose and more speed, Dinah made her way toward the large tent which Fernando used as his administrative headquarters; Christian and Muslim guards on duty surrounding the pavilion were wide awake and paying attention to their duties. In the last gloom before total darkness, everyone's nerves became a bit jumpy; an enemy sally could strike anywhere with lightning speed. Unconsciously, Dinah's hand crossed her body and she loosened the sword in its scabbard. It was not an idle gesture; in exchange for many fruitful lessons in the Qabala and the interpretation of esoteric books in Hebrew, Joseph had taught her to defend herself with great skill. In fact, he told her she had the makings of a champion swordsman.

The guards bowed to Dinah as she stepped through the entrance, gravely recognising this stranger, a Jew permitted to bear arms in the service of the sultan ... a strange thing in itself, but they had seen the official pass often enough. Thinking of this, she smiled slightly to herself. What it had taken to get that pass from Solomon! Finally, she had convinced him that she could not be kept locked up in Alcalá de Guadaira while he and Joseph imperilled their lives daily behind the enemy's thick walls. Finally, she convinced him she would be safer disguised as a man than on her own as a girl.

Officers of many different groups of infantry and cavalry moved about the large assembly area of the vast tent. Castilian, the local Iberio-Roman dialect, Catalan, Arabic ... the languages seemed to blend until she pictured a new Tower of Babel. Shamah, shamah, ha-Makon, she whispered silently to herself, invoking the God of Israel, let there be understanding, let there soon be peace. Even as she finished her short prayer, shouts of 'Ghalib, Ghalib' went up from many throats. Ahmar marched into their midst, his hands held high; he shouted even louder and more forcefully: 'La Ghalib ila Allah!'

At her elbow, a worried Christian knight in full armour, his helm under his arm, spoke softly, trying very hard to use Castilian rather than Catalan words.

'What did he say?' he asked.

'Crowds everywhere, even his own officers, call him Ghalib ... it is Arabic for Conqueror. His answer is always the same: "God alone is the Conqueror."'

A burly man in hose, short boots, a cuirass over his dark red tunic, doffed a velvet cap and approached the sultan, bowing low. He addressed a question to the sultan and there was a pause. Dinah moved forward, placing herself directly to Ahmar's left.

'May I help, my liege, I know the language.' As soon as she spoke, there was a smile of relief on the gentle, darkly bronzed face.

'King Fernando was to have been here much earlier.' Ahmar explained in a low voice. 'He has been speaking of visiting a special shrine inside the city. He is obsessed with a picture of a virgin there, one that is hidden behind a wall. More than once he has declared that if he can but worship there, the Christian heaven will espouse our cause.' Ahmar raised his eyebrows in a puzzled gesture of incredulity. 'I greatly fear that he may have tried to slip in there on his own tonight. Allah protect him if that butcher Sakkaf or his henchmen come upon him. The Christians and our people, of course, would protect him . . .' The imposing man waiting coughed in the most discreet manner.

'Sir,' Dinah smiled and addressed him, 'The Lord Sovereign of Granada informs me that King Fernando has not arrived. How can his majesty help you?'

'It is only that I am anxious to fulfil Don Fernando's commission concerning the bridge of ships across the river.' The man gestured apologetically. 'Forgive me, I am Ramón Bonifaz, Don Fernando's admiral of the fleet.' He bowed low, with a sweeping gesture of his arm. Not many ships to be called a fleet, the girl reckoned, but considering he has swept the river up to Aznalfarache, just below Seville, it is a better fleet than anything the enemy can muster.

When she translated all this for the sultan, he asked what they could do for the admiral in Fernando's absence.

'Good sir,' he answered when she translated the question, 'it is only that I wish to ascertain a date. The ships we ordered from Santander have arrived; they are the large ones we need to break the chains and destroy the bridge.' The man went on to describe the ships. He had agreed with Don Fernando that plating the bows with thick sheets of iron would improve their chances of rupturing the thick chains; those plates of iron had been mounted and the operation was ready to commence. To succeed, they needed a maximum flow tide and the blessings of a good wind. In five days, on the third of May, the conditions promised to be ideal. If they missed that date, it would be a while again before the offensive could be attempted with such favourable certainty. He was pressing for agreement as he needed all the time over the next five days to prepare the men and ships.

'Five days is not much time,' Ahmar mooted, 'and I have no idea what is in our overlord's mind about this. We spoke of attempting fire ships, using pitch as the Greeks did, but both the king and his admiral said it was too perilous, there were too few ships to risk it. If it failed, then our enemies would easily wrest naval superiority from us. And that would set us back a good deal, young — I am sorry, but I have forgotten your name.'

'I am David ben Immanuel, sire, the grandson of Solomon ha-Levi, newly arrived from Egypt.'

'Ah yes,' the sultan patted the shoulder affectionately at the mention of the chancellor's name. 'Your worthy grandfather is working very hard for our cause, risking much. Would you tell the admiral that I will arrange this with his monarch as soon as I can find him.'

'Sire . . . may I have a brief word with you first?' Ahmar nodded agreeably, having always benefitted from any parlay with the Levi family. She turned to the admiral and asked if he would indulge them for a few minutes while they discussed his proposal. Again, he swept the air before him and bowed deeply.

'My lord,' she whispered, not wanting to be overheard, 'it is almost certain that the iron-clad ships will be able to break the chain. However, my grandfather feels strongly that to destroy all the boats as well as sever the chain . . .'

'I couldn't agree more,' the sultan beamed, 'and that would be the opinion of Don Fernando, I have no doubt, but if this operation is to be successful, it needs to be executed at night. How can one destroy every ship under such conditions?'

Excusing herself, Dinah questioned the admiral. He agreed totally, that if there were some way to fire those boats without endangering his own ships, there was no question of the strategic advantage. The city must be cut off permanently from the rich farmlands which provisioned it. But the sultan was right, the peak of the flood tide would be near midnight, shortly after the crescent moon had set.

'You see,' the sultan said when she returned with this

information, 'it would be virtually impossible to coordinate such a plan in the dark.'

'Please, my lord, allow me to present our plan. My grandfather has discovered a secret and revolutionary powder, derived through exhaustive alchemical procedures. When this powder is confined in a tight place and ignited, it actually explodes violently before it burns. First the boats will be shattered and blown skyward and then what is left will burn fiercely.'

Ahmar was fascinated but Dinah pleaded with him not to ask her further questions. She was merely the messenger. If he would trust her and her companions, they would plan and execute everything. Surely, the King of Castile would agree?

Ahmar took it upon himself to approve the plan and the admiral went off the most pleased of men. He was absolutely certain that his fleet would succeed.

'If Don Fernando does not arrive soon, we shall have to send out a strong force to find him,' Ahmar rumbled after the happy admiral departed.

'Will your majesty hold those troops back until I have a chance to investigate?' Dinah asked. 'I am to meet my grandfather's assistant outside the Jerez gate in a short while. He will give me whatever news there is. If there is no sign of Don Fernando by then, I will ask this young physician to help me search inside the city. Surely, the picture he adores must be of the Virgin Mary and I suspect it is inside the great mosque somewhere. If you send in a large force, it is bound to create an alarm. If we find him, we will bring him out . . . but it would be nice if our soldiers could be near to hand . . . just in case.'

Dinah arranged, as soon as the sultan agreed, to meet the soldiers at the Guadaira bridge in less than an hour. Once she had bowed and taken her leave, she raced down one of the streets lined with stalls and tents until she found a large black one that was less conspicuous in the dark than its size would indicate. There was a large, well-armed eunuch standing guard before the closed tent flaps. The black tent was the banking headquarters for the family and their various associates in many merchanting activities. Yussel de Serota, a distant cousin of her dead mother, was here from León to take charge of the bank. When Dinah entered, she had not been warned yet that Yussel's wife had arrived from León with a large group of travellers earlier that day. Dinah's private quarters were in one wing of the tent. She had her own bath and two serving girls to take care of her needs. She had never seen Yussel's wife Sarah before. Sarah smiled as though she were on the verge of a swoon, tried to say something pleasant, then excused herself, making an excuse that the travel had exhausted her ... she became travel sick so easily ...

'I am sorry, dear cousin,' Yussel apologised, holding his hands palms up and shrugging with a conspiratorial wink, 'but Sarah is not capable of coping with a woman who looks like a man. She has not only taken to her bed, I'm sure she will stay there until this "insane war" as she calls it comes to a close.'

'Please do not worry, cousin.' Dinah returned the shrug of submission to the vagaries of fate. 'I will try to befriend her, the Lord grant that her humours improve and that I am allowed the time. Even now, I have hardly time to eat. If you can find Montse and Carmen, will you send them to me?'

While waiting for the girls, Dinah summoned Bubbi; she sat on the bed and jumped slightly when he cleaved through the earthen floor to create a great hump under the Persian carpet.

'Would it be too much to ask you to choose a spot where there are no obstructions?' he asked, somewhat testily for such an ordinarily good-natured creature.

'Sorry, I'm just terribly upset, little friend ... I wasn't thinking.' Dinah arranged the carpet neatly and invited the gnome to sit up on the bed with her. 'I guess I owe you another apology ... you look so annoyed I must have disturbed you once again in the middle of ... what did you call it?'

'"Blissies"?' he cocked his head enquiringly. She smiled and nodded. 'Certainly not,' he denied, still peevishly, 'I was just having an argument with Momo ... she's still at me about helping you with that eunuch ... she thinks we lost him his job.'

'If it's any comfort to her, you can assure her he has a new one ... much better, I think.' She paused and winked solemnly, then pointed northwards, toward the city. 'He's working for the captain of the Almohade forces.'

'Oooooo-hooo-hooo, does he know you and Joseph are here? With a war going on, it's bad enough ... but with Abu looking for you two ...'

'Why would he look for us, Bubbi? He doesn't know we were the ones, he was unconscious when it happened ...' She paused and looked down toward the rump poised on the edge of the bed next to her. 'You did that with your special gas, remember?'

'With or without those donkey's things, that Abu is a bad number, Dinah, I don't trust him. You just be careful.'

'I will. Now listen, the girls will be here to give me a bath and help me change any moment now. Do you remember that large bag of black powder Hutti tried to steal from Daddy's caravan and Aysha brought back to Granada for us?' The gnome thought for a moment, removed his pointed hat, scratched furiously in his thatch of pine-needle hair and suddenly beamed, bobbing his head up and down. 'Can you bring that bag here?' Bubbi looked shocked. 'Please, Bubbi? It's very important.'

'Have you any idea how heavy that bag is?' he cried. 'Momo and I and the two kids couldn't lift it ...'

'Stop that, Bubbi, you're just being contrary because you're annoyed with me. I'm not asking this as a personal favour, now. I gave my word to the sultan. We have to blow up those boats and we have only five days. Please, it may be the most important single thing needed to bring this siege to an end ...'

'... so we can all go home and enjoy life and live happily ever after,' he finished for her. 'At least I'll be pleased to get a little uninterrupted time for my family and my garden,' he added with a slight touch of sarcasm.

'Does that mean yes?' she bent forward and stared into his eyes.

Two short, pretty girls with black hair and brown eyes, struggling mightily with a huge cauldron of hot water, pushed through the curtains and laughed at their own awkward efforts. As they passed, each attempted a bow and murmured something which sounded like, 'Good evening, my lord.' To them, Bubbi was simply not there. He did hop down to the floor when a cloud of steam came his way, however, just in case one of them should turn and look back. Had she seen the gnome outlined by the steam, she might have dropped her burden.

'I'll need help,' he whispered, still being stubborn and uncooperative.

'You didn't need help when you made those two fabulous swords appear,' she reminded him with a triumphant grin, shaking an accusing finger under his nose.

'Oh, all right,' he relented, 'but I don't like to use up that talent . . . it doesn't replenish itself. I'll have to think about it very carefully while . . .' the girls appeared from behind the curtains which screened off Dinah's small bathing cubicle. She asked them to come back in a quarter of an hour with some cucumber, tomato, radish, any other fresh vegetables they could find . . . yes, if there was some rice cooked, a small bowl of that and fruit . . . oh, and a pot of soured milk. When the doorway curtain fell back in place, Dinah turned on the gnome.

'You'll have to think very carefully about what . . . while just what is happening?' she demanded, imitating Solomon's stern voice perfectly. In fact, it was only by keeping the image of him and his voice ever in her mind that she succeeded in passing herself off as a man. Bubbi turned away, blushed, did two or three rapid turns on the tips of his toes as though he weighed no more than a feather; but he studiously avoided her glance, to say nothing of the question very pointedly hanging in the air.

She stood, removed the belt, sword and scabbard, slipped a long, curved dagger from a belt under her robe and began undressing.

'You want to watch me in the bath, don't you? You're a secret dirty old gnome, aren't you? Happily married to a caring wife who gives you "Blissies" . . .'

'Stop! Why are you making me feel so guilty? I never eat anything that is not ritually clean, I always say my prayers and study religiously, everything, even the most obscure traditions . . . the Halakha, the Haggada, the Midrash. We always celebrate the sabbath properly . . .' He stopped and wiped a tear from the corner of his eye. 'I can't help it if I love you,' he wailed.

'I'm sorry.' She bent at the waist and kissed his cheek. 'Be a good friend and make the bag of powder appear. Then come in and watch me, if that makes you happy. I know it would make Joseph happy and I don't allow him . . . so consider yourself lucky . . . in fact, unique.'

She pulled the light tunic-blouse over her head and unfastened the loincloth, throwing that on the bed with the top. Bubbi gazed up at her cleanly-shaven mons veneris and giggled, his eyes darting up to the beard, down to the pelvis and back again.

'Just what is so funny?' she hissed, her fists digging angrily into her narrow, neat hips.

'I was just thinking,' he called back, skipping and leaping joyfully ahead of her toward the cubicle, 'while you get away with passing yourself off as a man in a Muslim army, you'd never pass yourself off as a Jew in the ladies' ritual bath . . . even without the beard.' His laughter goaded her but the well aimed kick at his rump missed by a long way. She swore he had eyes in the back of his head.

When she was dry and had a dressing robe wrapped about her in case the two girls returned with the food before she could get into her fresh clothes, Bubbi headed toward the outer curtain. As he passed the bed, he pointed underneath. Dinah bent over and, to be sure, the bag of powder was there. It was bigger than she had remembered it.

'Where are you going?' she asked, arranging a fresh loin-cloth.

'Home ... where do you think?' he laughed. 'There's your bag of powder.'

'Bubbi, please,' she ran to him and squatted on her heels, 'I'd like you to come with me to meet Joseph. I'm worried about the Christian king, I think he's on some mad religious lark inside the city. If Sakkaf and his men find him, every kingdom from Valencia to Paris will be held to ransom. I'd feel so much safer with you helping us find him,' she added, letting the robe slip down her shoulder a few inches.

'Dinah, Momo's going to cook *me* for supper one of these days ... oh, all right. Hurry up, I'll wait outside. I hate to watch you chew those vegetables.'

CHAPTER 4

Bubbi scampered through the gate, kicking at the earth and rattling some stray small stones. The duty guard's head came up and he ran out the gate, his lance drawn back; he looked in all directions but could see no movement at all. Stealthily, Dinah and Joseph slipped from the shadows and were immediately swallowed up in darkness inside the walls. When they rounded the next corner, Bubbi was skipping along ahead of them. The lane was narrow, the balconies of houses on either side almost blocking the sky overhead. The scent of flowers from those balconies as well as from the interior courts made the journey seem one through a perfumerie. As they passed the next crossing, Joseph pointed to the right, indicating the palace buildings; Bubbi was pointing straight ahead and she saw the Giralda Tower which was adjacent to the Great Mosque.

With the skill of an owl Bubbi guided them through the darkened mosque, around corners and eventually to a chapel wherein one lone figure kneeled, totally entranced. Even in the dark, Dinah recognised a state of religious ecstasy, reminiscent of the ecstasies described by dervishes. At that moment, the three newcomers saw a mysterious light shining through the wall before the kneeling king. It radiated outward from the centre of the wall in all directions; as they watched, this ineffable illumination moved across the floor and bathed the king's motionless figure.

Dinah felt more than saw a movement near her. She turned to see Joseph kneeling with his head bowed, no more able to look at the heavenly light. On impulse, though seriously questioning just what they were all doing when they should be spiriting this monarch back to his headquarters where he might hopefully recover his sense, she kneeled next to the silent Nubian.

'What is it you see and I don't?' she whispered.

'An unearthly effigy, a woman's face and form. I cannot prove it, but I am convinced she is blessing this extraordinary king.' He paused, shaking his head.

'You are terribly disturbed, my dear ... why?' she pleaded.

'You and I believe in God, in our religion. This man lives his totally. He is like a living miracle. He could easily make any religion miraculously manifest. I feel it is coming from him ... the power which makes the image glow and shed grace on him in return.'

The light began to dim and Joseph rose, moved forward and placed his hands under the king's arms, raising him gently. Between them, he and Dinah guided the somnambulistic prince out of the building and down the street they had taken on their way to the mosque. No one passed, they saw naught but an empty city; at the gate, they drew Fernando into the deep shadows while Bubbi again distracted the guard. Only then did they discover three more guards standing nearby. Bubbi created even more racket that seemed to issue from many places at once. In the ensuing turmoil, the three fugitives edged their way along the wall and made the outer walk, turning the corner when Fernando's sword became entangled between his legs; he stumbled, calling out as he regained full consciousness. The sword detached itself and came clanging to the stone roadway with the peal of a churchbell. Before they had gone another twenty paces, guards came racing out, followed by a number of knights and regular soldiers. Bubbi scampered invisibly ahead of the charging Moors with the sword the king had dropped. The guards nearly stopped in their tracks as they saw the sword apparently flying along ahead of them. In his panic, Bubbi made a slight error: he handed the sword to the king. The roar from the pursuers indicated they recognised their quarry and the physician's assistant accompanying the king.

'Get him out of here,' Joseph hissed, unsheathing his own sword. 'If you see any of our own men, send them quickly, but first get the king safely away. Bubbi, stay with me, you may be able to trip a few of them.'

Man and gnome ran speedily after Dinah and the king until the road was narrowed by a storehouse on the other side of them. Joseph turned, feeling sure he could prevent any of the pursuers getting by, at least until Dinah and the king were safe. Once sure of that, if the odds appeared impossible, he knew a path behind the storehouse that led straight to the river. Diving under and between the boats in the bridge, his pursuers would have a hard time finding him there.

Bubbi tripped the first guard and Joseph crowned him with the back of his blade, knocking him unconscious; even before that soldier hit the ground, the sword found its mark in another. The clashing was terrible, attracting attention from both the city and the camp of the besiegers; Joseph's sword was creating havoc and, with his eyesight, which was hardly affected by the dark, his opponents could do no more than thrash at a target which was never where they saw it a second earlier. From far away he heard Dinah scream, but it was too late. From behind him a mace came crashing down, aimed deliberately at that sword arm. Unnoticed, Abu had slipped around the storehouse to attack the rear. Bubbi pushed Joseph, but not quite hard enough. The glancing blow numbed the arm so the sword fell from the lifeless fingers.

Abu shifted the mace to his right hand and recovered the sword before Joseph could recover from the shock. The evil eunuch would have skewered the lad save for one small oversight on Abu's part. He never looked down. Bubbi shot straight up from between his legs, which were braced apart, and butted the donkey's gifts as hard as he could with his head. Abu shrieked, then groaned, sinking to his knees; but he never closed his eyes or loosed his grip on the precious sword. Joseph turned and the sword lashed out. It missed the neck it was aimed at, but caught the headcloth, tearing it loose.

'See,' he gasped, trying to control the pained voice, 'he is no Moor, he is a Nubian, a servant of the Sultan's Jew.' Abu regained his feet, forcing himself erect. 'I'll follow him, I have a blood score to settle ... get the Jew who poses as a Berber physician. Yusuf ibn Yakub of Murcia will pay his captor a handsome reward.'

In a near panic, Dinah popped her hexagram box in her mouth and sounded a note above the human hearing level. Bubbi was lifted off the ground and propelled towards her like a bolt leaving a crossbow.

'Thanks to the virgin in the chapel, we are saved,' the king announced to the knights now surrounding him.

'You should thank Joseph too,' Bubbi called out. The king blinked, staring uncertainly in what he thought was the direction from whence the voice came. In a swirl of cloaks and a clatter of armour, the knights sped toward the bridge with their monarch.

'You should never confuse a king,' Dinah admonished, unsheathing her sword and handing it to the gnome, 'it's considered very bad form ... here, bring this to Joseph, help him, Bubbi. I'll look for you both downstream.'

The gnome whirled and began running; Dinah sounded another, slightly different note through the box and Bubbi rose again to hurtle through the air, landing in the large river just ahead of Joseph, who was only a very short distance ahead of the pursuing eunuch.

'Let me catch my breath first,' Bubbi begged. Man and gnome were being propelled upstream by the strong tide, nearing the bridge of boats.

'Abu is going to give us no time to catch anything but him . . . here, hold on to me and breathe as much as you can,' Joseph advised.

'I'm sticking up too far, he'll be sure to see us,' Bubbi protested.

'Exactly. If he runs for the bridge as I think he will, here is what we shall do.' Even as he spoke and flung a quick look over his shoulder, Abu waded out of the stream and began running toward the bridge, Joseph's sword held high above his head, as though to paralyse his victim with fear.

Bubbi crouched down in the stagnant, unpleasant bilge after he and Joseph had wedged the wooden slat between his and the next boat. The loud slap of running feet on the boardwalk extending from boat to boat reached them. Joseph lowered himself between the two prows, which faced upstream, a slimy rope from Bubbi's boat caught in his left hand, Dinah's sword out of sight underwater in his right. He groaned loudly, then, in a plaintive, strangled voice, called for help in Arabic, interspersing the calls with terrified pleas to Yahweh in Hebrew.

'There he is!' Abu shouted with manic glee, waving the sword.

'Help me,' Joseph croaked, his nose hardly above water.

'Help you? O, in the name of the Prophet, will I help you.' Abu laughed like a demented hyena and raised the sword as high as he could, his face contorted, head bent forward to insure his aim.

Joseph rose high and clear of the water just before the blade reached the apex of its upward flight. A huge mouthful of water struck the eunuch in the eyes, momentarily blinding him and throwing him off balance. Before he could recover, the short oar in Bubbi's hands cracked against the tendons behind his heels, shooting his feet forward on the slippery boards. The sword flew to the side, clattering against the gunwhale of the next boat as his bottom dropped, dislodging the wooden slat holding the two gunwhales apart. Just as his shoulders passed the closing gunwhales, more than mere impact with the water arrested his plunge: the razor-sharp blade of Dinah's sword struck his crotch, neatly severing the donkey's transplant.

The scream of rage and terror was strangled as the heavy wooden boats clamped his neck between their gunwhales.

'You have nothing more to complain about, you rogue ... there you are, just as we found you.' Joseph gritted, levering himself up so his head was level with one of the prows.

'Yes,' Bubbi piped up, 'now you can get your job back and my wife can stop nagging ...'

'Bubbi, quick, hand me the other sword. His friends will be here any moment.' He slipped Dinah's sword in his belt and gripped his own firmly.

'What are you going to do?' Bubbi asked tremulously, watching Joseph measure the distance to Abu's head.

'What do you think? Gelded or not, as long as he lives we're all in terrible jeopardy, including our two kings.'

The moan was aborted in the gnome's throat. The thunder of the rest of the enemy soldiers echoed loudly across the boats as they came racing toward their quarry. Joseph quickly sheathed his sword and pulled Bubbi overboard.

'Wrap your legs about my waist, your arms about my neck ... leave my arms free, even if we plunge underwater ... shhh, here they come.' Holding a slimy line in one hand, Joseph eased the sword out of its sheath again and lowered himself in the water to just above eye level, steadying himself to plunge the blade into Abu's heart.

'There's the filthy spy,' an Almohade soldier roared, 'just about to lose his head!'

They saw the long robe swirl overhead, the right arm raised high in the approaching torchlight. The sword whistled as it came sweeping down. Abu's head flew up, flipped over twice, making a lazy arc before dropping into the stream below.

Once more Joseph sheathed his sword, thankful he was not forced to be the executioner, but shaken deeply by the strange turn of fate. Swimming underwater, he fought against the tide, finally reaching the shallows beneath a grassy overhanging bank which created a perfect shelter over the wet sand.

Just in time, Joseph clamped a hand over Bubbi's exuberant mouth. Holding the wriggling, protesting head between his strong hands, the youth eased himself up to chance a cautious look over the top of the bank. Not a sound, not a person in sight. Behind them, there was a great deal of commotion on the bridge, men running and shouting, torches bouncing and flaring.

'Whew!' Joseph dropped down, releasing Bubbi at the same time. 'That was some quiet, peaceful, lovers' tryst with Dinah, I must say.'

Bubbi huddled up to Joseph, feeling a bit chilled with his wet clothing and body. As an earth spirit, he was not too pleased with water.

'Was that his head? Did I hear his head hit the water?' Bubbi whispered, his skin feeling even more creepy. Joseph nodded. 'No longer attached to his body?' Smiling, but not happy, Joseph shook his head. 'Oooooo-hoo-hoo.'

'He was just about to cleave my head in half, Bubbi, why are you so upset . . . he'd have done the same to you if he had been able to see you.'

Bubbi shrugged, but he couldn't get rid of the uncomfortable feeling; he hated violence, particularly horrendous and visually shocking violence. To take his mind off it while they rested, he told Joseph about the king and his compliment . . . how grateful he was to Dinah. He added his own last remark about owing thanks to Joseph too.

The naive anecdote was just what Joseph needed to release the nerve-shattering tension. He rolled on the ground, gripping the heel of his hand with his teeth to keep from laughing aloud.

'And would Don Court Jester like to share the joke?' Bubbi minced the words, cutting each one off very clipped as Momo did when she was annoyed and calling him 'Don' something.

'You didn't understand, Bubbi, the king was not referring

to Dinah, he was referring to the mother of their prophet, the one who is called the Son of God.'

'Who?' Bubbi's chin dropped, his mouth hanging open.

'Isa ben Maryam, as he is called in Arabic . . . Yehoshua in Hebrew.'

'His father was God and his mother . . . was a virgin?' Bubbi's mouth still could not close. Joseph nodded seriously. The gnome thought about it for a few seconds. 'Does Dinah have any children?'

'Bubbi, don't be silly, Dinah is a virgin . . . oh, I forgot to mention, King Ferdinand probably thought you were referring to Jesus's father . . . his name was Joseph too.'

'You just told me . . .'

'I'm sorry, Bubbi, I've told you pretty much all I know. This is neither the time nor the place to pursue it further . . .'

'You can't do this . . . you can't do this to meffrrrmm . . .'

Joseph had his hand clamped over the gnome's mouth, worried that his crazed hectoring would be heard by sentries a long way off.

'One of these days, we'll engage Master Solomon in a discussion on comparative religions, he knows so much more. . .'

'What?' The gnome broke free, but kept his voice down to an hysterical whisper. 'In Torah, there *are* no comparisons . . . nobody compares, there is only Torah . . .'

'Peace, Bubbi, calm down.' Joseph hugged him, shaking him from side to side to distract his anger. 'We'll just talk about other people's religions, is that all right?'

'All right? Are you serious? You want me to take part in a discussion about heretics?'

'Oh, Bubbi, I am glad I don't run into fanatics like you in our world . . . I couldn't stand it.'

'You think *I'm* fanatical? You should listen to Momo . . . she thinks I'm in league with the . . .' The gnome shot straight up, shifted to one side in mid-air and came down on the opposite side of the Nubian, a finger pressed to his lips. '*Some* names you mention, guess who appears?'

Joseph shook his head and laughed softly. 'Come on,

Bubbi, things seem quiet now. Hold on as you did before. From the look of the water, the tide is turning. It won't take us long to reach the point below the Guadaira. Let's hope Dinah is waiting there. We've got to create a plan to get her grandfather free. You heard Abu, he told those cut-throats that ibn Yakub would pay dearly to get his hands on Master Solomon.'

'When we get in the water, I'll sit on your back as one sits on a horse . . . hooo-hooo, you're going to see something very fancy.'

True to his word, Bubbi managed to reduce Joseph's weight as well as his own to the point that Joseph rode on the surface like an inflated bladder. Using his hands as paddles, he skimmed across the river and down to Tablada, Fernando's headquarters, faster than a trim ship with a fresh wind.

When they were still one hundred or more yards away, they saw Dinah waving to them from the shore. Man and gnome sensed immediately that she was crying and miserable.

Ignoring the wet and slimy clothes, she threw her arms about Joseph and hugged him, sobbing as though her heart would break.

'Control yourself, dear princess, and tell us what is wrong,' Joseph pleaded, taking her shoulders and making her look up.

'That brute Abu told them all about Grandfather, I heard him shouting as he took off after you. The sultan is planning a rescue, he has already sent squadrons of cavalry to block every road, but . . . but . . .'

'Well, then, that will give us time to plan for his rescue,' Joseph interrupted.

'No it won't.' She sobbed again for a short while; when she'd calmed down a little, she described the scene she'd witnessed. Only by accident, she thought, had she looked up when Ahmar had spoken. For the briefest part of an instant, she saw her grandfather on the easternmost parapet of the palace. He shot up and, just as she had witnessed those times on the astral plane, his body seemed to cut its way through an invisible black curtain. Even as brief as the flicker of vision was, she saw the head, followed by the body, then by the feet and there was nothing!

'A Djinn!' Bubbi rumbled, his stomach making incredible sounds as it always did when he was upset. 'Would Hutti do that? Why?' He tugged at Dinah's robe. 'This Yakub ... is he a magician, by any chance?'

'I don't know ... why?' She looked at Joseph; he shook his head.

'Don't you see? Who wants your grandfather? Yakub! Who told them all exactly who was hiding behind the black beard, the Berber braids and clothing? Yakub's spy! In less time than it takes to tell, Yakub has the information, he commands a Djinn, your grandfather disappears. To where? To just where Yakub wants him, that's where.'

'What will we do?' Joseph asked. 'Have you any ideas, Dinah?'

'Yes, the first one is to get away from here as quickly as possible. For all we know, Yakub might want us for good measure. He must know we would try to rescue Grandfather ...'

'Right!' Bubbi agreed, so excited he broke into her explanation. 'Get to Alcalá as fast as you can ...'

'That's what I decided too,' Dinah interrupted him. 'There is a tremendous power source there, the springs underground, the magnetic forces ...'

'Exactly ... get going,' Bubbi urged. 'I'll be there long before you, plotting things. First, I have to go home and calm Momo down ... and have something to eat, I'm starving.'

CHAPTER 5

'I don't like it, Dinah, I simply do-not-like-it!' Sitting cross-legged in the centre of the twin circles, Joseph balanced his sheathed sword on his knees. He was dressed in slightly tattered, and very unclean-looking clothes that only a lowly slave girl in a poor kitchen would wear. The cowl covering his head, the veil across the bridge of his nose, left nothing of Joseph recognisable. He was still the nutty brown colour; his large black eyes had been enhanced with kohl and other cosmetics to enlarge them while slanting them alluringly. Bubbi, pacing up and down the plain, large unfurnished room in a tower of Alcalá fortress, could not help admiring what an attractive woman Joseph made ... even if a startlingly tall and powerful-looking one. Dinah sat on a large table up against the wall under an archery slit of a window. Dressed like Joseph, her sword lying next to her on the oaken surface, she drew up her feet and wrapped her arms about her knees, her face turned down toward the floor as her mind worked furiously.

'Look, Joseph ... now, don't misunderstand me, I am not belittling your objection, but how many choices have we? If we try to summon Musa, then we will cross the astral plane, we will not be able to avoid Hutti ... he is a busy-body as you well know. And now, it seems, he's working for both sides, Merciful God in heaven alone knows why.'

'Dinah!' Bubbi jumped up and down like a weightless gourd, banging his pointed hat with both fists and gnashing his teeth. Startled, she looked up.

'Bubbi ... what is it? Are you ill?' She was half off the table when he landed on his feet and held up a hand.

'Dinah, I just wanted to get your attention. Listen. That world you call the astral plane is like a universe of its own. You couldn't count the Djinni there if you spent a thousand years at it. Hutti is not the only one ...'

'I know that, Bubbi, but he's the only one ...'

'No, he isn't the only one you know,' Bubbi contradicted her, 'or, I should say, not the only one who knows you. How about his young friend called Hawwaz? You'd be surprised how the news of what you did to Hutti and Musa got around. Hawwaz is so keen to insinuate himself, to see if he can accomplish what Hutti failed ...'

'Ah-ha!' Joseph ejaculated. 'One more rears its ugly head ...'

'Joseph, will you stop thinking like a typical possessive, jealous male? We're trying to rescue Grandfather, remember?' Joseph continued to smoulder. 'Why are you so against Bubbi trying to get me to Murcia with the underarm method?'

'You heard Bubbi ... he admitted it was the way he and his wife made the twins ...'

'How many times do I have to tell you,' Bubbi shouted, bouncing up and down again even more furiously, 'you can also use it to make instantaneous journeys between the two planes ... no Djinni, no demons ... no ...' he stopped speaking aloud, but with hideous gestures and facial expressions, he gave a very clear impression of Azazel, the Archduke of Hell. Calming himself, he sat in the triangle Joseph had drawn and faced the youth. 'Joseph, only two gnomes, one male, one female, are properly constructed to create what you're so worried about. Look, you ca right next to the table and watch. If I look the least bit happy, shout and we'll stop right then and there . . . but my friend, you and your stubborn fixity are costing us precious time . . .'

'Exactly!' Dinah jumped to her feet, smoothed her tatty raiment, and faced Joseph. 'Will you stop being such a simple child?' She drew her magic box from inside the robe and held it up. 'I'll leave here a virgin and return in precisely the same condition. Well?'

Joseph shrugged his defeat and lowered his head. In the final part of any argument with Dinah, he felt he would always give her her way.

'Come on, Bubbi, let's get going. Remember, this is only an exploratory trip. All we want to do is discover exactly where my grandfather is being held . . . we assume he was spirited off to Yakub in Murcia. We get the information and come straight back. Then, if we have to call upon Musa, then Musa it is. Can you imagine what I'm going to have to put up with from *that* one if I have to give a couple more treatments of The Ultimate?'

'Dinah!' Joseph warned loudly.

'Yes, dear,' she answered meekly. She stretched out on the table, slipped the sword and scabbard up under the tatty garment and under a heavy leather belt fastened about her waist underneath. Bubbi slid across the table on his rump, stretched out in the opposite direction and presented his bared underarm. With a fastidious sniffle under the veil, she raised her arm and closed her eyes.

To Joseph, watching intently, the two bodies rose as one, hesitated in seemingly weightless levitation, then shot sideways. Not through the thick wall, of that he was sure. They slipped between two 'somethings' — perhaps two 'nothings' — and were gone before they reached the wall.

For Dinah, the first and only reality was standing on the uppermost rampart of a huge fortress. She assumed it was the outer castle wall of ibn Hud's Murcian stronghold. When she turned to look out over the landscape, she gasped. The fortress was high above a ridge in mountainous country, barren and harsh, sand blowing. It certainly was not Murcia. She doubted it was Spain. Looking down, she found Bubbi lying on his back, twitching, the silliest grin on his face. She also heard shouts from below, then the pounding of feet on stone stairs.

She bent over and began slapping his face, increasing the force of the blows until his eyes opened, he shook his head and leaped to his feet. When he looked down, he squeaked, appalled by the terrain.

'Hurry,' he pulled her down on the roof, arranging himself at her side. 'We have to get out of here . . . fast.'

'Where are we . . . do you know?'

'Hadjar an-Nasr,' he whispered, raising his arm. His tone indicated something fearful.

'The Eagle's Rock? Where is that?'

'Near Ceuta . . . North Africa . . . where all the Moors are. Belongs to the Edrisi princes . . . one of them used to bring anyone he didn't like up here and throw him off . . . oooooo-hooo-hooo . . . down there. Quick!'

'How did we get here, Bubbi, what went wrong? Tell me!'

'A little mistake, Dinah, I couldn't help it . . . it's just that I love you so and lost my head. Somehow, I lost control and went straight to the Golden Caverns . . . please don't tell Joseph . . . please?'

'All right, but get us out of here before those savages find us. I'm not trying this crazy method again, I'd rather deal with Musa and his impossible father, Hutti.'

'Well, what did you find out?' Joseph asked. He was on his feet, standing next to the table. 'You weren't gone very long. Say something!' He stared at Dinah's blinking eyes.

'Well, did you know there was a fortress named the Eagle's Rock . . . near Ceuta? Well, there is.' Joseph glowered at Bubbi suspiciously; the gnome simpered.

Dinah levered herself erect and dropped to the floor. 'Come on everyone . . . we have to summon Musa.'

An hour later, Dinah looked at Joseph and they both looked at Bubbi sitting opposite in the triangle. Dinah had worked the ceremony three times; each time she added more incense to the charcoal brazier.

'I *know* it's right,' Bubbi piped up before either of them could ask a question. 'I just don't understand . . . Ooooooo-hooo-hooo!' Musa was standing over him, having materialised from apparently nowhere, with one muscular leg on either side of the gnome.

'Where were . . .' That was all Dinah got a chance to say. The room shook violently and the walls appeared to press in so forcibly their ears felt ready to implode. Even as all three pairs of hands flew up to protect their ears, the effect ceased abruptly.

'Don't you become insufferably bold with me, young woman,' the demon warned fiercely. 'I've been having enough trouble on your behalf without inconvenient summonses . . . and then that face and imperious manner on you when I don't arrive at the snap of your fingers.' He snapped his fingers. The sound was like a thunderclap . . . but confined inside the room. Dinah screamed and held her ears again.

'I'm sorry,' she whispered, unable to retrieve her voice easily.

'Trouble?' Joseph asked, scratching his rather painful ear. 'What sort of trouble?'

'Hutti and Hawwaz were having a terrible fight . . . over you,' Musa inclined his head toward Dinah. 'My father Hutti is your champion, of course, your ardent admirer, he never stops talking about you and — what was it — oh yes — The Ultimate. Hawwaz, on the other hand, is insanely envious. I know what you are going to say: it is absolutely childish. I know. In that mood, Hawwaz was easily swayed to do something . . .'

'It was he who spirited my grandfather away, wasn't it? He did it at the bidding of that horribly evil man, ibn Yakub.'

'Absolutely right, my dear,' Musa agreed affably. 'You must be doing your esoteric studies quite religiously . . . very good. Now, I suppose, your little friend here is going to enlist my aid to get the old fellow back, is that it?' He caught Bubbi's head between his flexed knees playfully; but the pressure was enough to make the gnome's bottom bounce up and down frantically.

'Stop that, you big bully, or I'll do something you won't like!' The minute Bubbi said this, the demon stood up straight, a worried look on his face giving the impression of chastised schoolboy.

Bubbi stood and glared up at Musa, totally fearless. 'How is it *you* were stopping a fight between Hutti and Hawwaz? You're allowed to use that dimension only to pass through ... not to do anything in ... just like the Djinni cannot visit your underground palace ... they'd never get out, they'd go straight down to ...' he left it unfinished, just pointing and grimacing.

'Bubbi, Bubbi, Bubbi,' the demon remonstrated good-naturedly, bending down to straighten the conical hat which had slipped askew, 'a lot of those rules have changed, don't you ever listen or keep up with things?' A slightly sad reflection passed over the green face. 'My father can visit me any time he wants. He just doesn't.'

'Do you have any suggestions?' Joseph asked, worried about the time they were losing. 'I mean, about rescuing Dinah's grandfather.'

'I suppose you know you're up against a rather potent magician in Yusuf ibn Yakub. Potent and very nasty. He'll stop at nothing. He's the kind who'd sell his soul if he wanted something badly enough. If we get Solomon free, he'll *want* something badly enough. To some extent ... because of you, young woman, and don't take offence ... that will fit in perfectly with one unholy entity who wants all his powers back. You let his foot in ... Yakub has it in his power to free the rest ... to loose that horror on your world.'

'What can we do?' Bubbi squeaked with pent-up frustration. 'We have to do something, we can't just stand here borrowing trouble.'

'Right!' Musa agreed. 'Let's go rescue the old fellow.

Dinah, in your reading, did you come across the making of a clay effigy, then animating it to do some task? Sort of a powerful animated statue which can't be stopped?'

'Yes . . . yes, I have,' she answered, animated herself now. 'You create the ritual and then put the instructions on a piece of paper and pop the paper in the statue's mouth.'

'Exactly. That may be the one thing Yakub will not be able to deal with. A perfect guard for a perfect prison. One who never sleeps, one all weapons are useless against . . . yes, I think we'll try that one.'

'You will imprison Yakub?' Joseph asked, his hand playing restlessly with the hilt of his sword.

Musa shook his head disapprovingly. 'I see you'd like to make it easy by simply removing his head . . . hmmmn? So far, you have been blameless, let's keep it that way.'

'But, think,' Joseph protested, 'if you leave him powerless, it is sure to force him into the bargain you mentioned but moments ago.'

'Precisely,' Musa agreed with an infuriating smile. 'It would happen sooner or later. Isn't it better to precipitate it? Have it happen with haste, being forced so that we may be ready . . . knowing the direction and having a fair idea of timing?'

'He's right, Joseph. The sooner the better,' Dinah affirmed.

'Do I have permission?' Musa pointed to the protective circle. 'Very clever, you two,' he added, 'going as a pair of scullery slaves.' He was laughing when Dinah intoned the permission for him to cross the chalk circles. The smile seemed to come at them with the speed of lightning. With Bubbi caught up between his ankles, Dinah under one arm, Joseph under the other, they tore through the fabric which separated the dimensions of the two different worlds.

This time, the girl had hardly any impression of the plane she was flashing through. It seemed she merely tried to catch her breath and she was standing at the end of a garden, facing the kitchens of a very large castle. Only a few fruit trees stood close to the out-buildings housing the kitchens, pantries and abattoir, along with enclosures for chickens, geese and more exotic game birds. Most of the garden was devoted to table vegetables.

Musa and Bubbi were seated on two weathered tree stumps which had never been dug out. An older woman wrapped in a shapeless black garment which reached the ground stepped out of the door and stared at the two 'scullery maids'. She shouted that they had better hurry if they wanted something to eat. Dinah caught the softer slurring of the Andalusian patois of Murcia and chanced just a yes and a thank you. The woman turned a bit ponderously and disappeared.

'There you are,' Musa smiled agreeably, 'accepted as a pair of the household's slavies . . . fortunate, you'll be able to move around everywhere without creating suspicion.' The demon cocked his head and scrutinised Joseph. 'One of you will,' he corrected himself.

'Don't we have to make an effigy?' Bubbi asked. Musa looked down at him and pursed his lips, as though he might pat the gnome on the head as a reward for showing such colossal intelligence. Then he pointed to a bare patch at the very end of the garden. Light was failing so fast, it was difficult to ascertain just why he was indicating the spot.

'Joseph, there is a well just over there, next to the large outer gate. Start bringing some pails of water, please.' Musa turned to Dinah and beckoned her with his finger. 'Shall we start digging up some of the earth over there? It has a very high clay content. If we get a move on now, it should be soft enough to fashion the effigy before the air gets too cool. Then, before the night is out, it should be firm enough to animate.'

* * *

'Well, what do you think?' Joseph sat back and looked at the weird conglomeration. Discomfitingly, the ridiculous, human-like mass of clay and stones looked back at him, no more impressed with Joseph than was Joseph with it . . . him, he corrected himself. Dinah had insisted on very life-like genitals; how was he to effect the sort of male courage necessary if he were not fully 'male', was her argument. Still, she didn't have to be all that precise, down to the heroic proportions and the circumcision.

'I can tell, just looking at you,' Dinah breathed hotly, 'you are still worked up about . . .' she stopped in mid-sentence. The large clay sculpture had folded his hands over his groin protectively before she finished. She and Joseph exchanged glances.

'Your agent serves no purpose just sitting there,' Musa reminded her. 'Get him moving about, give him some orders. He has to get used to moving, he looks all stiff still.'

'Creature,' she addressed him, 'go to the well and fetch me a dipper of water, please.'

The creature opened his mouth slowly, much like a rusty toy, raised his arm jerkily and poked one finger into his mouth.

'Very good,' she congratulated him. 'Yes, water to drink. A dipperful. From the well. Over there.' She pointed. 'See?' The thing's head turned slowly, pausing for a moment while his eyes, made of bright red pebbles, checked the alignment of her pointing finger. He nodded, turned back and pointed to the inside of his toothless mouth.

'Stop showing me what I intend doing with the water and go fetch . . .'

'That's not what he's doing, Dinah, he's letting you know you have to follow the arcane directions precisely. Write the instructions on a piece of paper and put the paper in his mouth.' Musa allowed himself an exasperated sigh.

When he did bring the water back, the dipper was almost in Dinah's hand when the creature noticed some water still left in a pale puddle on the ground. With a delighted, toothless grin, he poured the dipper on the spot, then splashed his heavy, stony foot in it. In the deepening gloom, she tried a few more exercises and, with each one, the foolish character devised an unexpected twist at the end.

'This isn't going to work,' Joseph muttered. 'He'll capture the wily Yakub and turn him free at the door of the dungeon.'

'Seems that way,' Musa agreed. 'Dinah, what did your unimpeachable text tell you about these creatures?'

'That they are not very smart, I'm afraid.' They watched Bubbi climb up the large creature and sit on his shoulder. The gnome stuck his finger into the clay cheek and the mouth shot open. Bubbi took the piece of paper out and looked at it. It was the one about fetching water. Of course, Don Smart-boy had emptied the dipper over the puddle again. Bubbi shoved the paper back in and waited. A big foot started to slap the water on the ground happily.

'"Thing" is certainly not very smart,' he agreed, climbing down with great agility. 'If I could only climb inside and make him do things right . . .'

'He thought of the perfect solution,' Musa informed them.

'Can Bubbi actually do that?' Joseph wondered.

'No, but Hutti can. It would be more than wise to obtain his services, considering we have no way of stopping Hawwaz if Yakub should call on him.'

'And have Dinah do that . . . whatever it is that drives him sex-mad . . . is that what you're suggesting?'

'I'm suggesting, dear devoted Joseph, that we get Solomon out of here as fast and efficiently as we can. We can think of the price later!'

'He's right, Joseph,' Dinah added, 'please stop acting like I'm an unfaithful wife. I'm not a wife and I'm not unfaithful.'

'Can Hutti really get inside the "Thing",' Bubbi asked.

'Bubbi,' Dinah scolded, 'stop calling him "Thing", it's in very bad taste. You'll hurt his feelings.' To their amazement, the creature stamped heavily on the puddle, splashing them. His face wore the petulant look of a small boy.

'She's right,' Joseph said. 'Well, what *is* his name, then?'

Dinah closed one eye, pursed her lips and concentrated; the others watched her, waiting silently. Finally, the creature leaned forward as if to listen.

'Golem. Yes, that's a good name, it describes him rather well.' She smiled, pleased with herself. Facing the creature, she said the word slowly and clearly, four times. 'That's your name, understand?' She pointed to his mouth. 'Golem, you still have the pieces of paper about the water. Fetch some more, please. And this time hand the dipper to me. Do not spill it on the ground.'

Golem tilted his head, as though weighing the instructions, perhaps sifting them in search of some minor breach of form. At last, he turned slowly and, more slowly still, began his ponderous journey to the well.

'What does that word mean, Dinah?' Joseph asked. 'Most of the Hebrew I know is not much use outside the synagogue.'

'Oh . . . it has more than one meaning. Shapeless mass might be the most descriptive. But blockhead is pretty descriptive too . . . especially in this case.'

'Dinah, do you think I should summon my father now?' Musa donned his pained smile again. 'It would be nice to leave here before morning.'

'I'm sorry, yes, of course.'

The words were still in the air as Musa was no longer with them. Joseph had heard a very faint Pop! Whether the flash of blue light was real or imagined, he could not tell. To his surprise, the Golem was coming toward them at a fast and lively pace, the dipper waving about perilously, yet not a drop being spilled.

'That's better,' Musa muttered, back at Joseph's elbow. The Nubian jumped with surprise.

'Here, my dear, drink this and let's get going,' Golem stated blithely, thrusting the dipper at Dinah. 'Oh, are we going to make beautiful music together when this job is done . . . hmmmn?'

Dinah spilt half the contents on the ground and Joseph's mouth fell open. The only one beside Musa who showed no surprise was Bubbi.

'How is it in there, Hutti, can you breathe all right . . .

aren't you a bit cramped?' the gnome asked with a touch of mischievous glee.

A cloud of thick vapour was ejected from Golem's mouth; it instantly surrounded the small gnome. His screams were so muffled they hardly carried. And less than a second later, the cloud was reabsorbed and the muffled screams and shouts now came from inside the large clay creature. Just as Dinah was about to scream herself, the vapour shot forward once more, depositing the gnome on his bottom in the middle of the puddle.

'Does that little visit answer all your malicious questions, you miserable little mole?' a slightly stifled Hutti's voice enquired with feigned sweetness. Huffing, Bubbi jumped to his feet and started wiping his wet bottom with his hands.

Candles and lamps started moving about in the kitchen and pantry areas. Like a ghostly dance, the flickering lights moved away from the watchers, seeking passageways and stairwells in the interior; up since before dawn, the servants and slaves were retiring.

'Let's go,' Hutti ordered from inside his new and ponderous clay garment.

'Will you have to stay here all the time?' Bubbi asked, making an attempt at reconciliation with the Djinn.

'No . . . once I see to it that my Little Brother, as I call him, keeps out of the way, this invention of Dinah's will do what he is supposed. Perhaps with a good deal more cleverness, thanks to his association with a superior being.'

They drifted silently through the darkened hallways, surprising no one en route. Dinah thought about the fact that neither she nor Joseph had any notion of the palace's layout, yet there was no hesitation in the turnings they took. A clay hand, heavy and clammy, dropped on her shoulder; she could tell from the startled movement next to her that the same had befallen Joseph. They halted and Golem moved the few paces to the next corner. With a motion of his hand, he first indicated the troupe was to wait. Then, without looking back, he gestured to Joseph to join him.

Joseph peered around the corner. Four guards stood at

attention outside the heavy oaken doors to what he supposed to be the central audience chamber. Just then, one of the doors was pushed open and two gigantic eunuchs stepped out. One of them rounded another corner on the far side of the doors and returned a moment later leading a pure white ass. At the door, the two eunuchs grabbed the halter from either side to restrain the agitated beast. One whispered something to the nearest guard, the doors swung open and the strange entourage entered. In that brief instant, Joseph heard gasps and one stifled scream. He saw at least ten girls, some of them hardly advanced into puberty, all sprawled on lush carpets, all of them totally naked. As the doors slammed, he saw the flash of a whip. Had his hearing not been amplified by Hutti, he would not have heard the next scream through the solid wood.

'Is that the harem?' he whispered. 'I thought it to be the audience chamber.'

'You are right, it *is* the audience chamber. Yakub, that pleasant fellow, is giving a special audience to some very youthful inmates of the harem. If we move smartly now, we may be able to save some of them a rather painful, if not fatal, introduction to the pleasures of life.'

'You don't mean . . .'

'I most certainly do, Joseph. Did you bring your sword?'

The young man brandished the fabled blade even as Hutti's voice asked the question. Without another word, Hutti moved Golem forward, but so lightly the huge feet made no noise on the exquisite tiled floor. Two guards levelled spears and sprang forward, the other two drawing their swords. Golem ignored them, walking steadily towards the panelled doors. The shafts of the two spears snapped, the heads springing away from the impervious body to clatter harmlessly on the floor. Before the other two guards could raise their swords, Joseph disarmed them with his speedy, accurate blade. One collapsed on the floor, the other rushed the ridiculous apparition in a kitchen maid's attire. Joseph darted to one side, tripped him with his sword, cracking the back of the blade down on his head. The two lancers pressed their bodies into the wall. Joseph pointed to their swords. With frantic fingers, they undid the belts. Swords and belts struck the floor with a loud clatter. The Nubian kicked them all across the wide hallway, beyond the corner where his companions waited. From Golem's red pebble eyes, Hutti looked on with open admiration. Grunting, the clay hands grasped the door handles, there was a quick flex of the knees and a snap upward. The doors were torn loose from the hinges with a terrible squeal, falling inward and crashing to the floor. Girls screamed, sliding across the floor, scampering on their hands and knees as rapidly as they could. All of them had their ankles hobbled together by stout hempen rope.

A man, his face filled with inhuman hate, stood quaking with anger before a throne on an ample dais. Cushions and carpets were scattered about the throne, a table with many varieties of delicacies and a number of flagons of wine stood to one side. Before the dais, the donkey's hooves had been chained to rungs secured to the floor. As the doors had burst in, one of the eunuchs had been stroking the ass's member, the other sliding a low table on wheels between the beast's front legs. On the table, strapped down on her elbows and knees, her pitiful young bottom aimed at the donkey's enraged part, was a young girl hardly thirteen. It was her wailing which had brought the others running. Dinah's furious scream of anger joined the girl's as she drew her sword defiantly.

Golem moved forward with studied casualness, knowing the entire company was momentarily paralysed. He grabbed one eunuch's head in one hand, grabbed the other's and dragged him from the donkey. The sickening crunch of the two skulls smashed together made even Joseph swallow hard to contain the contents of his stomach. Lifting both dead bodies high, Golem flung them at the immobile picture of hate and evil on the dais.

Yakub crashed backward, striking his head on the gilded arm of the throne. Dinah mobilised herself, cutting the hapless young child free with her sword. Bubbi unfastened the chains and shooed the willing ass out the gaping doorway. Kneeling on the floor, Dinah gathered the hysterical girl to her breast and rocked her, cooing to her calmingly.

'Do you girls know where your clothes are?' Joseph asked. 'Go and find them, get dressed and run home as fast as you can.' They didn't need a second invitation; frantically they began unbinding their ankles. He then turned and signalled the guards. All four came forward, walking with an air of lassitude which belied their former ferocity. The eldest of them, a man with a beard liberally laced with silver and quite a bit taller than his companions, tried to speak. He seemed unable to.

'Where is the king?' Joseph asked. The soldier looked at him blankly. 'Ibn Hud . . . your liege lord . . . where is he? Answer me, man,' Joseph's voice hardened and the sword began to rise. The clammy clay hand arrested his arm.

Golem's hand slid under the immobile head, lifting the man up by his jaw. He raised him as high as he could, then began to shake him, the oscillations becoming faster and faster until the others could see nothing but a vague blur. Without warning, Golem brought the guard down on his heels with shocking force.

The guard grimaced with pain but did not cry out. He shook his head and looked about, as though seeing the room for the first time. He jumped back, reaching instinctively for his missing sword.

'Who are you?' he asked Joseph. His glance took in Golem and he blanched. 'And what . . . what is that?'

'If you'll look up on the dais, you will see what "that", as you so rudely refer to Sheikh Golem, can do with his bare hands.'

'But . . . but . . . he is made from earth . . . from clay,' the bewildered soldier cried.

'Look carefully in the Qur'an. Then you can check with Torah and the Christian scriptures . . . they all say the Lord created Adam out of clay. Why should we try to improve on Allah?' Joseph smiled the smile of sweet reason. 'Now, where is ibn Hud . . . you are wearing my patience thin.'

The man looked toward the throne, at the bloody eunuchs, at the unconscious vizier, Yakub. His face revealed the furious efforts of his mind. His lips opened, closed, then opened again.

'You were held under a spell by that evil magician,' Hutti's clay-encased voice told the guard. 'We have released you . . . think hard, where is your king?'

The man's face underwent another change mirroring whelming revelation.

'The king? The king? Did you not know? He is long dead . . . but I cannot tell you how long . . . I have just awakened from a nightmare. I once knew, I'm sure I once knew . . .' he licked his lips with uncertainty.

'Are you recovered enough to join your companions?' Dinah asked the young girl. 'They are finding their clothes and going home . . . you'll join them, yes?' The girl nodded, wiping her nose with the back of her hand like a child. Impulsively, she kissed Dinah and ran. Dinah took the guard by the hand and led him to the dais, easing him down.

'Sit and think for a few minutes. Will you promise to wait here for us? We will be back soon.' He displayed such gratitude in his expression, giving proof that her gentle concern had touched the right responses.

Golem threw the sacklike figure of Yakub up on his shoulder. The ornate turban fell to the floor as the head hung upside down. He had stringy, sparse bits of beard near his ears, the ears large and shaped like jug handles. The head was shaved and there was an ugly gash in the back of the scalp, crusts of dried blood adhering to the skin. The whole aspect of Yakub filled her with loathing, but she forced herself closer and bent forward to peer more carefully. What she read was frightening. Though certainly no older than fifty odd years, she instinctively sensed him to be completely impotent . . . not as eunuchs are, but through some mistake of nature — or, she thought, nature's vengeance. That is why he tortured the innocent with outrageous versions of what he was incapable of performing. Did he see himself as the rampant ass, huge, tearing young bodies apart? And his evil practice of magic . . . did that compensate for the prowess he was denied?

'Your thinking and insights are improving, young princess,' Hutti's voice informed her. 'Want to help us release the old fool in the dungeon?'

Her head shot up; suddenly, it seemed, she had come back to this room. Joseph was talking to the guard and pointing.

'Have them drag these two corpses out to the kitchen courtyard,' he told the man.

'You want them buried there?' the man asked with surprise.

'No,' Joseph answered amiably, 'just cut up for the stable dogs. People who would do such things deserve no better.'

Solomon blinked under the lights of the torches his rescuers had brought with them. Yusuf ibn Yakub, still unconscious, was chained to the wall where Solomon had been, the heavy iron collar about his neck, the feet and hands in irons, suspended from chains also secured to the thick stone wall. Sitting next to the Murcian who claimed descent from Tariq, the conqueror of Spain, was a huge, powerfully shaped man made of clay. As he watched, fascinated, a thick cloud of vapour stormed from the conglomeration's mouth and settled in a solid ball on the floor. At a speed defying any passage of time, a splendid, beautiful Djinn stood before him.

'Well, you old fool, it seems I must make a career of rescuing one after the other of your careless family, doesn't it?'

'It does indeed look that way, Hutti. I apologise for the inconveniences we have caused you.'

'From what I hear, he gets very nobly rewarded,' Joseph scowled. Hutti's burst of laughter shook the walls.

'Hutti, I'm dying to find out what happened to the king,' Bubbi shouted up at him, tapping his knee with his knuckles. 'Do you think he'll be able to find the memory.'

'Let's go find out, you little mudball,' the Djinn answered with another burst of laughter.

Bubbi looked down and a tear fell on his foot. Hutti saw it before the others, swooped down and threw the gnome up on his shoulder.

'I was just teasing you, we're friends again. I'll give you a ride back to the audience chambers . . . hmmmn, what price can I exact from you? You're certainly not edible . . .'

'Hutti!' Dinah stood in front of him, angry fists planted on her hips. 'If you make him cry . . .' Hutti was no longer there and the two young persons helped Solomon toward the door. Even his brief time in prison had damaged his health. With great will power and pride of spirit, he soon forced his legs to do their own work, making himself keep up with the young ones.

'. . . and that was it. All of it,' the guard assured his rapt and appalled audience. 'The king was here, he was arranging for the troops that he was obliged to send for service with the Christian king and then one night he was drinking with one of his oldest and dearest friends. He became terribly drunk and fell asleep. No one has ever been able to explain why this old friend drowned the noble king in a vat of water. Before anyone in the palace could say anything, the vizier told us the king had gone with the troops. Something happened. Everyone forgot the drowning . . . it was as though a day had been removed from history . . . oh, yes! That day all the blackened shields and banners fell from the walls of the mosque.'

'Blackened shields?' Joseph asked.

'When ibn Hud was a young man, he had the mosques cleansed when the Almohades were driven out of here. And all their ensigns blackened out. An old Almohade sorcerer had predicted an evil death for the king. When it happened, he predicted the shields would fall . . . and they did. That means, he had foretold, there would thence be no Islamic king on Seville's throne. Sakkaf, ibn Hud's Almohade captain there, was really put there by ibn Yakub. And Sakkaf is no king. It seems the dire prediction is coming true.'

'And all this time, Yakub gave you reports of the king's

successes far to the west, through to the western ocean?' Solomon asked. The man nodded.

'We have all been in some state of sleep, and we do not know when it started.' The guard shrugged his shoulders with great sadness.

'And it is true that you are the king's cousin and you were given such a lowly job by Yakub for that very reason?' Dinah asked.

'Ask the other guards when they return. Abdullah ibn Muhammad ibn Hud I was born and so I shall die.'

'Then the administration will be in your hands. No matter who tries to go near the prisoner, warn him that he will be destroyed. Sheikh Golem is not vulnerable to mortal man. You might take a lesson from your noble cousin, Abdullah. Cleanse this house and see that no evil practices are permitted again.'

Abdullah bowed, trembling, before the awesome appearance of the Djinn.

With sparks flying from her eyes, Dinah looked Hutti up and down, her eyes hesitating for a moment on the great ranji and its pearly sphere. Evil practices? Little girls of thirteen subjected to such horrendous appendages . . . why you pompous, hypocritical . . . But Solomon's warning glance and raised forefinger stopped the words before they could leap out.

CHAPTER 6

'Are you sure these are waterproof?' Joseph asked, running his hand gingerly over the hardened clay cases. He and Bubbi were practically buried in wet sand on the west bank of the Guadalquivir, about half a mile below the bridge of boats. Though it had been quite hot during the day for the Third of May, as Fernando and his knights referred to the date, the night was becoming quite chilly.

'I guarantee it,' the gnome replied hotly, 'do you think I lack such simple skills?'

'Let's not argue,' the youth suggested reasonably, 'let's save our energy. I have a feeling we'll need all of it before the night is through.' He patted Bubbi's shoulder. 'What about the candle?'

The gnome ran his arm along the ground, pulled back a strange contraption and indicated Joseph should touch it. The Nubian pulled his hand back with a startled intake of breath. Bubbi had fashioned a box-like container which, by using alternate panels, allowed air in to the flame while concealing the flame perfectly.

'Remember,' the dwarf said with a pedantic change of pitch, 'you slide the wick through here and . . .'

'I thought the Master said it should be called a fuse,' Joseph interrupted.

'Call it a shayghellah-lum-de-dooh adah, if you wish, don't interrupt. You slide the end of the fuse in through this hole. It is channelled to guide the thing to the flame. Then move on. Now ... you have all these cases on the raft, I go from boat to boat. You hand them up one by one, correct?' Joseph nodded wearily. It was the third time this evening Bubbi was rehearsing the manoeuvre. As Dinah had wisely said, put Bubbi in charge of any operation and he's worse than a petty officer in Admiral Bonifaz's fleet.

'And you slip one of your guaranteed leak-proof boxes of black powder down in the deepest part of the bilge. On the way back, we push the raft along and one by one we ignite the fuses with the candle,' Joseph sing-songed like a schoolboy. 'Each one is that much shorter than the last so, if *you* have done your calculations correctly, the whole line of boats should blow up simultaneously ...'

'... just as Admiral Bonifaz's two iron-clad ships reach the beginning of Triana's walls,' Bubbi finished for him.

'... and we are trying to run downstream along the bank and not get hit by the shower of missiles which will be flying in all directions ...' Joseph added.

'... but mostly in the poor admiral's direction. Still, it is possible the explosions and fire in all the boats will paralyse the archers with fear. To them, this totally unknown substance from Cathay will seem a miracle.'

'If it works.'

'Did we not try a few experiments under water in Alcalá?' the gnome asked testily. 'They all worked. We were eating trout for three days ... the shock killed dozens of them.'

'A good thing, too. Poor Master Solomon is still so ill he can eat but the lightest and most delicate food. Trout is ideal, but I am so worried by his slow recovery ... at times I doubt he is making any progress.'

'Stop fretting, Dinah will surely bring good news with her.'

Across the river, one shout became two, then thousands

of voices blended to become one terrifying roar. Horses screamed and the telltale crash of sword against shield added another dimension to the awful din. Poor Joseph could not contain himself. They had buried themselves in sand to remain inconspicuous — not that such an effort was necessary for the gnome — but with the sound of an unexpected battle of major proportions, the youth plowed his way out of his burrow and started wading into the fast, in-coming tide.

Bubbi got so excited his burblings were totally unintelligible for the first two seconds. Then the staccato became recognisable. What did Joseph think he was doing? The admiral would be sending up the signal lantern any time now, they had to load the raft and move upstream . . . how else would they co-ordinate the explosions with the smashing of the chains? Over his shoulder, in a few terse and rather rude words, the youth made his priorities perfectly clear: there was a major attack on Fernando's forces . . . it was the largest sally which had ever left the city from the sound of it. If the king suffered irretrievable losses now, what good would the destruction of the bridge do them? Last but not least, Dinah was at this very moment approaching from the southeast; headstrong as ever, she would run straight into the thick of the fight. Bubbi should watch the mast of the lead ship. When the lantern was run up, signalling the upstream onslaught at the peak of the tide, if Joseph had not been able to return, then Bubbi would have to summon Momo to help him.

As the youth battled the fierce tide, his muscles straining to their limit to force his body across the stream in a direct line, he dimly heard the gnome's outraged belching explosion: 'Momo? Are you serious? Are you mad? She will immediately demand we do the entire operation *her* way . . . straight out of the Talmud!'

On the opposite shore, Joseph cast aside the dripping robe, baring himself to just his loincloth; he had never worn armour or carried a shield. His shaman in the interior of Nubia had always insisted that each addition beyond one's weapon was more an encumbrance than a help. Speed, fast change of pace, cut and thrust and appear to disappear only to reappear in another quarter, delivering the blow that pierced all defences, far outstripped any succour offered by shield or bulky armour.

True to these hallowed principles, he roamed the field like a blazing will o' the wisp. Murmurs rose among the soldiers and knights of the Christian king's forces: who was this spear of lightness who vaulted over an armoured knight to disarm his opponent and move on before anyone could describe him ... beyond saying that he blended perfectly with the night. One bystander, a man famed for setting such battles scenes to verse, later described the Phantom of the Field, the Terror of Tablada, the Scourge of Seville, his progress followed only by carefully listening to the running erratic line described by the screams of the wounded and dying.

Unaware of this romantic legend already forming, Joseph paused to draw breath on the bank of the smaller Guadaira River near the one bridge across which all the bold garrison troops had crossed. With a soft laugh of triumph, he saw Ahmar's perfectly disciplined cavalry appear as if from nowhere on the far side of the river ... the sultan himself in the boldly exposed lead. No sooner had Joseph witnessed this splendidly conceived and lightning-like execution of a masterly tactic, when a cry of dismay went up from the Almohade attackers. It was matched by a roar of triumphal challenge from Fernando's infantry.

Those who made for the bridge were quickly and effectively dispatched by the waiting cavalry. The rest were relentlessly pushed into the river by the surge of rallied infantry. Knowing the sultan and the king, Joseph felt sure that any and all unwilling citizens in that adventure from Seville would be spared. Only the North Africans would suffer. His chest rising and falling like the bellows in a forge, Joseph knelt, cleansed the uncanny weapon on the grass and offered thanks to the Lord for his salvation and the strength which had been given to his arm. Even as he thought that word, arm, a hand rested on that very limb.

'Joseph ... my love ... are you all right?' Dinah's voice sent a wild and hitherto unknown thrill through the young man. Till now, he had been unaware that the taut and dangerous excitement of battle can produce a response similar to sexual desire. Only as she touched him, called his name, did he realise that his loin cloth had been accidentally shed by the wild passion sweeping through him. He twisted his torso, reached up and encircled her waist, pulling her down to him. She was caught so by surprise that she lost her footing, sprawling on the ground awkwardly. Momentarily demented, Joseph was on top of her like a ravenous cat.

The cry that seemed to come from her heart broke the spell. Even as the apologies poured from him, she threw her arms about his neck, kissing him with eager passion. Falling on her, he inadvertently parted her robe, his plunging passion out of control; the mere touch of her virginal thighs released the floodgates. Holding him more tightly still, Dinah felt the inundation overtake her, happy that she had been here when he needed her most.

A sudden shift in sounds indicated that Fernando's men were falling back; if the young lovers didn't move quickly, they might easily be overrun. As they ran toward the river, crouching low to create minimum silhouettes, Dinah noticed for the first time that Joseph wore nothing but the harness of his sword over his shoulder ... the loincloth was gone.

Reaching the river, she shed her own robe and loincloth on a mad and inexplicable impulse; even as she plunged into the water with him, her mind entertained the notion that she would swim easier unencumbered. They no sooner reached the opposite bank when Bubbi literally flew from his burrow, pointing excitedly downstream. The second lamp had been hoisted on the mast: Bonifaz was about to begin the attack. As though to affirm that thought, the sails began to unfurl, snapping taut on the still freshening breeze from the south. They pushed the small raft into the water, piled the explosives on it along with Bubbi and his concealed candle.

The tide, sweeping grandly up the river, bringing the

memory of a salty tang with it from the tidal marshes below, took them along speedily with minimum effort, Joseph and Dinah holding the stern and kicking underwater so that they would bring no attention to themselves. When they reached the line of captive boats rocking and straining against the chains with the force of the tide, they could hear excited shouts passing back and forth across the river from high above. The garrisons of Triana and the city were aware of the oncoming ships.

Dinah concentrated on moving the raft along the line of boats while Joseph passed the hardened clay containers up to Bubbi. Each one was rammed underneath the loose floor boards, well immersed in the bilge water. Solomon had told them the added constriction of the water would assure the bursting of the wooden hulls when the charges exploded. The way back across the river to the western bank once more was much faster. Joseph lapped fuse after fuse over the boats as he grabbed and lighted the next. When they reached the last one, a half dozen vicious tearing sounds announced the piercing of wood by crossbow bolts from above. And the last fuse looked dangerously short.

Crouching low, Bubbi ran down along the bank; Dinah and Joseph, being too tall to take advantage of the embankment, at its lowest here, stayed in the water up to their shoulders, straining against the tide to make headway. Soon they were panting, Joseph's right arm about Dinah to help her along. They were hardly out of range of the archers when the first huge ship passed them, its sails filled and the sheets protesting. Feeling they could safely come ashore now, they plunged on, bending as low as they could and trying to keep up with Bubbi who was bounding along the sandy shore with the leaps of a giant hare. A shout from the second boat was followed by a roar. This in turn was answered by a startled cry from Dinah. Her hand clamped itself over her left buttock. Just then, Joseph saw and heard two arrows plunge into the sand just before him. He turned and shouted the only phrase he could remember at the moment in the Castilian language. It had something to do with having illicit and incestuous relations with one's mother. This was answered by an outraged roar from the ship. But the flight of arrows stopped.

They threw themselves to the ground where the burrows had been dug in the sand. Joseph turned Dinah over on her stomach and examined the wound the best he could in the dark. Once more, he silently thanked Hutti for his amazing eyesight. It was a grazing cut, made by the blade of the arrowhead, but not deep at all and little blood had been lost, thanks to the razor sharpness of the arrowhead. With no other resource to hand, Joseph bent forward and began sucking the wound to cleanse it. Bubbi and Dinah gasped in unison. Hers indicating shocked surprise, Bubbi's inclined a bit more to wordlessly voicing a low opinion of human intimacies.

'Yes, Bubbi,' Dinah murmured, 'you can go home to Momo now. And thank you so much. Don't be unkind to Joseph, he is merely cleaning the wound as best he can. Just think, that arrow could have been tipped with poison.'

'Oooooo-hoo-hoo,' the gnome wailed just before he disappeared under the sand.

'Jo-Jo-o-o-seph? I'm not wounded *there* ... ahhh!' She flung her body about, forcing herself up to rest awkwardly on the good buttock. 'What ... I mean, just exactly what do you think you are doing?'

He put his arms about her, kissed her warmly and pressed her down into the sand next to him.

'We both know what I was doing, the only question is, did you like it?'

'That is irrelevant,' she slapped him. 'You are getting terribly bold and what's more, making my singleness of purpose much more difficult than it should ...' Suddenly, her voice stopped short. She sat up abruptly and gazed across the river; not toward the victorious herding of the captives by Ahmar's cavalry, but toward the spot where she had left her clothes. Only now did she realise she had left her precious talisman behind her. Once more you have been stupidly and hopelessly careless, she reprimanded herself.

Then she saw a glow hovering over the clothes, but had no time to stare; Joseph gripped her arm.

The first ship struck the line of boats, smashing two of them and tearing one of the rungs halfway from its mooring in Triana's wall. The second and largest boat struck, bursting the chain and sweeping upstream in a terrible hail of missiles. As the first ship fell back, slackening its sheets in preparation for a quick retreat, the blaze of fiery bursts and the ear-splitting sound of explosions racked the large boat precariously as the river responded to the violence of clay containers going off almost simultaneously.

Joseph and Dinah held hands, delighted with their tremendous success, watching the splinters of wood flying up and shedding light across the river. Now, not only was the chain broken, but there would not be enough left of the boats for the Almohades to repair. King Fernando could safely say the siege would not last much longer.

As her eyes left the darkening scene of carnage, they passed the spot where her robe had fallen with her loincloth. She could no longer see them. Startled, she put out her hand to steady herself and felt cloth beneath it. There was her robe, Joseph's, the loincloths and her sword. Only then was she aware of another presence, one Joseph was obviously not aware of. She felt his hot hands coursing along her body and turned away, seeking to identify the presence which had made their things materialise on this side of the river . . . surely not Bubbi, he was never that subtle.

A soundless voice inside her mind directed her gaze to the southeastern horizon. There, where she knew the fortress of Alcalá de Guadaira rose above the river's bank, something in the dark sky had a definitely unhealthy aspect. Yes, her grandfather was ill, there was no questioning that, of course. He was comfortable if not vastly improved. And well cared for. But something was threatening him and the stronghold, something more evil than any of them had ever faced in the full manifesting of its baleful powers. If she did not get there soon and take on this horror, Yakub would be able to break his chains, destroy Golem and end the two kings' victories here before they were won.

As Dinah strove to rise, the voice asked her if she could not detect the end of an era, the end of her strengths built on one premise ... yes, if she now changed that, it would be a fundamental change. However, the strengths she would develop no doubt would eventually exceed the ones she would lose. The art of creating The Ultimate through her purity and the magic box would be no more. Through her own efforts and researches among the arcane arts and sciences, she would find new and wonderful capabilities in that little, exquisitely wrought box. However, until the fundamental change was made, she would not be able to thwart the evil now threatening her house.

An invisible hand patted her arm encouragingly and Dinah knew Aysha was gone. She thought about the words which had been pounding through her mind; she watched Joseph's hand stroking her thigh, moving across the shorn part and up along her belly to cup one of her breasts. She sighed and shrugged. She could not lie to herself and say it didn't feel nice. It was exciting to feel him engorged and out of control ... and the violence of that explosion! Even the charges which blew up the boats had no greater potency.

'Make love to me, Joseph. Don't gawk, don't say "Huh?" and don't ask questions, just do it.' She slipped her hand inside her robe and closed her fingers over the little magic box.

She could hardly keep the stars in their right places. How romantic he is, refusing to obey me until I painfully removed every last bit of my beard. How, she wondered, could he make love to me with a beard? He even commented on how much shorter this beard looked than the last one. How fast did he think a woman's 'beard garden' grew?

The hand, opening her wider still, finding her innermost bells of happiness, caused the heavens to alter course erratically once more ... his lips were hot, finding more and more, wanting more and more, making her feel grateful for how much he loved and desired her and then ... gritting her teeth she waited for the pain but it never came ... just a breath-taking expansion, growing and growing as so much of him became part of her, filling her, moving her as nothing ever had before. Just as her senses were leaving her, the ground lifting her as the sky plunged down to meet her, she wondered idly how The Ultimate could be any more wonderful than this. Her hand tightened on the silver box of hexagrams and, as it did, everything about her exploded with a thousand times the force of smashing boats . . . wiping the stars out of the skies, leaving her in a profound swoon.

* * *

Wheeling his simply caparisoned horse about to face his brother monarch, Fernando raised his sword in salute. Ahmar answered the gesture with his light scimitar and veered off, leaving the cavalry in charge of the more than two thousand prisoners they had taken. Even as he rode off, his men began roaring after him: 'Ghalib, Ghalib' and he rose in the stirrups, turning to tell them that God is the only conqueror.

The two kings dismounted, Fernando with more difficulty and needing the help of two foot-soldiers because of the heavy suit of armour. In the middle of the field, they embraced as two actual brothers might, had they been long separated.

'I have called you cousin as a mark of respect,' the Christian said, his hand on Ahmar's shoulder, 'but from now on, the only appropriate term is brother. Will it please you to be as a brother to me?' he asked shyly. Ahmar knelt and kissed his overlord's hand as an answer and to show his profound respect for the Castilian who was already recognised as a saint by his own people. Before Ahmar could rise, Fernando touched each of his shoulders with the huge, two-handed sword, pronouncing him Don Mohammad.

The king's armourers arrived to relieve the monarch of his ponderous suit of metal, then the two walked together, arm-in-arm, to the sultan's tent which was closest.

'What advice do you give me regarding the prisoners, Brother?' Fernando asked. His regard for Ahmar was such that he took no major decision in this campaign without consulting the measures with the sultan.

'Simplicity is not in it, Brother Fernando, for we have two types of prisoners. Nearly two thousand of them are hapless townsmen forced into service by their Almohade rulers. That is to say, Captain Sakkaf and his officers. There are less than two hundred of our actual enemies among them.'

'I believe you will suggest two different solutions . . . why should we always believe one solution serves any given problem?' Fernando smiled and accepted a cool cup of very light white wine he had discovered in the area. He passed that cup to Ahmar and accepted the second from the servant's tray. 'How kind of you to keep my favourite wine on hand.'

Ahmar shrugged diffidently, embarrassed that the king should even comment on such basic things. However, this king never took even the smallest favour or service for granted.

'The solutions I would offer, sire, are in themselves simple enough. As you know, we lost the good offices of my chancellor, Solomon ha-Levi and his slave, the youthful and very talented Nubian, behind the city's walls.' Both men heard the thunder of two horses leaving the camp but did not take any notice. 'If we return all the townsmen, most of whom are my Yemenite followers, they will undoubtedly be impressed by the generosity of the king who comes here to free them and defeat their oppressors. And I feel sure they will be even more effective champions of our cause than were Solomon and his apprentice.'

'And you would execute the others?' Fernando asked, making a strong effort to disguise how distressing that solution seemed.

'With all proper respect, good brother, would that not give the lie to a very noble gesture?'

'You would send them back to North Africa . . . after extracting an oath of honour that they would never return!'

exclaimed the king enthusiastically.

'Exactly, sire. Even to the very words I was about to say. Our minds are indeed as one.' Ahmar raised the cup, his face suddenly relieved of anxiety; Fernando answered the gesture. Ahmar proposed an elaborate and flattering toast to the health of the courageous admiral who had run the gauntlet, faced a veritable hail of missiles, to destroy the Sevillians' bridge of boats. Then Fernando proposed the quiet heroes who had created an unexplained inferno among the boats themselves, with startlingly accurate timing. When he asked who they were, al-Ahmar mentioned a tall and powerful dark youth and his companion, a small soldier with a flaming red beard.

'But Brother Mohammad, I saw such a youth, near naked and black, flying among the Almohade host like an avenging angel. He was never in one place for more than a blink of the eye; he wreaked havoc among our enemies.'

'That is Joseph, the slave apprentice of Solomon, our Hebrew slyboots. Solomon would tell me no more about the explosions but that he would, this once, open one of nature's secret and terrifying troves. And he extracted a promise from me that it would never be discussed. May I put that obligation upon you as well?' Ahmar asked; the king, of course, nodded with a smile.

When Fernando asked about Joseph's companion, Ahmar acknowledged what he suspected to be another well-kept secret. Fernando was aghast; did not Islamic law punish a woman with death for impersonating a man? Countering the question, Ahmar wondered would that be justified if the 'soldier' fought so well and so hard for her liege and that liege's overlord. Each raised his cup again to toast the young couple.

* * *

'I don't know how I could ever have considered you to be a brother of mine,' Hutti shouted, hammering his fists against the tall, broad-boled tree in impotent fury. Showers of fruit dropped to the ground. In a typical way aimed at goading the speaker even further, Hawwaz stooped down and scooped up a few of the fruits, which resembled apples save for the deep blue colour which made humans take them for sapphires, and nodded an indifferent thank you.

'Did you hear anything I said at all, you ignorant, thick-headed, stubborn fool?'

'Have some of your harvest,' Hawwaz suggested, tossing a sapphire apple to his big brother. 'And yes, before you fling that back at me, I heard everything. Including your last interesting, if inaccurate, description of me. I don't know what you are going on and on about. Did anyone tell you not to help that bunch of clumsy, inept fools in Granada . . . or wherever?'

'That's different!' Hutti stormed, pummelling the tree again. This time, two of the blue apples bounced off Hawwaz's skull.

'You did that on purpose, you superior, arrogant . . .'

'I'll give you purpose, I'll knock that thick skull right off your shoulders . . .'

'You and who else?' Hawwaz roared back, clenching his fists and flexing his knees into a crouch. 'Well, you and who else? I asked. Did you bring your army with you?'

Both Djinni were now so furious they didn't even notice the two youthful figures approach, stop, exchange horrified glances and turn away. No taller than the shoulder height of the two battling Djinni, these were the sons of Hutti and Hawwaz; unlike human children, the young Djinni, now a mere four hundred years or so old, seemed more like small adults. Each resembled his father exactly. They had hardly taken ten steps when a fabulous creature materialised before them. It was Aysha in the guise of an angel, her favourite impression, complete with huge feathered wings and a long, diaphanous garment that draped back over the purple grass where she had landed. She took each of her children by the hand.

'Can you two stop threatening each other for a moment?'

she called. The shouts were unabated. 'CHAUVINISTS!' she halooed so loudly the tree dropped another shower of fruit, crowning both contestants painfully. They whirled and gasped.

'No, no,' Hutti pleaded, running toward her. 'Please don't take mine away, it's all Hawwaz's fault, just take . . .' He never finished. Something shining from Aysha's eyes, resembling a solid beam of light, struck him and knocked him flat on his back. Hawwaz, who had taken only two steps, halted in his tracks.

'I know the mischief you've been up to, you,' she accused Hawwaz. 'And until you wash your hands of it, neither of you will see these boys again . . . don't bother begging!' she warned.

'But that's unfair!' Hutti was now on his stomach, pounding the soft grass with his fists. 'All I'm doing is trying to help your friends . . . that Dinah you like so much . . .'

'Do you think I'm so stupid I didn't know anything about that little astral-shaking experience of yours? The Ultimate!' she laughed mockingly. 'You're helping *my* friends, indeed.'

'Well, I am,' Hutti protested weakly, an unaccustomed dark green blush suffusing his cheeks and ears. 'You're right about that idiot back there, he's really making trouble, he's trying to help Dinah's enemies . . .'

'I'm fully aware of what he's doing. You talk him out of it, you're supposed to set a good example, you're the eldest, remember? Not that it means much with males, you stay children all through eternity anyway.' Hutti started beating the grass with his fists again. 'And stop that right now.' she boomed at him. 'Have you no respect for your environment? Shaking all the fruit out of the trees, ruining the grass . . . it's people like you who give a place a bad name.'

'It's so unjust, so unfair . . .' Hutti howled like a wounded wolf and, turning on his back, began to pound his own chest. 'He went down there and climbed into that clay thing Dinah made, he's going to get it to smash the chains and carry that dirty old man Yakub all the way to . . .'

'You rotten sneak, you big-mouthed . . .' Hawwaz

bounded off the ground, hands outstretched for Hutti's neck; halfway there, he seemed to smash into a wall. He dropped to the ground, writhing in pain.

'Is there no reprehensible display you two won't put on in front of these impressionable children? I'm warning the pair of you, not only do you sort yourselves out and undo the damage you're up to in Murcia, but you do it immediately. If not, you'll never see the lads again.' The great wings extended and a split second later, Aysha and the youngsters vanished.

'Now look what you've done, you contemptible idiot!' Hutti stormed, pounding the grass again.

'Don't you think it's about time we figured out a way to resolve this mess? Fighting obviously hasn't helped much,' Hawwaz reminded his hysterical colleague sensibly. Hutti sat up and blinked. Their ranjis extended themselves and shook tips in a gesture of reconciliation.

'What do you have to do save put that clay thing back ... I don't mean put it back, you know ... just make it like it was when you found it.' Hutti vaulted to his feet and stretched.

'It's not that easy, something is going on down there that I have been unable to identify properly. You have to see that Yakub ... humans are not normally frightening, but this one is. He seems to be getting stronger and stronger ... didn't you tell me that your old man got weaker and weaker in that dungeon?'

'He's not "my old man", if you please and yes, it was a very debilitating experience ... how old is your one?' Hutti asked.

'Good heavens, who can tell a human's age? He has a greying beard, not much of it either ... and his head was shaven ... that's growing in fairly grey too ...'

'I'd say somewhat younger than Solomon. And you feel he's building up his strength there? What are they feeding him?'

'It isn't that. I have this terrible premonition we're not the only ones involved there ...'

'I'd rather not start another argument, Little Brother, but I don't believe "we" is the operative term.'

'All right. Still, something else I can't detect is going on. Have you ever seen a human possessed by a spirit ... a powerful entity from a non-human dimension?' It was apparent that Hawwaz was not only serious, but disturbed deeply as well.

'If you think something like that is going on, you're going to have to do the exorcising ritual,' Hutti pronounced sternly, implying great disapproval for Hawwaz's negligence.

'Surely ...' Hawwaz halted, colour draining from his face. He looked down at his ranji. It curled up just enough for the tip to aim itself at his face, as though returning the stare in a one-eyed fashion.

'I most surely do,' Hutti finished for his semi-paralysed friend. 'There is only one appropriate exorcising ritual.'

'That's not true!' Hawwaz objected. 'Humans do exorcising rituals ... and they are nothing like ...'

'And they don't work most of the time ... why are you wasting your time and mine? You know that we are morally and legally obliged to undo whatever has created such a situation. You simply go down there, you straighten out that clay dummy. He sits on the straw next to that dirty old thing, doesn't he? Isn't that what you told me?'

'Yes.' Hawwaz replied desisting from biting his lip just long enough to snap the answer.

'Look, young fellow, don't get in a huff with me. You got into this all on your own. Get the dummy to turn him around and hold his bottom up. You know the appropriate words as well as I do. You banish the dybbuk, or whatever it's called, then you ram your ranji ...'

'Stop! I can't do it. I can't! It's all right for you, you haven't seen this one lately. I mean, we've been pretty naughty at times, I agree, but this human is *really* evil. He knows it too, he wants to be evil.' There were shimmering tears in the younger Djinn's eyes. 'Hutti, won't you *please* help me?'

'I'll do whatever I can for you. Do you want me to hold

him for you? Would that — uh — firm up your purpose?' Hawwaz compressed his lips and shook his head vehemently. 'No? What then?' Hutti asked, an edge of impatience creeping into his tone. Hawwaz looked mutely but meaningfully at the older Djinn's ranji.

Hutti stepped back, placing his fingertips very deliberately on his hips; he eyed Hawwaz up and down, his jaw muscles bulging, the edges of his pinched nostrils blanching.

'You actually mean you want me ... you mean you are actually trying to tell me *you* should hold that dirty old man and *I* should be the one ... oh-oh, no ... I don't believe this, Hawwaz. You've been very cheeky and demanding at times, but this takes the date. Of all the nerve ...'

'All right! Don't go on and on about it.' Hawwaz turned away to hide his confusion; his voice had broken with emotional strain.

'Sorry about that, dear brother.' Hutti strode over and put an arm about the unhappy Djinn's shoulder. 'Leaving that aside, is there anything *else* I can do?'

Hawwaz looked down, ran one powerful though exquisitely formed foot back and forth over the soft grass. He looked sideways: Hutti's ranji had rolled a diamond-like fruit over the grass and the tip was drawn back. His own ranji quivered, ready to bat the diamond back. He looked up at Hutti.

'I suppose lending me your ranji is out of the question?' he chanced. Hutti withdrew the arm and stormed off, spoiling his ranji's aim.

CHAPTER 7

Hawwaz began to stop every few paces as he neared the steps to the dungeon. When he appeared atop the royal palace at Murcia, invisible to anyone who might have been looking up in the middle of the knight, his size was greater than that of the building. Then, with a snap of his fingers, he reduced his size to one more suitable for travelling through the building. He encountered no one in the long corridors and down the flights of steps. He could see two guards asleep near the door of the dungeon and wondered at the continuing formality. As long as the clay dummy was there, who needed other guards? Yet ... he sniffed, turning the smells round and round, trying to identify, give some recognisable form to the one which had been baffling him. He knew he should know it, that it was not alien ... and yet?

For sheer deviltry, as he passed the two sleeping guards, he glared at the leg of the stool of the man nearest the door. The wood broke just where the leg had been fitted into the planed and polished section of tree trunk. With a gasp of dismay the man hit the floor, yelping as the tender joint of his elbow sang against the solid stone. By this time, Hawwaz was through the door and holding back an impish giggle. As he had foreseen the commotion wakened the victim of his next assault. What he had not foreseen was the look on the face. It was one of sheer hatred and . . . it . . . was directed at the Djinn himself. Even as Yusuf ibn Yakub glared venomously at him, Hawwaz blanched seeing the gangrenous shade the man's skin had turned, that and the blackened areas about his ears, eyelids and mouth, the edges of his nostrils. What had originally caused him to think of the man's aspect as an unhealthy one, combined mysteriously with burgeoning strength, now appeared more readily identifiable: unwholesome, corrupt. Gazing back, he throttled his momentary fear and wondered at the human race. Entities of other realms, such as his own, could do things men would term evil, but only because humans dealt in these definitions. A Djinn was never evil in such a sense because the term did not have the same value to him. That is why a human who knowingly immerses himself in evil begins to reflect his own decaying concept, the corruption showing. Yes, he warned himself, but he is not doing it all by himself. As soon as he thought that, ibn Yakub laughed in such a foul way the Djinn's skin crawled slightly. The man could not only see him, he was reading thoughts.

Immediately, Hawwaz cleared his mind. He walked over to the seated Golem and lifted him to his feet, opening the slack mouth as wide as he could. Slipping inside the robot, he formed a new pattern of instructions for him to follow. Then he slipped back out. Golem turned, reached down and lifted Yakub, flipping him over and tucking him under one arm. With the free hand, he lifted the filthy robe, exposing a none-too-clean bottom. Yakub laughed again, this time even more chillingly. Hawwaz had to drum one thought through his head over and over: this is the man who was about to do that dreadful thing to a little girl hardly thirteen . . . and with a donkey! And even as he kept that image without legible pattern in a secret compartment of his mind where Yakub's newly acquired skills could not locate it, another thought formed there: was Hutti not trying to do that to a girl of exactly the same age when he got so knotted? Ah, yes, but that was different. Donkeys . . . Ugh!

With a slight gesture, the Djinn indicated the dummy should lower the target an inch or two. Just right, stop there, his next gesture halted the downward progress. Now, let us see how hard he will laugh at the next stage, Hutti thought unscreened. A laugh was his answer from Yakub. Unnerving, the Djinn admitted, but this was all bluff on the man's part. He could do nothing to thwart this ritual and whatever was giving him the strength and the occult powers would be on its way to wherever it came from . . . but Hawwaz did not carry that thought to its obvious conclusion, unfortunately.

In an archaic and no longer known language that predated Arabic by millenia, Hawwaz grandly and sonorously intoned the incantation of exorcism. When he was nearly at the end, Golem dropped Yakub on his face in the straw and walked toward Hawwaz as though totally fascinated by the words. With an angry snarl, the Djinn lowered his ranji and dived at the robot, and down his throat. A split-second later, ibn Yakub was on his feet, his body expanding to a degree that defied the laws of physics for humans; the face was contorted, the mask of evil it had become bearing no relationship to his own features. The arms extended in the direction of Golem and from the fingertips a bolt of something dark red, fiery and horrendous shot out, creating a suffocating stench in the chamber. Golem was shattered into such fine particles even the dust itself disappeared; there was also an ear-splitting tear as the very fabric of space parted momentarily to permit Hawwaz's shattering passage at a speed not admissable in the universe he was leaving. And he left it without a trace.

As though exhausted by the brief but intensive labour, the body of ibn Yakub shrank back to its normal size, the features regaining their familiar pattern as the man sank, trembling, to the straw. His eyes closed for a few minutes and, when they finally opened, they revealed a baleful presence lurking behind them, renewing its energies and searching ceaselessly for the exit to that world which surrounded the newly-created energumen; ibn Yakub's possessor was obviously no insignificant dybbuk, as had been suspected.

* * *

Hutti sat against the bole of his favourite tree and wept shamelessly. Aysha and the two children stood at some distance from him, respecting his grief.

No one had seen Hawwaz's passing. Such things are not normally visual on the plane inhabited by the Djinni and now and then visited by extraordinary humans. But the disaster had communicated itself by means much higher than the sensory ones.

'Where is he ... do you know that?' he sobbed, swiping at his eyes with the backs of his hands like a lost little boy.

Aysha walked to him and knelt down, the huge wings opening partially to accommodate the gesture. She took his hands in hers and held them to her cheek, then kissed them softly.

'Not a universe known to many, I fear,' she answered sadly, deeply shaken by his abject misery. 'However, I've had no time to make enquiries ... we shall see.'

'Somehow, it's all my fault ...'

'Hutti, stop that,' she scolded, drawing him to her and resting his head against her lovely bosom. 'You know perfectly well he stirred all that up because he was envious and jealous. He simply could not bear to be less important than you ... or anyone.'

'And I was fighting with him, shaming him into going back there to do the exorcism ...'

'Hutti, what is the matter with you? It is the law. We are not allowed to manipulate humans to the point where they are vulnerable to possession by unscrupulous spirits and entities; if we do, we are obliged to undo the harm ... you know that.'

'Yes, *I* know that, but did *he* know what he was facing? We are not talking about some dybbuk, some pipsqueak vampire soul looking for a body, we are talking about an Archduke of Hell.'

'True, so what do you think you could have done about it? Gone with him?' she asked frankly. 'Neither of us know exactly what happened there, but I'm very sure of one thing. Had you gone with Hawwaz — which, if I may remind you, you had no business to do — there would now be two of you floating about like atomic dust in some unimaginable universe.'

'Aysha, I should have remembered, I should have guessed, I was the one who knew that Azazel was up to something. I never said a word to that boy, I just let him go to face . . . that!'

'Did you realise that was what awaited him when you sent him off?'

'No, of course not . . . we both thought it was a simple ritual.' He hesitated, looking down shyly, then guardedly toward the children; they were quite busy with their own discussion.

'What can't you bear to tell me?' she asked, displaying the first hint of a twinkle in her eyes.

'He wanted me to do the . . . you know, forcing the invader out, sort of thing for him . . .'

'Ridiculous! That is simply not permitted. The one who has caused the problem must resolve it . . . and on his own . . . with his own . . . hmmmn . . . resources.'

'He even wanted to borrow my . . .'

'Stop! No more loathesome details, if you don't mind. Do you want the chilren to hear?' She laughed wryly. 'Dear, dear, still and all, how typically Hawwaz. Borrow someone else's.'

'Is there any way of getting him back, Aysha? You know everybody . . . is there no one who can help?'

'We'll see. I can't promise anything now. In fact, I'd like to speak with Anwar about it. Now, pull yourself together, what do you imagine the children will be thinking . . . one of their heroes reduced to tears?'

He sniffled and held his head high.

CHAPTER 8

'The Lord Yahweh is my shepherd, I shall not want; though I wander in the valley of the shadow of death I fear not; His rod and staff shall comfort me.'

Solomon's deep and melodious voice seemed to calm the candles themselves, making the flames steadier as the storm built greater and greater atmospheric tension; wind howled through the river valley below the fortress of Alcalá, lashing the Guadaira against its banks; it shrieked in the ramparts above, playing eerie tunes in the serrated top of what here was also known as the Sultan's Turret, directly above the old man's tower chamber. When the wind passed the narrow apertures used by defending archers, a moan became two and three and dozens, a voice of hell rising in the night, punctuated regularly by brilliant flashes from the lowering sky and the ever closer rumble of thunder.

When the last word of the psalm died on her grandfather's lips, Dinah took it up, repeating the words slowly, giving vital reality to each and every word. Joseph looked at her adoringly; she was not just speaking those words, he realised, but living them. Just as Joseph took his turn in the recital accompanying the third night of their vigil, a strangled groan rose from the floor near Solomon's bed. Farida's head rose, her body prone from the neck down, her belly pressed into the thick carpet. She swept the room with what appeared to be unseeing eyes, still their flight was arrested at each face. The head went back at an angle akin to a lowering ox; indeed, she had the quality of a dumb beast awaiting the ritual knife. In tune with the rising wind, her voice rose, the sound inhuman, challenging the night.

Joseph's recitation came to an end and, when it did and before Solomon began anew, Farida's head came crashing down, the face buried in the carpet. Dinah gripped Joseph's hand, her fingers nearly frozen with foreboding. No human head is pulled back like that through its own muscle power. Nor cast down with such force, enough to smash the poor woman's nose had the deep silken pile of the carpet not been there to absorb the shock.

As his recital ended, Solomon held up his hand. They all listened for any changes in this dreadful night which seemed to be heralding the end of the world. The old patriarch adjusted the small skull-cap and drew his prayer shawl more tightly about his shoulders. As he did, the candle light bounced off the large ring cut in the Seal of Solomon. How often, as a small child, Dinah remembered, she had believed the ring had a life and soul of its own. It still seemed that way, the power reaching out to her. Unthinkingly, her free hand slipped under her robe to grasp the box made of the same hexagrams as Solomon's ring.

'It is a terrible struggle,' the patriarch advised them, his head shaking slowly. 'And none of us can know the pain, the torture she is going through. See how valiantly she fights, letting no measure of terror change her resolve. She is denying "shemad" with every ounce of her will,' he declared, using the Hebrew word for apostasy.

'Will she survive such an onslaught?' Joseph wanted to know, but the old man shrugged.

'If loyalty and faith are enough, then she will. As you know, we are dealing with something so powerful, there is no adequate rule, no accurate scale to take its measure. We will wait and we will pray and in this way give force and reinforcement to each other.'

'Why Farida?' Dinah moaned miserably. 'Poor, simple, addled Farida with her fantasies and queer notions ... I was the one who made the careless error ...'

'Silence!' The old man's voice boomed so loudly it drowned the fury of the approaching storm. 'Are you trying to offer another target, expose a weakness to exploit?' he demanded at the top of his voice. 'Farida was chosen for the very reasons you suggest. A presumed lump of jelly with no will of her own. Well, that was a miscalculation ... faith was not considered. Farida will fight for her God while there is a breath of life in her body.'

Solomon looked down at the now slender form writhing on the floor, slowly, painfully, like a wounded reptile. His heart ached, a pang of memory striking him ... had she not indeed been as Abishag the Shunammite, the comfort and warmth for his many years, a balm for the frosts of age.

A tremendous flash illuminated the room, paling the candles and quelling the fire. The inmates were momentarily blinded, hearing the crash of huge stones as part of the Sultan's Turret fell away. The stench of electrical fire seeped into the room, but there was another, even more fell odour beginning to overpower the first. Another and yet another flash of lightning stabbed down at the fortress from the sky directly overhead, answered by crashes from the tortured building below, the rent heavens above. One last blinding chain struck the building, this time tearing a hole in the bed chamber where the ceiling joined the outer wall. Now, the stench of unmentionable pits, the cesspools of the damned, burst in on them unbridled.

The two young people flew from their chairs and stood by the bed, each holding one of the old man's hands. Joseph's naked sword was in his free hand, the silver box clasped tightly in Dinah's.

The hole in the ceiling widened with no apparent loss of stones, no sound of altered dimensions; something like a bulky, filthy bag of cloth began oozing through. A moment later, an hideous replica of Yusuf ibn Yakub stood learing before them, shapeless nearly, and that undulating, emphasising the lack of solid, material form.

'Up, slave,' a strange, inhuman voice sounded, hardly seeming to originate from the mass representing Yakub. Farida moaned, her body trying to squirm away; something very powerful crossed the floor, vapourous and rufescent, intensifying the terrible stench and causing the three facing the terror to experience painful electrical vibrations through veins and sinews.

Like a wooden toy held together by strings, the body jerked straight up to its knees, then turned, pivoting on the carpet as if pulled by those invisible strings. Then the knees, with no motion of their own, started to slide toward the expanding hulk which was beginning to fill the whole far corner near the exposed sky. Little staccato cries broke from Farida's lips, cries that combined deathly fright, sobs of endurance and something more . . . almost the moans of passion . . . or anticipation, Dinah suddenly realised.

She looked down toward her grandfather. He had the fringe of his prayer shawl in his left hand, pressed to his lips. The palm of the right was pressed flat against his brow; Dinah noticed the ring was turned in, the hexagram out of sight.

When Farida was almost to the lowering apparition, hardly resembling ibn Yakub now, it took on more solid-looking form. With indescribable anguish, Solomon saw the first hints of the beautiful, angelic aspect of Azazel, Archduke of Hell.

'Bow your head that I may bless you and anoint you as my bride,' a sonorous voice ordered, echoing like massed trumpets off the walls. A phallus like in unearthly sculpture of ivory, mother-of-pearl and pale pink marble rose majestically over the bowed head.

'The Lord Yahweh is my shepherd, I shall not want,' three voices rose in a triumphal chant, filling the room with their wholesome sound. Farida's body trembled. 'Though I wander in the valley of the shadow of death . . .' When that last word reached Farida, she forgot herself and thought only of the man she worshipped, the father, grandfather, husband, lover, brother ... all those things she needed and didn't have. Like a suddenly transformed gazelle, she flew to her feet and, in one great leap, threw herself across his body. Even as she reached him, muttering the name of Abishag over and over, covering him with her, protecting him, Azazel struck, the phallus now a fiery spear. The three defenders braced themselves, the blow striking Farida and through her to Solomon ... but not before his hand shot out, the ring burning the apparition's brow so strongly the smell of sizzling putrefaction saturated the room. The box clenched in her hand, Dinah drove her fist into the looming chest as Joseph's blade came down on the base of the phallus-turned-spear. There was a terrible screech, but it was drowned by Solomon's words.

'Damned and accursed for ever, as my ancestor so bound you over to eternal damnation and imprisonment, so do I in his name and with his Seal, the Seal of Solomon, and you shall come forth no more until the Judgement Day.'

The shrinking mass squirmed, squeaked and made vile obscenities, but on and on it shrank, finally no larger than a mouse and then ... it was gone. Immediately, Joseph circled the room, intoning the prayer of purification and asking God's grace and benediction. When he returned, Dinah had rolled Farida off her grandfather's chest. Unabashed tears rolled down the old man's cheeks.

'Adonai, look kindly upon this child who gave so much and asked so little, even sacrificing her life that an old man might live a few moments longer. If Abishag the Shunammite was half so kind and generous, then her memory is twice blessed.'

Dinah turned to ask Joseph to help her carry the girl to another room for the balance of the night, but Solomon shook his head.

'Make her comfortable here next to me. I will keep the vigil overnight. Soon enough, on the morrow, she will be gone from me for ever.'

Dinah sat on the edge of the bed, holding Farida's cold hand and weeping. Solomon reached under his pillow and extracted a small piece of paper and a key. He handed the paper to Joseph. There were two letters written there, L and V in Hebrew.

'Lamed Vav?' Joseph asked. Solomon nodded. Joseph pondered, then remembered the values in Gematria. 'Thirty-six?' Again the old man agreed with a nod.

'There is a tradition that there must always be thirty-six Nistor in the world, Joseph. They are supposed to be saintly men, guardians of their people, those who take the punishment and the burdens of much and many upon themselves. Strive to be chosen ... though some do not even realise they've been chosen ... you have the qualities needed.' He turned to Dinah, taking her shoulder to make her face him.

'This key is for you, my child. It is the key to the key. You will find it ... that key which is not, like this, a material object. With that key, you will make a journey and you will learn how to prepare yourself.' He held up his hand, showing the blackened surface of his ring.

'This ring is for your son ...' he smiled, pointing to her abdomen ... 'he who already seeks life inside you.' Dinah blanched, then flushed deep crimson. Her grandfather pretended to look past her. 'Two years before he died, the great Sufi master Abdul Qadir Jilani predicted the birth of he who was to be known as the greatest Spaniard, El-Arabi. Some of the most wonderful things I learnt were in the days with El-Arabi, when I was young. While it is terribly immodest of me in terms of my own great-grandson, I predict he will be a great man on that very path. When you come in here in the morning, you may remove the ring.'

'What do you mean ... Grandfather?' The last word was on a rising note of panic.

'Joseph, comfort your bride-to-be. You hereby have my permission, I give you your freedom and, as quickly as you can, communicate this to Dinah's father in Carmona ... yes, and to the sultan. I believe he and the Christian king will make you a knight shortly. You may like that, it is probably uplifting for young men.'

Dinah tore free of Joseph's protective arms and threw herself into her grandfather's.

'You're not going to die, it's not fair . . .'

'Joseph, would you go downstairs and see if you can find us a flagon of decent wine and some cups that I may toast your health and future? Besides, I need a few moments to talk some commonsense into this girl.'

When the door closed, Dinah became aware of another presence in the room. She lifted her head and stared; something seemed to be creating a current of air over Farida's face, making the ringlets of her hair tremble. Without even thinking of why, she reached in for her silver box and held it before her. Immediately, the splendid angelic form of Aysha was visible, perched on the bed next to the dead girl. Aysha was stroking her brow gently.

'I've come to help him home, Dinah, so please don't spoil this, the most wonderful journey of all time. Someone who has admired him for years, one of those Sufi saints your grandfather always talks about, is waiting to meet him. Solomon has had a very full life, he has carried an enormous burden further than most men . . . there are only one or two such men each century, my child.' She pointed to the small key in Dinah's hand. 'It is up to you now.' Aysha leaned over and patted the girl's arm. 'Go off and join your Joseph, I'll look after Solomon. No tears. Be happy for him.'

As in a trance, Dinah rose and walked toward the door. She turned, just before leaving. She could no longer see Aysha but Solomon was smiling. His head was on the pillow and his eyes closed. Tenderly, he held Farida's hand in his.

CHAPTER 9

Dinah sat in her study, surrounded by books. Your grandfather's study, she corrected herself. Before her was a small wooden chest. In the lock was the key her beloved grandfather had given her the night he died.

Dinah shifted her weight on the high stool; each time she tried to lean forward, that huge belly got in her way. Easy enough for a man, some star-rocking ecstasy on the bank of the river, half in water, half in sand, then he goes off to be knighted and fight a few more battles, but what happens to the woman? I should never have taken off my beard! Ever! A movement inside that swollen abdomen changed her expression completely. She glowed with the movement of new life.

Shaking her head, she placed all the slips of paper before her in a new arrangement. At the very top she put the number 5040. Product of the numbers one through seven, also of seven through ten, and divisible by all ten of them. Surrounding the Tree of Life with its ten sephira, were the magic squares of the planets. Month after month she had been seeking that elusive key her grandfather had told her about.

Meditate, she ordered herself ... you spend too much time trying to reason, to find precise mathematical formulae ... it isn't like that! As you watch these numbers, send them out into the macroscosm ... follow them, see how the stars and planets arrange these numbers. Solomon's papers here are very, very clear about the final knowledge man seeks. It is a realisation, a revelation ... enlightenment that comes not to the mundane part of the mind. If you discover the Ba'al Shem Tov, that elusive thing of being Master of the Good Name, that opens the door, say some. Solomon thought it could be expressed as the Lost Commandment. Find it and everything falls into place. In the Sufi writings he left me, it is always called a Path. *The* Path. An inward route to enlightenment, which is unending love for God, the desire of nothing but unity. Neither hope for heaven nor fear of hell. Just love of God for no other reason.

Something clicked and to Dinah's surprise she was not just sitting meditating now, entranced and removed from the world. She was sitting on the steps of a great building, one of the largest she had ever seen. Sitting next to her and one step higher, was one of the most wonderful men she had ever seen. His skin was deeply tanned, his hair a deep tawny gold, the eyes startlingly blue ... and yet ... she wondered at the familiarity ... he was like her grandfather too. And ... yes, that very ancient man she had once seen in another world, the one who protected her, Aysha's friend, Anwar.

'... so, you see, my child, this world is gone and in another sense it will always be ... forever supported by man's race memories, those that tell him once there was an idyllic time, once there was a land like Eden. And so it was. Here, we would build great edifices with mighty stones, hewn seemingly by magic and lifted into place as though they weighed nothing. Our knowledge was based on our attunement with all the forces of the universe. We knew all those cosmic secrets man has lost. Still, there are those rare ones who seek and find, as the human race once more evolves, striving to be still a higher form of being, capable of the wisdom and miracles of the ancient pantheistic gods they worshipped. And in and through all the ages since, the chain of transmission of such esoteric wisdom has been unbroken.'

'What am I to do, how will I find these things . . . I don't think I am justifying my grandfather's faith in me.' Dinah looked up and then quickly down; it was too overwhelming to look into a face that contained the cosmos.

'Time is not wasted on the study you are doing. Add to it, as your grandfather told you, a study of the works of great Sufi masters. El-Arabi and the woman, Rabi'ah Al-Adawiyah, who lived for the pure love of God, asking nothing. then, go to Persia and study with Jalaluddin Rumi.'

'But I do not want to convert, will these teachers not require adherence to Islam?' Dinah lamented.

'They teach that theirs is the secret meaning, the knowledge contained inside every great religion; that the outer garment conceals the inner, like a series of veils. In choosing, you choose only the outer form, isn't that correct?'

'And the selection is up to me, is that true?'

'Absolutely. That's why a Sufi is truly free.'

'That is why . . . ?' Dinah slipped halfway off the stool in her excitement. She was back in her grandfather's old study, the sun was blazing down on the wide, almost endless vega to the west, glistening on the snowy peaks of the Sierras to the south and, across the river and etched against the snowy peaks, the splendid palaces of Alhambra sparkled, the Sultan's Turret ablaze.

All Futura Books are available at your bookshop or newsagent, or can be ordered from the following address:
Futura Books, Cash Sales Department,
P.O. Box 11, Falmouth, Cornwall

Please send cheque or postal order (no currency), and allow 55p for postage and packing for the first book plus 22p for the second book and 14p for each additional book ordered up to a maximum charge of £1.75 in U.K.

Customers in Eire and B.F.P.O. please allow 55p for the first book, 22p for the second book plus 14p per copy for the next 7 books, thereafter 8p per book.

Overseas customers please allow £1.00 for postage and packing for the first book and 25p per copy for each additional book.